Redemption of Love

EXODUS AND PAXTON'S STORY

AUBRY J.

Redemption of Love: Exodus and Paxton's Story

Copyright 2023 by Aubry J.

Published by Grand Penz Publications

All rights reserved

This book is a work of fiction. Names, characters, places, and incidents either are the product of the author's imagination or are used fictitiously and are not to be construed as real. Any resemblance to actual persons, living or dead, business establishments, events, or locales or, is entirely coincidental.

No portion of this book may be used or reproduced in any manner whatsoever without writer permission except in the case of brief quotations embodied in critical articles and reviews.

Want to be a part of the Grand Penz Family?

To submit your manuscript to Grand Penz Publications, please send the first three chapters and synopsis to info@grandpenz.com

Synopsis:

Fresh out of a failed relationship, Paxton Littlejohn gave up on the thought of falling in love. The fearless beauty focused on her social life and running her business with her brothers. Tragedy strikes and it has Paxton ready to shoot her way through any situation to get revenge. It also leaves her with a wave of emotions she's sure she can control—all except the one of desire when she reaches out to the bloodthirsty menace himself, Exodus DeCorte.

The thrill Exodus received from hunting and torturing those on his radar had the streets prudent in how they moved. No man should enjoy death the way Exodus does, but it was for that reason Paxton knew he was the only person to accompany her on the road to revenge. The one act of mercy he ever showed was a prayer for your soul, and you could only hope you'd ended up above instead of below.

The only problem with Paxton's plan was the steep price Exodus intended to charge. One look at Paxton's finger around a trigger ready to take a life had Exodus hooked. She's his, and he would stop at nothing to prove that they belonged together.

It's easy to hate and even kill. But love will prove to be the biggest obstacle for Paxton Littlejohn. Will this standalone end in revenge or redemption? Or both?

Before you read:

Paxton and Exodus's story started as a fun, quick story I wanted to tell. It doesn't have the full details of my other novels but has drama and even a few surprise visits from some older characters. You've met Paxton and Exodus in *Wait for Me*. You don't have to read that before starting this. Their story is just that—theirs. Enjoy! I hope you love them as much as I loved writing them.

Also, one last thing: Paxton is not a hitta. Yes, she has a gun and will shoot whoever, but she is not a hitta. If you are looking for a female hitta story, you should read Trenches if you haven't already.

Aubry J

CHAPTER 1

Paxton

"PAXTON!" Mama yelled my name, but I didn't give a fuck about what she was talking about right now. I had to get to Naeem and see that he was okay. My daddy stepped into my path, grabbed me by my arm, and pulled me to him. I fought for a few seconds, ready to go to war with my blood, but I didn't care. I needed to see Naeem and look at him to ensure he was still on this side of the earth. My baby brother was my heart, and knowing he was lying in a hospital bed, fighting for his life, had me fucked up.

"Chill, baby girl," Daddy said into my ear. The tears I held back threatened to drop from my eyes, but I wasn't about to let it happen. "He's gonna be all right; you just gotta stay strong."

"What happened, Daddy?" I asked him as he hugged me.

"He was shot," he answered. And I swear if my daddy's arms weren't around me, I would've dropped to the ground. "The doctors said that he was lucky that no major organs were hit, but he's going to be out for the count for a bit."

"Who shot him?"

"Be calm when I answer that," Daddy said. He reared back and looked at me in the eyes. "I'm not telling you shit until you promise me you'll be calm." I diverted my eyes to look around the waiting room, and Daddy gently shook me to get my attention. "I'm serious, Paxton."

"All right." I nodded.

Daddy stared me down for a few seconds before looking over at Mama. She gave him a quick nod; then he let out a small sigh. "Yalonda shot him. He went to pick up the kids, and she was mad because he wasn't trying to deal with her. You know, he said they were over with, and I guess he meant it this time."

"So, she got mad and shot him?" I asked, confused. In my opinion, Yalonda and Naeem always had a fucked-up relationship, but to my knowledge, they were never violent. "That doesn't make any sense."

"That's what Xavi said when we got here."

"I want to talk to Xavi," I said, and Daddy nodded. I couldn't stand Xavi since the day Naeem started bringing him around, but I didn't dictate who my brothers dealt with as long as they didn't interfere with me and my money.

"He's not here right now, but he said he was coming back," Mama said. Daddy let me go, and I sat beside Mama in the waiting room. When I got the call about thirty minutes ago that my brother had been shot, I'd dropped everything I was doing and came straight to the hospital. Naeem didn't live here; he stayed in Vegas, but Yalonda and his kids did, so he split his time between the two places. Xavi was his right-hand man; wherever Naeem was, he was beside him.

"Explain to me everything that happened." Even though I wasn't looking at either of my parents, they knew I was talking to my daddy. My right leg bounced up and down as I tried to keep my temper under control.

"I told you everything we knew." Daddy sighed as he came to sit next to me. He gently touched my right leg to stop me from moving, but it wasn't helping. "Naeem and Xavi went to pick up the kids. Yalonda was upset and shot up their car."

"That shit doesn't sound right," I replied. I ran my hands over my face and let out a deep breath. "I just need to know all the details."

"Why?" Daddy questioned. I cut my eyes at him, and he shook his head. "You're not killing that girl, Paxton."

"If my brother doesn't make it out of this alive, I will." I shrugged.

"You don't gotta like it, Daddy, but it will happen. If that doctor doesn't come from the back saying he's going to make it, then her family will be planning her funeral just like we're planning his."

"What about the kids?" Mama weakly argued. "You'd leave them orphaned." I shrugged, and she looked over at Daddy with pleading eyes. I knew my parents didn't agree with our lifestyle, more so me than my brothers, but they didn't interfere with it either. They'd raised hustlers, and we found our lane. We didn't always keep our hands clean, but we kept the drama from their doorstep.

A short, very pregnant doctor came from the back and looked around. I could tell from my parents' tense look that she was Naeem's doctor. Daddy stood up and walked over to her while Mama held tight to my knee. When his head dropped and the doctor patted him on the shoulder before leaving, I knew my brother hadn't made it.

"Patrice," Daddy said, walking over to Mama. The fact that he used her name instead of calling her baby was all I needed to hear. I pushed up from my chair and stepped past my grieving parents. The first person I would look for was Yalonda; after I laid her out, I would find Xavi. He was supposed to be my brother's right hand, and this nigga was walking about, uninjured, while my brother was gone. Something wasn't adding up, and I wanted to know the truth.

CHAPTER 2

Exodus

"SHIT STUPID," I said, sitting down. The crowd was thick for a Tuesday night, but I wasn't about to complain as long as I was making money. I could hear niggas yelling from the back, begging for help, but I wasn't a forgiving ass nigga. I collected my money, did what I did, and disposed of the bodies. When niggas saw me coming, they knew it was a problem, and I planned on fixing it.

"It's not stupid," Krude replied, wiping his hands on a towel. He threw it in the burning barrel in the middle of the room, then turned to look at me. "I have been tellin' you for a while that I want to lock her down. This is the only way I can do it."

"You think getting her pregnant is the way to go?" I asked, without looking up from my notepad. I was a simple nigga and didn't believe in putting shit on anything digital. It was a million times easier to get rid of the evidence by burning it than trying to wipe a system clean. I'd see niggas think they were untouchable because they had someone on their payroll who was good with computers. The thing was, no matter how good you thought you were, there was somebody better that could get your ass.

"It's that or kidnap her ass, and I ain't in the mood to fight with Megan." He chuckled.

"You think her getting pregnant ain't gonna cause no fight?" I questioned, and Krude shrugged. "That girl gonna fuckin' kill you, lil cuz."

"Nah, she loves a nigga too much for that," he replied, and I waved him off. Megan and Krude's relationship was crazy as hell, in my opinion. Half the time, I didn't even know if they were together, and when I knew for a fact that they were, it was because either Krude or Megan were showing their ass over something the other did. "I can see that shit now. Her wobbling her ass through the house, cleaning, and shit. It's going to be dope as hell."

"It's gonna be hell, all right," I mumbled and shook my head. "The whole dope part is still up in the air."

"Fam, I can't wait for you to get a girl," he said, and I sucked my teeth. "For real, yo' mean ass gonna be out there doing crazy shit just to keep her."

"Never that." I stood and stretched my arms over my head. "It ain't a woman alive that can get me to come out of character for her ass." I grabbed my machete off the table and headed toward the back, where my next victim was waiting. I could hear Krude laughing and mumbling some shit under his breath, but I didn't give a fuck about what he was talking about. My mind was on my next kill and how it would make me feel. Some niggas smoked weed or drank to get that high, but not me. I killed. Don't get me wrong, though, I smoked weed, too, but it was to calm me down after I killed a nigga.

The hallway down to my next kill was short, but that didn't stop me from taking my time. I'd spent two days looking for this bitch ass nigga, only to find him hiding in an abandoned school on the other side of town. I snatched him from his sleep and dragged him kicking and screaming to my warehouse. I was paid damn near forty thousand to kill his weak ass, but I probably would've done it for free. He had a thing for touching little kids, and muthafuckas like that always deserved to die. If it were going to be by my hands, then his death would be slow, painful, and worth every dime the person who paid me was spending.

I cracked my neck before dropping my head. When I lifted it, I pushed the door open to see Pauly tied to a chair in the middle of the room. Pauly's eyes bugged out his head when he saw the machete in my hand. "Don't worry about this," I said, stepping into the room.

"Ay, Ex," Krude said from outside the room. I turned to look at him standing there with his gun. The playful grin my cousin typically wore on his face was gone, and his eyes were cold. He slowly blinked before turning to look at me. "Make that nigga bleed."

"Say less," I replied with a nod of my head. I kicked the door closed and turned to Pauly. A slow smile pulled at my lips as Pauly wildly shook his head. "And do not fear those who kill the body but cannot kill the soul. Rather, fear him, who can destroy both soul and body in hell. Mathew 10:28."

My phone rang, and I pulled it out of my pocket to see Paxton's name flashing across the screen. I sent her to voicemail, and she called again before I could put my phone back up. I let out a small sigh and swiped my finger across the screen.

"Yes?" I greeted her as I walked around Pauly. His eyes bounced from me to the machete in my hand. Nigga was so scared that he'd peed on himself and was sitting in it. I didn't doubt that if he weren't tied up and gagged, he'd run and scream, trying to get out of here.

"I need your help," Paxton replied, and I stopped moving.

"What you need?" I asked.

"Your services," she answered.

"All right," I said, then hung up. I turned my attention back to Pauly and shook my head. "This is about to hurt, Pauly." I set my machete on the floor next to the door, walked over to him, and grabbed the chain above his head. Pauly was tied to a bunk when I reached down and connected the chain to his ankle. "Aye, bitch, be still." I smacked him in the face hard as fuck, and he groaned. With ease, I kicked the chair from under him, and he fell over, hitting the back of his head, but I didn't give a fuck. The lever to activate the pulley to lift Pauly was on the other side of the room, but I had to go over there, grab the water hose, and drag it across the room. His stupid ass was upside down, swaying side to side by the time I walked over to him. I pulled a pair of gloves out of my pocket, put them on, and then grabbed Pauly by the neck to make him stop moving. He was naked, looking like a damn fool, but it worked to my advantage. With no remorse, I shoved the head of the water hose into his asshole, then pushed it a good six inches inside him. Pauly screamed, but I had no sympathy for him. His bitch ass liked to touch kids, so he deserved everything he was enduring, plus more. I whistled as I walked back to the wall and turned on the water. Pauly screamed at the top of his lungs for mercy. I grabbed my favorite machete off the floor and left the room.

CHAPTER 3

Paxton

"YOU DIDN'T HAVE to come and check on me." I opened the front door to allow Mahogany and Shaka into the house. I wasn't surprised that they had shown up. I knew they would show their faces when I called them from the hospital, saying Naeem was shot. Shaka waddled her seven-month-pregnant ass over to the couch and dropped down while Mahogany and her baby bump sat across from her. I loved that both my friends were pregnant and happily in love. At first, I thought it would change the dynamic of our friendship, but it didn't; if anything, it increased our love for each other.

"Miss ma'am, your brother was shot," Mahogany replied with a roll of her eyes. "What kind of friends would we be if we didn't?"

"Right," Shaka agreed. She reached the coffee table, picked a fry off my plate, and ate it. "You are there for us whenever something goes down; why wouldn't we be there for you?"

"I'ono." I shrugged, then sat down next to Shaka. I grabbed my plate off the table and returned to eating, even though I wasn't hungry. "I'm just used to handling shit on my own."

"Which you need to stop," Mahogany sighed. "You got us, and we got you. Now tell us what happened."

I broke down the story that my parents told me to them and ate my food. My daddy was on my heels when I stormed out of the hospital. He didn't let me leave until he explained Naeem wasn't dead, but was in a medically induced coma. The fact that my little brother was still alive put a little peace in my heart, but I still had questions I needed answers to. I went back inside the hospital, and seeing him lying in the bed, with tubes and an IV connected to him, broke my heart. I was close to Naeem. He was born when I was five, and our oldest brother, Cade, was seven. We did everything together, and to see him down and out had me ready to go to war.

"Have you spoken to Cade?" Shaka asked.

"He'll be in town later tonight." I nodded. When I spoke with Cade earlier, he was torn up about Naeem. He blamed himself since he was the one who introduced Yalonda and Naeem years ago. Yalonda was the sister of his boy, Mike. Mike was in jail for several robberies, but Cade kept money on his books and looked out for Yalonda. "He said he would call me when his plane landed."

"How are your parents?"

"Doing as best as they can," I answered honestly. Mama was a wreck, but I was more concerned about Daddy. Our parents started a family late, having us when they were in their forties and Naeem at damn near fifty. Now they were in their seventies and dealing with their health problems. Naeem getting shot didn't help with the stress. "I sat up there with him while they got some rest here. They didn't want to drive back to their house way up north when my spot was closer, and I agreed. They have clothes and stuff here, anyway."

"What do you need from us?" Mahogany asked with a small, sad smile. "And if you say nothing, I'm going to cry and call Tobias, and you know how he is when I cry."

"Lawd, please don't do all that." I giggled. "I don't want to hear his mouth."

Since becoming pregnant, Mahogany was extremely emotional and would burst into tears without provoking. Focus was her fiancé, and child's father was going through it. Whenever she dropped a tear or even looked like she was going to, he tried to fix the problem. He didn't care what he was doing or whose nerves he was getting on; he was going to take care of it.

"Then tell us what you need from us." She laughed.

"Yo, she so damn spoiled," Shaka said, and I nodded in agreement. "But she's right; tell us what you need."

"Nothing." I shook my head. "It's going to be taken care of."

"Hell, Paxton, what did you do?" Shaka sighed. "Because that tone of voice and sneaky ass look on your face is already giving you away."

"Nothing." I shrugged, then took a bite of my food. Shaka and Mahogany shared a look, but neither pressed the issue further. I knew neither believed me, but there wasn't shit they or anyone else could say to stop me.

———

"Answer the damn door, Bridget!" I yelled as I knocked on the door with the butt of my gun. Bridget was Yalonda's cousin. They were always together, so I knew if anyone knew where Yalonda was hiding out, it was her. "All I wanna do is talk!"

"Talkin' doesn't involve a gun, Paxton!" Bridget yelled from behind me. I turned around and smirked before shaking my head. I flipped the safety back on, put the gun in my purse, and set it down. Yalonda's house wasn't big, so her yard was small, but it was big enough for me to knock her around.

"You are absolutely right." I chuckled as I walked down the three stairs and got in Bridget's face. "This ass whoopin' you're about to get involves only my fist." I popped Bridget in the mouth before she realized what I had said. I wasn't a sneak a bitch type of fighter; I believed in going head up, and Bridget was about to get every drop of anger I was feeling right now. She stumbled back, failing miserably at catching her footing, but it didn't matter because I wasn't letting up. I grabbed Bridget by the hair and repeatedly slammed my fist into her face. Her eyes were swelling, and she was screaming for someone to help her, but niggas weren't about to move to help her ass. I slammed her head into the driver's door of her car and let her fall. "Where the fuck is your punk ass cousin?"

"I don't know!" Bridget cried as she lay in the fetal position; her hands covered her head as I kicked at her face. "I don't know!"

"Not good enough, bitch!" I shouted. I grabbed her by her raggedy ass weave and drugged her to the porch. Like the weak-ass bitch she was, Bridget cried and begged me to let her go. "Get on your knees, bitch!"

"Please, Paxton." She cried, but did what she was told. Bridget looked fucked up. Her hair was all over her head, her eyes were swollen, and her nose and mouth were leaking blood. I didn't even think I hit her that hard, but I was wrong. "Just let me go."

"Nah, big shit talker." I laughed. I grabbed my purse from the spot I'd set it down before I beat her ass and grabbed my gun out of it. "You pulled up on me like you were going to do something, and now you are begging for your life. Make it make sense."

"I was just looking out for my family," Bridget cried. She wiped her nose with her hand and shook her head.

"Me too." I chuckled, then flipped the safety off my gun. "I'm just lookin' out for my brother." I emptied an entire clip into Bridget without an ounce of regret. She fell face forward into the grass. I put my gun back in my purse, stepped over her body, and got in my car.

"Yeah?" Exodus answered. My body reacted to his deep voice, and I shook my head. Exodus was my best friend's best friend and was fine as fuck. Tall, standing maybe six foot six, muscular but not too much where it looked like a muscle head. Skin the color of raw honey covered with tattoos from his neck to ankles. Full, pink lips, flared nose, dark brown eyes, thick brows, short but full beard, and tapered fade with a crispy line.

"Clean up," I said as I drove down the street.

"Drop the address." Exodus chuckled, and I could picture him shaking his head with his all-knowing smirk. I stopped at a red light and did what he asked. "Cool."

"Let me know the cost," I said. Instead of replying, he hung up the phone.

CHAPTER 4

Exodus

"YOU DIDN'T HAVE to pick him up from school," my cousin Corinthian said as I stepped through her shop. I looked around, shaking my head at all the thirsty ass niggas that were watching her move before I sat down in her chair. Her son Judah ran to her, and she quickly kissed his forehead before he ran off to the back office.

"Those damn people get on his nerves," I half-ass replied, not giving a fuck what she was talking about. I picked her son up any damn time I felt like it, and we both knew it. Judah was my nigga; from the second he was born, we'd been rockin' and hard. Judah was with me whenever I stepped and wasn't on no killin' shit.

"He's three." She laughed and shook her head. "How is he supposed to get used to being around kids his age when he's always with you?"

"Kids his age are bad as fuck." I shrugged. Corinthian rolled her eyes as she snapped her barber cape and placed it around my neck. To be truthful, Judah was bad as fuck, too, but I wasn't about to admit that to her ass. "My boy good with rollin' with me."

"What happens when it's time for him to go to kindergarten? You can't just pull him out when you want company."

"Yeah, you gonna have to home-school then." I shrugged, serious as hell. Corinthian cut on the clippers and tightened my lineup instead of responding to me. She knew I was serious as hell, and my cousin wasn't about to not work because my ass probably needed more friends. But like I told her, Judah was my lil homie, and if he said he didn't like school, then shit, he wasn't about to be there.

Thirty minutes later, she pulled the cape back off me, and I checked myself in the mirror. Corinthian was cold as fuck with the clippers and was the only one I let touch my head since I was fourteen. Without thinking, I dropped two hundred into her Venmo, which covered my cut, tip, and then some, and pulled her into a hug.

"What you about to get into now?" Corinthian asked after she pulled back and started cleaning up. Her next client stood from his seat and dropped down in the chair. I stepped into her path when I noticed him checking out my cousin's ass, and he sucked his teeth. When I turned to look at him, his weak ass quickly turned his head. *Bitch ass nigga.*

"Running some errands, then going to check on the laundry mats." I shrugged. I owned about seventeen laundry mats throughout the city. It allowed me to move freely without having to check in with anyone, and my income was amazing. I had my hand in a few other things, one being a restaurant with Focus, but I enjoyed being the sole owner of my shit. "Probably grab some food after that and chill at the house."

"You not going to the hospital?"

"Who in the hospital?" I reared back.

"Naeem was shot a few days ago," she answered. I shook my head and wiped my hands down my face. My mind raced, thinking back over the last week. I'd been working my legal and illegal jobs and not worried about shit else. I let out a small laugh and nodded my head. Now Paxton calling and asking me for my services and the other day for a cleanup made sense. "You didn't know?"

"Nah." My phone rang, and I checked to watch to see a text from a female I fucked with from time to time. I wasn't in the mood to deal with her mouth, so I ignored that shit and looked up at Corinthian, who had a mug on her face. "I didn't know."

"Yeah." She nodded her head. "His baby mama shot him. Cade has been in town for a few days, and I have been checking in with Paxton to make sure she was cool."

"I'll hit them up when I leave here," I said, and Corinthian nodded. Her client let out an impatient grunt, and I turned to look at him. I smirked, then grabbed the collar of his shirt, lifted him out of the chair, and pulled him close to my face. "Lil nigga, do we have a problem?"

"N-n-no," he stuttered.

"I didn't think so," I said, then dropped him back in his chair. "Don't rush her when she's speaking to me."

"Was that necessary?" She sighed and shook her head. I shrugged, not taking my eyes off the bitch ass nigga in her chair. "Get out, Ex."

"I'll see you later." I chuckled, then left the shop. I knew my cousin could and would handle herself if need be, but I didn't like niggas rushing her. She was supplying their bitch ass with a service. Her shop stayed packed, and it wasn't just because she was pretty. But they had to know they wouldn't disrespect her, either. Snatching a nigga up from time to time was necessary.

After leaving the shop and running a few errands, I headed to the other side of town to see Paxton. I'd meant to hit her back up and see what she needed, but now I knew, so there wasn't any reason for no small talk. I parked in her driveway and headed to the porch. Paxton lived in a cool neighborhood, wasn't much shit going on, and it was peaceful, from what I could tell. I rang the doorbell and stepped back when the porch light came on.

"What up?" I said when she opened the front door. I let out a small chuckle at the gun she had in her hand. Paxton was forever packing, so I wasn't surprised. The crazy thing was, it was sexy as fuck to me. I was all for a woman being able to protect themselves, but to see Paxton pull her gun without a second thought had my dick bricking up way too many times in the past. "You can put that shit up."

"Can't ever be too sure," she said, then stuffed the gun into her yoga pants. My eyes roamed over her from head to toe. Usually, Paxton dressed in jeans and t-shirts, but to see her in a pair of green yoga pants, matching sports bra top, and fluffy socks had a nigga wanting to see her like this all the time. Paxton was fine as fuck and knew it with her pouty lips, small, slanted eyes, and deep dimples. Her ember-colored skin was blemish-free, and I swear I wanted to run my hands over it whenever we were around each other. My favorite thing was Paxton was considered a BBW, and every time she walked past me, I saw how fat her ass was, and a nigga had to thank the man above.

"Understandable." I nodded. She backed up and let me into the house. The smell of fried chicken hit my nose, and my stomach growled. I hadn't eaten since breakfast, and it was damn near ten at night, and that shit was starting to catch up with me.

"Hungry?" She lifted her brow and smirked.

"Yeah." I nodded, then licked my lips. She was talking about food, and I was talking about pussy, but I didn't say that shit out loud.

"Come on." She waved for me to follow her, and the entire walk back to the kitchen, my eyes were on her ass. My dick started to brick up, and I adjusted my shit in my pants. I sat down at the small island, and she quickly made me a plate and put it in the microwave. Once it was warm, she sat it in front of me, leaned against the counter, and crossed her arms over her chest. "So, what are you doing here?"

"I heard about Naeem," I said in between bites of food. The food was good as hell, and I started smashing it. "I wanted to reach out to see how you were doing."

"I'm good." She shrugged. The sports bra she wore held her titties in place, but they still had a little jiggle to them.

"And yo' people?"

"Mama and Daddy are stressing like always, and my oldest brother is here trying to get some answers, but you know Yalonda people ain't talking like that," she replied.

"It doesn't help that you already poppin' niggas." I shook my head, and she shrugged. When she called me saying she needed a cleanup, I didn't think twice about sending out a crew. I knew she was leaving a message to somebody because she left the body in the middle of the yard, but I didn't ask any questions. Now that I knew it was connected to her brother being shot, I completely understood her doing what she did. "Was it necessary?"

"Yeah," she replied, and I grunted. "What's the problem?"

"Shit was messy," I said, then wiped my mouth. "Why?"

"Cuz that bitch's cousin shot my brother. Naeem is lying in a medically induced coma because of her. And when I catch his bitch ass best friend, I'm going to do the same thing to him."

"Why are females so quick to pull a gun on some revenge shit?" I said, more to myself than Paxton. Don't get me wrong, I knew how niggas moved, and at times it was more reckless than a woman, but for this instance, I was only speaking Paxton's short-tempered ass.

"When niggas do it, nobody bats an eye, but when a bitch does it, it's a problem?" Paxton chuckled. "If that ain't no double standard shit, I don't know what is."

"I didn't say all that." I got up and scraped my plate before taking over to the sink. "I would tell one of my niggas that was being messy too if they left a body in the middle of a yard and pulled off. What if I wouldn't have answered the phone when you called?"

"I would've called somebody else." She shrugged, and I cut my eyes at her. "The shit would've been taken care of."

"What nigga you callin' to take care of shit?" I couldn't stop myself from asking. I knew of one nigga that Paxton fucked with in the past, and from what I knew, that shit didn't end well. Nobody told me the full details about their breakup, and it was probably best that I didn't.

"Don't worry about it." She smirked. The little comment had me ready to fuck shit up because what nigga did she trust to handle anything for her? "Just know it would've been handled." She grabbed a small sucker off the counter, opened it, then put it in her mouth. Paxton had a sweet tooth and was forever eating some candy. How she had such a pretty ass smile was beyond me, but she did. "No questions asked."

"Ay, look." I washed my plate and set it on the rack next to the sink. "Don't call no other nigga for no cleanup but me." I grabbed a napkin off the counter and dried my hands. "Matter of fact, don't pop nobody else from here on out."

"Yeah, that's not going to happen." She laughed and shook her head. "That bitch shot my brother, so I'm coming after her."

"Not if you gonna be messy with it," I grunted. Paxton rolled her eyes and tried to walk away, but I grabbed her arm. "Legit Paxton, you are not about to be messy with the shit. If you are going to run off straight emotion, then step the fuck back and let somebody else handle it."

"First off, let me the fuck go," she said and snatched her arm from me. "Second, you don't run shit over here, but your damn mouth, so watch how you talk to me." She had a fire in her eyes that had me wanting to snatch her ass up, but I kept my cool. Paxton was used to talking to niggas like they were crazy and getting away with it. I wasn't one of those weak niggas, and she knew it, so for her to try me, let me know she wasn't thinking clearly. She mugged me up and down, and I had to bite my bottom lip to keep from saying what I wanted and having her ass go off on me. My dick started to brick up, and I smirked. Her ass was too fuckin' sexy, and that shit was a problem because I didn't let anybody talk to me crazy like she was.

"Let's get something straight right now." I stepped into her space, pinning her against my body and the counter. "I ain't gonna do shit, but stay black and die. And if and when I tell you to do something, understand I'm not saying that shit to hear my voice; I'm saying it to protect you because I see shit you don't. You understand me?" I knew she could feel how hard my dick was against her stomach, but I didn't give a fuck. She wanted to talk to me like I was a little nigga, then she would feel how big my shit was.

I half expected her to argue with me, but she stubbornly nodded. I stepped back, grabbed the sucker from her hand, and put it in my mouth. "Cool, I'll be in contact." The taste of cherry hit my tongue, and I wondered if hers tasted like it, too.

"Contact for what?" she questioned as I walked away.

"You'll see." I threw over my shoulder and then stepped out of her house. A plan was already formulated in my head. She was about to see how a real nigga took care of shit.

CHAPTER 5

Paxton

"AY, boss lady, how's it going?" one of the drivers called out when I moved through the warehouse. I threw my hand up in acknowledgment but didn't stop moving. I was running on fumes between going to the hospital to check on Naeem and running the business. Cade being in town didn't help because all he was worried about was some bitch. He'd barely stopped by to see Naeem, and that shit didn't do anything but piss me off.

After getting to my office, I dropped into my chair and kicked off my heels. To the outside world, 3 of a Kind Transportation was an established trucking company run by my brothers and me, and it was the truth. We also had a street connection as well. We ran guns and drugs from one coast to the other. And while the shit was great money, it was a headache that I didn't want to deal with. I worked through emails for the rest of the day and ensured that routes were good. We had over twenty trucks on the road moving from one part of the country to the other. By the time I was done reviewing reports, it was damn near seven at night, and I was ready to go home. I quickly packed up and headed home. I hadn't been home since last night and desperately wanted to lie in bed. My parents stayed with Naeem since I'd spent the morning with him before coming to work.

"Hello?" I answered the phone as I drove. Even though I wanted to grab something to eat, I decided against it. I had food at home that I could warm up after I showered.

"Where are you?" Exodus questioned, and I cut my eyes at the dash as if it were his face. I hadn't seen or heard from him since he left my house two days ago. A part of me wondered what he had up his sleeve since he said he would contact me, but I wasn't going to push it.

"Heading home," I said.

"Cool." He hung up, and I laughed. Exodus was rude as fuck majority of the time, and I didn't see a problem with his attitude. It was annoying, but at the same time, I understood why he was the way he was. As the oldest of all his cousins, he was used to being in charge and people falling in line with his words.

I pulled into the driveway and shook my head at the sight of Exodus's big-ass truck parked on the other side of my driveway as if it belonged. He got out and came to my door. After shutting off my car, he opened the door and helped me out. Even though he was a complete asshole, I could say he was a gentleman who never let me or my girls touch a door if we were with him.

"What are you doing here?" I asked once we were in the house.

"Go get changed," he stated as if that answered my question.

"For?" I lifted my brow in question and waited. "And where do you think we are going that I can't be dressed like this?" Usually, at work, I wear jeans and a T-shirt with the company logo, but today, I had a few meetings and had to dress up. The pin-striped hunter green fitted suit and gold heels that I wore today were cute but also gave off the boss bitch vibe that I wanted.

"It's cool for work, but not for where we goin'." He looked down at his phone and then up at me when my feet didn't move from their planted spot. "Why are you not moving'?"

"Because you didn't answer my question." I crossed my arms over my chest. He was dressed casually in joggers, a fitted tee, Jordan, and a fitted KC hat. Like always, he was in all black. "Where are we going?"

"The hookah club," he replied.

"Why?" I wasn't a smoker, so going to a hookah club didn't interest me. The hookah club was a mixture of a club and a hookah bar. You got the vibe of a club with the music and dance floor but then got the vibe of a hookah bar with the relaxed setting, obviously the hookah, and good food.

"Just go get changed so we can go." He sighed, and I debated if I wanted to argue with him. Deciding I didn't, I went to my bedroom, grabbed a cute all-white maxi dress from the closet, and quickly showered. I returned to the living room a little under an hour later, dressed and ready to go.

"Ready?" I grabbed my purse off the couch and ensured I had my wallet and keys before looking up to see Exodus staring at me with an unreadable expression. "What?"

"Nothin'," he replied, shaking his head. He stood up, adjusted his joggers, grabbed his hat off the table, and walked to the door. "Let's go."

"I'll follow you," I said once we left the house and headed toward our cars.

"Nah." Exodus unlocked his truck and walked around it to open the passenger door. "I'll drive; we got some shit to talk about on the way."

"What do we have to talk about?" I laughed. He stood next to the open door with a mug on his face.

"Get in," he said instead of answering my question. I knew Exodus was stubborn, but so was I. I stepped into his space and shook my head.

"Not until you tell me what this is about," I said, loving that I was so close to him. Up close, I could see the tiny sprinkle of freckles lining his nose that I'd never noticed before. My eyes wandered over his face, trying to see if I could find something else that I'd never seen.

"We are going huntin'," he finally said. "Now get your fine ass in the car before I have you bent the fuck over and screaming my name so loud that your neighbors think you're out here getting murdered."

My pussy instantly started throbbing at his words, and I had to swallow the moan threatening to roll off my lips. I could feel my nipples harden up and press against my bra. Exodus looked me up and down, his eyes stopping momentarily at my breast, and he licked his lips. He stepped into my space, closing the little distance we had between each other, and stared down at me. "I'm not them niggas you used to fuckin' with, Hitta; now get your ass in the truck so we can go."

"Hitta?" I questioned with a laugh. "Isn't that technically your title?"

"Get in the truck," he said, stepping back instead of answering my question. Immediately, I wanted to be back under him, but instead, I did what he said and got in the truck. Exodus waited until I put my seatbelt on before nodding and closing the door. I watched as he confidently walked around his vehicle and then got in. My mind raced back to his words. He'd never spoken to me like that before, and instantly, I knew his words would always play over in my mind. He was too damn fine, and I was too damn horny to play with fire. Exodus was, if nothing else, a man of his word, and those words he'd spoken and how he looked at me told me he was playing no games.

"So, what do we have to talk about?" I asked once we were on our way to the hookah bar.

"We gonna do this shit my way," he said, like that was supposed to mean something to me. When we got to a stoplight, he looked over at me. Every time a car passed us, their headlights hit his eyes, making them sparkle. This man was so fucking fine that it had to be a sin. "You got your gun on you?"

"Always." I nodded.

"Get it out." He nodded. I picked my purse up from resting between my feet, got my gun, and showed it to him. He reached over, took it from me, and put it in the side panel of his door. "From here on out, you not carrying that shit when you with me."

"What?" I laughed, not understanding what he was saying. I'd been carrying a gun since I was fifteen, and he was talking about how I wouldn't be bringing it when I was with him. He had to be out of his damn mind. "Exodus, give me my damn gun."

"Nah." He shook his head, then started driving. "When you are with me, I don't care what we are doing. Driving, eating, chillin' doesn't matter; you are not carrying a damn gun. You don't need to be there if I can't protect you."

"I can protect myself. I don't need you to do it," I argued, and

Exodus grunted. "I'm serious! I will shoot your ass without thinking twice about it."

"With what gun?" he teased and looked over at me. I opened my mouth to tell him I had another gun strapped inside my thigh, but I thought twice about it. The way he looked at me, I had no doubt he'd reach right under my dress and take my gun. And my fast ass would gladly throw my legs open and let him find it, plus whatever else he might want. "Yeah, I thought so."

"You win," I replied, and he nodded. "Now, tell me about this hunt we are going on."

"You lookin' for somebody, right?" he inquired, and it was my turn to nod. "All right then, let's find their ass."

"You're going to help me without knowing the entire situation?" I asked, slightly surprised.

"Ain't shit to know." He shrugged. "You are looking for the bitch responsible for shooting your brother. You're on some revenge shit, and I get it. She shot your brother, and you want answers. I'm going to make sure you get them."

"How much is this going to cost me?" I wasn't worried about the price because I had more than enough money put aside, but I knew Exodus services were expensive.

"Did I say I was charging you?" he asked, mugging me.

"No, but I know you have a fee for what you do," I answered.

"Then shut up," he said.

CHAPTER 6

Exodus

IT DIDN'T TAKE MUCH to figure out what Paxton was up to once I
had minimal information. Naeem being shot and then her killing his
baby mama cousin was a dead giveaway. As I told her in the car, I
understood she wanted revenge because I did. Any fuck shit that made
its way to my family's doorstep was met with death. I didn't particularly appreciate how she was going about it. She could knock anybody
off that she wanted, but she would be smart with how she was
moving. Leaving a body in the middle of a yard in broad daylight
wasn't smart. There wasn't shit in me that didn't think she'd killed
plenty back in the day, but she wasn't Monica, a.k.a. Trenches. What
she was doing and how she was moving would have me calling in
favors to clean up more than just a few bodies here and there.

"So why are we at a hookah club?" she asked, looking around. We
were tucked off in the corner; the bar / club was packed with niggas
and bitches trying to impress each other. A few were just vibing and
enjoying the person they were with, but I could probably count them
all on two hands.

"How was your day at work?" I asked instead of answering her
question. My eyes roamed her, sitting across from me. Paxton was fine
as fuck. From the moment I met her a few years back, I had wanted

her, but because of her friendship with Mahogany and my friendship with Mahogany, I decided to step back. It wasn't on no noble shit, either. I knew crazy when I saw it, and Paxton was crazy as fuck, and I moved too freely to have somebody doing crazy shit because they were pissed off. I reached over, picked up my Hennessy glass off the table, and drank some.

"What does my workday have to do with my question?" she asked. The sexy-ass look on her face had my dick brickin' up, and I had to open my legs more to keep my dick from pressing against my joggers. She unknowingly was playing a dangerous ass game with a nigga like me.

"I can't make conversation?" I asked, then drank some more of my drink. "A nigga trying to show you he got manners."

"I never doubted you have manners, Exodus," she replied. I loved how she said my name. Most folks called me Ex unless they were upset, but not Paxton. She always called me by my full name, like she was reprimanding a nigga or something. "But that doesn't change the fact that I asked why we were here."

"Tell me what you know about your brother being shot." I nodded. "He's still in a coma, right?"

"Medically induced," she said, then licked her pretty ass lips. I know I should probably feel like shit for checking her out while she was sitting there stressing over her brother, but I didn't give a fuck. I rocked with Paxton because of Mahogany. I knew she had two brothers and was the middle child. They ran a trucking company that was a front for some other shit, and she was part of operations. I also knew they were close, but that was it. Any personal information I wanted to know about her would come from her. "He was getting his kids from his baby mama, and something happened; words were said, I'm guessing, and she shot him."

"That's all you know?"

"That's it." She nodded. "Which is why I went looking for her. Yalonda knows I don't play about my brothers, so her hiding out shows me she was trying to kill him."

"Or somebody is after her because of him," I suggested. I don't have proof of shit right now, but it was just an observation.

"I doubt that." Paxton shook her head. "No one would have a reason to go after Naeem. He stayed low-key, cared for his kids, and ensured his business side was handled. If anyone had beef with him, then that shit was one-sided."

"That's all a beef is sometimes is a one-sided issue," I said, and Paxton shrugged. I could tell she didn't want to hear the shit I had to say, which was cool. I relaxed, pulled a blunt from my pocket, and lit it. "Look at that shit that happened with Mahogany and ole girl."

"True, but that doesn't change the fact that my brother was shot by her bitch ass," Paxton stubbornly said. I took another pull of my blunt and nodded. She wanted justice, and I understood and respected it. "So again, why are we here?"

"You ever heard the name Jax?" I asked. My eyes were low from the weed, but I was still on alert and looking around. Paxton shook her head when I brought my gaze back to her. "Well, he fucks around with a bitch named Niecy; you ever heard of her?"

"Too generic of a name to know for sure." She shrugged. "Why?"

"Well, that's the Niecy I'm talkin' about." I nodded toward a little chick sitting near us at another table. She was cool, easy on the eyes but didn't have shit else to offer a nigga. Niecy stayed jumping from dick to dick, hoping to get a nigga with deep pockets would get her pregnant.

"Okay," Paxton said, turning around to look over her shoulder.

"Come to this side so it doesn't look like you are trying to be nosy." I laughed. Paxton looked at me with a mug on her face but did what I asked. When she sat down, I wrapped my arms around her waist and pulled her closer. I didn't have to, but something inside of me wanted to. I have wanted to be under her since our little exchange at her house. I wasn't sure if it was because I knew she was affected by my words or because she held her ground with me and didn't back down. "All right, Niecy always has the information when a nigga needs it."

"So, you fuckin' her, in other words," Paxton said with a slight attitude.

"Nah." I chuckled and shook my head. I offered the blunt, but she shook her head, and I shrugged. "I ain't fucked Niecy, and just so you know, it ain't from lack of trying on her part, either. I just don't fuck with desperate ass females." I looked Paxton up and down, loving how the all-white looked against her pretty ass skin. "Plus, she ain't got enough meat on her bones for me. A skinny bitch can't do shit for me."

"Okay," she softly said, like she didn't believe me. Paxton didn't give me jealous vibes, but the way she stared down Niecy, who was now looking over at us, had me ready to bend her ass over my knee. "So why is she staring at us like she wants to swallow your dick?"

"Shit, she probably does." I shrugged and lowly laughed. Paxton cut her eyes at me, and I smiled at her ass. Yeah, it was official; when I dropped her ass off at her spot later, I was fuckin' the shit out of her. This little cat-and-mouse game I was playing at first was done with. I wanted her ass, and bad as fuck.

Out of the corner of my eye, I saw Niecy say something to the group she was with before getting up and heading to our table. I relaxed my hand against Paxton's waist and shook my head. This girl would show her damn ass if Niecy said the wrong thing. "Check your temper before she makes her way over here."

"Fuck her," Paxton replied, then sat back and crossed her arms over her chest. I moved my arm from around her waist and put it over her shoulder. Lazily, I rubbed my index finger over her bicep. Her skin was soft as fuck, and I loved that shit.

"What's up, Ex?" Niecy said, coming to stand just outside our area. She was bold, but not bold enough to step into a space she wasn't invited into, especially my space.

"You don't see my guest right here?" I asked her. Niecy glanced over at Paxton, mugged her like she wasn't the baddest in the damn club, then turned her attention back to me. I shook my head when I felt Paxton get tense. "Niecy, don't be rude, Mama; speak before we have a problem."

"Hi," she said to Paxton, who mugged Niecy instead of respond-ing. Niecy sucked her teeth and then turned to face me. "You got a minute to talk?"

"What you gotta say to me can be said in front of her," I said with a shrug. Paxton's foot started tapping against the floor, and I smirked. Her temper was about to get the best of her. Niecy didn't even realize how much danger she was in. It was good that I took her gun from her before we arrived.

"It's about the information you asked me to get."

"Speak on it," I sighed. Paxton's face twisted up, and her body was tense, so I did the only thing I could think of, which buried my face into her neck. I felt her shiver, and her body slightly relaxed. I kissed her neck and then spoke softly into her ear. "Chill so we can get the information she got." I dropped another kiss on her neck before turning to Niecy. "What you know, Niecy?"

"The streets not talkin'." Niecy shrugged with a mug on her face. The fact that her stupid ass felt like she had the right to be jealous was comical as fuck. She had a nigga or two yet was mad I was showing Paxton affection. "Whoever was after that young nigga wants to keep that shit under wraps."

"That young nigga has a name," Paxton replied.

"Check your side piece, Ex," Niecy said without looking at Paxton. "I wasn't speaking to her."

"Yet bitch, I spoke to you." Paxton moved quick as fuck from her spot under me to being right in Niecy's face. I watched with fascination as she grabbed Niecy by the neck and pushed the gun barrel into the side of her head with the other hand. "The next time you want to get smart, make sure the bitch you talkin' to cares about if you live or die."

I patted my pocket to ensure Paxton didn't steal my gun and stood up. Her ass had another gun on her, and I was impressed as fuck. Where did she hide that muthafucka?

"Ex, help me," Niecy pleaded with tears in her eyes. I shook my head, and a lone tear dropped from her eye. "Please?"

"She's not wrong, you know." I shrugged, then picked my glass of Hennessy back up and drank some. "Next time, you need to be more careful." I turned to look at Paxon. "Let her go, Hitta; she's not worth the bullet."

Paxton debated with herself before finally pushing Niecy away from her. Niecy stumbled back and fell into a group of niggas. They looked down at her, then over at Paxton. The gleam of her gun at her side had their punk asses backing up. But only for a second. A woman, especially one as fine as Paxton, holding a gun was a hot commodity around here.

"Damn, Mama, what did she do to piss yo' fine ass off?" one nigga said. He stepped over Niecy and made his way toward Paxton. I chuckled, then set my cup down on the table. If this nigga thought for one second he was about to step to her, then he was the second dumbest person in here. The first one was Niecy for stepping to Paxton wrong. "You fine as fuck, you know that?"

"She knows it," I said, stepping next to Paxton. My gun was already in my hand as I mugged his ass. "Why do you think she has been by my side all night?"

"I ain't talkin' to you, homeboy," he said, mugging me. His punk ass nigga was right behind him, and I chuckled. He must've thought they were supposed to put fear in my heart or something. "This between me and her sexy ass."

"Unless you ain't tryin' to make it home tonight, I'd advise you to take a step back from her," I said. "She is spoken for."

"It's six of us and one of you. All I gotta do is give the word, and you'll be dead before you realize what's happening." He chuckled, then nodded toward my gun while he lifted his shirt. "And you ain't the only one with a gun."

"It could be a hundred of y'all, and I would still bet on me." I smirked. I looked over to see Paxton staring at my empty hand and chuckled. "It ain't there, Hitta." Paxton looked up at me and lifted her brow in question. I knew she was looking for my rosary that I usually kept on me. I had it, but it was in my pocket. I cracked my neck and turned to look at the stupid niggas that were still standing in front of me. "Then shall the dust return to the earth as it was: and the spirit shall return unto God who gave it. Ecclesiastes chapter twelve, verse seven."

"Are you praying?" the same stupid nigga from earlier asked with a laugh. He turned to look at his boys, who all laughed with him. "This ain't no damn church! What the fuck are you praying for, nigga?"

"The prayer was for you." Paxton laughed. I watched as her finger softly flipped off her safety, and before any of them realized it, she started shooting. Their bodies dropped, and people around us started yelling and running. Paxton didn't seem to give a fuck as she bent down and grabbed Niecy by the front of her dress and dragged her across the dead bodies that lie around her. She threw her into one of the empty seats in our area and sat on the table across from her. Her gun was set between her legs, and I couldn't front. I was probably in love with her ass right then and there. Blood was splattered across her clothes and face, but she looked sexy as fuck. "Now we are going to talk about how you decided to speak to me because I don't tolerate disrespect very well."

I chuckled as I pulled my phone out of my pocket and requested a clean-up crew. Paxton was not about to be the one to fuck with, and I loved that shit.

"I didn't mean to disrespect you," Niecy cried.

"Yes, the fuck you did cuz you did that shit without a second thought." Paxton mugged the shit out of Niecy. "That's beside the point right now, but please don't think we won't discuss that later." My ears perked up at that. I would be surprised to see Paxton let Niecy live.

CHAPTER 7

Paxton

THE WEAK-ASS BITCH sitting in front of me worked my nerves for multiple reasons. The first was because she had dismissed me when she approached Ex and me sitting here. The second was how she looked at him while speaking to him. No Ex didn't belong to me, nor had we ever stepped over the line, but she didn't know. I hate bitches who think stepping to a nigga while he is with a female is okay. Like hoe, I know you saw me and all my fuckin' glory, so stop playing with me.

"Stop cryin'; that shit makes you look weak," I said, shaking my head. Niecy sucked up her snort a few times, and that shit disguised the fuck out of me. She was sitting here swallowing her damn boogers like that was okay. "Now explain to me what the fuck you heard about the young nigga." I rolled my eyes at what she called my brother. "That was shot. Word is it was his girl that did it."

"It wasn't." She cried and shook her head.

"Then who was it?" I asked, surprised. It wasn't my intention to kill any of the niggas I had thrown her into, but they were a causality of my short temper and need for answers. Niecy took too long to answer my question, so I pushed the barrel of my gun under her chin.

"You saw me drop them without a second thought. Don't think I won't drop you."

"Xavi," she said, and I shook my head. I knew this nigga had something to do with my brother being shot. "He shot Naeem."

"Why did you lie when I asked you about it earlier?" Exodus asked, and I wondered the same thing.

"Because." She started to cry again instead of answering my question. Annoyed as fuck, I stood and shook my head. It didn't matter why she lied because now I had a name. "I don't want to die."

"It's cool." I patted Niecy on the head with my gun and smiled down at her. "You are good, Niecy. Go on and get out of here." Niecy's eyes bounced from me to Exodus before she quickly got up and headed toward the exit.

"You gonna let her just go like that?" Exodus asked.

I turned and watched as Niecy raced out the door, and I laughed. Yeah, she was going to live for right now, but that didn't mean I wouldn't be visiting her later on. "I'll catch her around sooner or later." I walked back over to where we were sitting and grabbed my purse off the couch where I'd left it. "You ready to go?"

"Yeah." He nodded. As we moved through the club, I noticed a small crew coming through the back door. "The cleaning crew will handle all this before the night ends."

"I wasn't worried about it." I chuckled. We got outside and walked to his truck. Exodus opened the door for me and helped me in.

"Of course, you weren't," he replied with his laugh as he shook his head.

"Thank you," I said, then he closed the door. I watched as his fine ass rounded the truck and then got inside.

"Where did you get the gun from?" he asked me once we were halfway back to my house. I looked up from my phone to find him staring at me as we waited at a red light. "I know you heard me."

"I did," I replied. "I'm just trying to see if you can handle the truth."

"Never lie to me, Hitta." He shook his head. "Even if you don't think I will like the answer, don't lie. That's the quickest way to get a bullet in your dome."

"You'd shoot me Exodus?" I asked. I knew Exodus was a killer; shit, I'd seen him kill on more than one occasion. I don't think I'd ever see him go after a woman before.

"Would you shoot me, Paxton?" he questioned with a lifted brow. I wanted to tell him no, but I knew I would choose myself if I had to pick between me and him.

"Without a second thought," I replied, and he nodded. He pulled off, and I relaxed back in my seat and enjoyed the ride.

"You know you never answered my question, though," Exodus said once we returned to my house. We walked from his truck to my front door.

"What was your question?" I looked at him, pressed the code to unlock my door, and pushed it open. I flipped on the light switch for the living room and then turned to look at Exodus.

"Where did you get the gun from?" he said, and I nodded.

"These thighs," I replied and patted my leg. Exodus stood over me with a hungry look as he licked his lips.

"What else is between them?" He traced his index finger along my throat to my titties. Exodus's touch made goosebumps form on my skin and my nipples hard. Instantly, I thought back to the club and him kissing my neck and ear. I wanted this man for years, and from the look in his eyes, I could tell he wanted me to. "Huh, Hitta, what else you got?"

I wasn't a woman of words; the back-and-forth shit would annoy me after a while, so instead of answering him, I grabbed Exodus by the collar of his shirt and pulled him to me. Our mouths crashed into each other, and we fought for control. He slammed me into the wall, and I gasped at the sudden impact, which gave him the upper hand and control of the kiss. My hands were under his shirt, and I scraped my nails against his chiseled stomach. I made my way down to the waist of his joggers and stuck my hand into them. His dick was long and thick, just like I loved, and I prayed this man knew how to use it.

"Back up," he said, pulling his mouth from me. I looked over his shoulder to see that the door was still open. I nodded and moved, and Exodus slammed the door closed behind him. "Take off whatever you don't want ripped the fuck up." He pulled his shirt off, and my mouth watered at the sight of his chest. Beautiful skin, muscles, and tattoos. I knew he was a work of art, but seeing it made me want to see the rest. I walked over to the couch and sat down. "The fuck you doin'?"

"Enjoying the show," I answered. "You can finish."

"I ain't a stripper," Exodus said, shaking his head.

"Scared?" I teased with a smirk. "You think you'll bore me?"

"This dick ain't ever had that complaint." He smirked. He gripped his dick through his joggers, and I licked my lips. Exodus was a cocky ass nigga, but there was nothing about how he acted that told me he couldn't or wouldn't be able to back up what he was offering.

"Big talk, Exodus." I playfully rolled my eyes. "That's all you are doing right now is talkin'."

"Bet." He nodded. Without breaking eye contact, he kicked off his shoes, dropped his joggers, and stepped out. He stood before me in boxer briefs, socks, and a black beater, and I loved it. "Come out that shit before I have to buy you a whole new dress."

"It's ruined, anyway." I shrugged.

"You're right." He nodded, then licked his lips. He bent down, grabbed something from his pants pockets, and approached me. "Stand the fuck up." His rough voice had my pussy throbbing, and when I stood, I could feel my juices running down my legs. "You better not move, either." The sound of a knife being flicked open made me look down at his hand, and that's when I saw the small blade in his hand. Exodus easily reached up and cut my maxi dress open, and it fell from my body. His eyes roamed over my body, and he licked his lips; when he noticed my gun strapped to my thigh, he chuckled. "You 'bout that life, huh?"

"I ride for those who ride for me," I answered with a shrug.

"Understood." He nodded, then closed the knife and threw it back on his clothes. "But right now, you 'bout to ride my face." He moved around me, grabbed a pillow off the couch, and dropped it on the floor. He laid down, got comfortable, then looked up at me with a mug on his face. "The fuck you waitin' on?"

"You want me to ride your face?" I asked with a laugh. I was a big girl, not sloppy big, but I had meat on my bone, my thighs jiggled, and I had love handles. In the past, I always laid down to get head; I'd never ridden a man's face. His dick, yes, with no problems but never a face. "You see me, right?"

"Do I look blind to you?" he questioned with an attitude.

"No." I laughed.

"Then do what the fuck I said do," he fussed. "I ain't a nigga that likes repeating himself. Drop them draws or push them to the side. I don't give a fuck which one you do, but bring your fine ass over here so I can eat your pussy like I have been wanting to do for years."

"Ex-"

"I'm hungry as fuck right now, and you are interrupting my fuckin' meal," he said, then got up from the floor. Exodus pushed me; not hard, but forceful enough that I sat down on the coffee table, and he sat down and then pushed my legs open. I watched as he ripped my panties off and threw them on the floor. "Fuckin' childish ass girl talkin' about, do you see me?" He kissed up my thigh when his face got to my pussy; he kissed each lip. "Fuck yeah, I see you, been seeing yo' ass." He looked up at me with a twisted face. "When I say something, I mean that shit. When I say ride my face, that's what the fuck I mean. Don't talk to me like I'm a weak nigga no damn more. Don't fuckin' question me. You understand?" I nodded because I was so fuckin' horny from the rough sound of his voice to the way he gently traced his finger up and down my folds to the hungry look in his eyes. "Open your damn mouth and answer me. Do you understand me?"

"Yes." I nodded.

"Good." He smirked as he looked at my pussy. "Now let me have my meal in peace. If you interrupt me with some bullshit, it's going to be some problems. You understand?"

"Yes."

"Good." He nodded. "Now leave me the fuck alone."

The moment Exodus's tongue touched my pussy, I knew it would be a problem. He pushed his face into me, and my head fell back. He took no mercy on my poor little pussy, and I swear on everything I saw stars. He licked, slurped, sucked, and nibbled on my clit to the point that not even five minutes into getting head, I was about to cum. I tried to push his head away, but Exodus shook my hand away, and the movements had my eyes rolling into the back of my head.

"What I tell you?" He stopped and looked at me. He licked my juices from his lips and shook his head. "Stop fuckin' pushin' my head away."

"It's too much," I moaned. "You gotta slow down."

"You don't run shit," he said. Exodus went back to work eating my pussy. He stuck two fingers inside me as he sucked on my clit, and my legs started to shake. I wanted to push his head away from me so badly, but I loved the feeling that he was giving me. A second orgasm swept over my body, and my back arched off my back.

"Exodus!" I moaned and, this time, tried to push away. He wasn't having it, though; he grabbed my thighs and pulled me back toward him. Not once did he let up on my pussy. The aggressiveness turned me on more, and another orgasm was starting to build up. I'd never cum this many times this quickly from just head. "Fuck!"

CHAPTER 8

Exodus

THE TASTE of Paxton's pussy had me ready to bust a fuckin' nut, so I knew once I was inside her, it would be a wrap. I flicked my tongue over her clit faster, and just like I knew she would, her back arched off the table, and she moaned my name. Her orgasms were intense, but I wasn't coming up for air until she squirted. I didn't even know if she could squirt, but it was my mission for it to happen before the night was over.

"Exodus!" she sobbed, and I looked up to see her looking at me. That was probably the sexiest shit in the world. To know that I was giving her so much pleasure that the only thing that she could do was call out my name and drop tears. "Ohhhhhh, my God!" Her legs shook, slapping me in the ears as they moved back and forth, but I didn't let go. I sucked hard, pulling her clit into my mouth, and flicked my tongue back and forth. "Shit!" her nails dug into my scalp, and I kept working when her body tensed up; I knew she was about to cum again, and when she did, I got my wish. Her juices sprayed out of her body, and I drank every drop.

"Pretty ass pussy," I said, finally pulling back. Paxton lay on the table, eyes closed, arms over her head, breast rising and falling as she tried to catch her breath. I wiped my mouth and beard and stood over her. My dick was pushing against my boxer briefs and hurt so damn bad that I had to reach down and pull it out and stroke it a few times to try to relieve the pain. "Get the fuck up."

Paxton opened her eyes and glared at me. She looked down at my dick in my hands and back up at me. "You gotta give me a second." She moaned and licked her lips.

"Nah, ain't no second," I said, shaking my head. "Get the fuck up, bend over, and grab your ankles." Paxton acted like she wouldn't move, and I started to sit back down. "Fine, I can eat some more."

"Wait!" She crossed her legs and pulled them close to her.

"Then do what I said."

"Okay." She nodded, then uncrossed her leg. She stood on wobbly legs, then turned around and braced her hands on the table.

"Nah, grab your damn ankles," I said, smacking her ass. The sight of them jiggling had me biting my lip. Paxton looked over her shoulder at me, and I knew right then that would be a sight I wanted to see again. "Grab your fuckin' ankles, Paxton." I pushed my draws down and stepped out of them. Paxton moved away from the table and grabbed her ankles, and that had me had a nigga ready to propose. Her bald pussy was swollen but glistening with her juices, and I had to bite my lip to keep myself from moaning. "Good girl."

I lined my dick up to her opening and slowly pushed inside. She was hot, warm, and tight as fuck. If I were a young nigga, I would've busted before I got to work, but I wasn't. I grabbed onto her hips when I felt her start to shake.

"Ooohhhh," Paxton moaned. I started long stroking her, making sure I hit every damn spot in her pussy. "Shit, Exodus!"

"Take this dick," I said when Paxton tried to reach back and push me away. I grabbed her wrist and pinned it against her lower back. "Take this shit." Paxton used her other hand and reached for the table to help her stay up. Every time she cried out, I felt the vibrations in my balls, and it had me pushing into her harder. Her ass smacking against my stomach and the sound of her wet ass pussy was the best thing I'd heard all day. "Pretty ass tough in the streets, but now yo' pussy suckin' a nigga in. Shit too fuckin' good!" I reached up, grabbed her ponytail holder off her hair, and let her curls. I loved a natural woman, and Paxton had some pretty ass hair. She took good care of it, too, so when I grabbed a handful, I wasn't worried about it being brittle when I pulled it. "Throw that ass."

"Damn it, Exodus!" she moaned when I switched my rhythm and started beating up her pussy. I could feel the tip of my dick knocking against her G-spot, and her legs began to shake. "That's my spot!"

"Yeah, I feel this pussy getting' tight." I reached around and started teasing her clit.

"Exodus!"

"Stop screaming my fuckin' name and cum," I growled into her ear. "You got this good-ass pussy that you have been holding back from a nigga." I smacked her ass cheek, then rubbed away the sting I knew my hit caused.

"Baby, please," she moaned, then started fucking me back. I chuckled, then let go of her waist. Paxton looked over her shoulder at me before turning around and dropping her head. Her pussy clamped down on my dick so hard that I knew she was about to cum again. "Fuck! I'm about to cum!"

"Then cum shit!" I growled. Her ass so damn turned me on that she could have asked me for anything, and I would've given it to her. "Stop playing around and get that nut!"

"Shit!" she shouted, then her pussy started spazzing. I bucked against her ass, keeping up and pushing her toward her nut. Her pussy clamped down, and my toes dug into her carpet floors as I pushed inside her. "Exodus!"

"Shit!" I moaned as she came. Paxton squirted all over my dick as she came. I pushed into her more, my nuts tightened, and I came. I didn't even try to pull out as I nutted all inside her. After I knew I was good, I pulled out of her, hating that I wasn't wrapped in her warmth anymore, and dropped down on the couch behind me. Paxton dropped to her knees and rested her head against the table. We were quiet as we tried to get together.

"I'll be right back," she said, then pushed herself up. She came back about five minutes later, wrapped in a satin robe with a small hand towel in her hand.

"I appreciate it," I said, taking the towel. I cleaned myself up then handed it back to her. My dick was slightly partly hard and sensitive as fuck.

"This was cool," she said, taking the towel from me. "I'll call you later, though."

"What?" I chuckled and looked up at her.

"I don't do sleepovers, Exodus," she sighed and shook her head.

"So, you putting me out?" I asked, standing. Paxton looked me up and down, her eyes stopping at my dick for a few seconds before meeting my eyes. She shrugged her shoulders, and I nodded. I wasn't a nigga that begged. Without any more words, I grabbed my clothes and put them on. I didn't even rush as she stared at me with an unreadable expression on her face. After I was dressed, I grabbed my keys and phone off the floor and left. To be a little childish, I left her front door open.

————

"She put yo' ass out?" Krude asked with a laugh. I looked over at my cousin through the phone and stopped chopping the onions I had. "Like put you out after you dicked her down?"

"Yeah, nigga," I replied, making him laugh harder.

"Yo' dick game must've been weak as fuck!"

"What?"

"That's the only thing it could've been," he said after controlling his laughter. He wiped the tears that fell from his eyes. "Because I ain't ever had a woman put me out after I fucked her good."

"Didn't you say Megan put you out after the first time y'all fucked?" I asked.

"Nigga, Megan fucked me that first time," he argued, like that shit was supposed to make sense. "And I left her ass after that shit because, ma'am, how the fuck do you think you gonna fuck me and think that shit was okay? I felt like a straight bitch! Had me ready to cook her breakfast at three in the morning, take her car to be detailed, and fill it up."

I stared at my cousin's serious ass face and hung up on him. Fuck him. He could figure out how to cook a meal on his damn own. He wasn't about to talk shit to me like I wasn't helping his ass and not the other way around. I finished chopping up my onion and then threw it in a pan. I wasn't in the mood to eat, but I had to walk Krude's simple ass through each step and show him, and now I wasn't about to let this food go to waste. Without my cousin distracting me, I finished cooking quickly and put it in the fridge for later.

After finishing, I showered and threw on some clothes to work out. I knew showering before working out was a damn waste of time, but I hated walking around smelling like food. I usually went to the gym on the other side of town, but I used the ride to chill out. I hadn't heard from Paxton in two days, which wasn't abnormal for us since we didn't talk on the phone before the other night, but now a nigga was annoyed. I'd given her some good-ass dick; I knew that from how many times she'd cum. I usually had females blowing up my phone after I fucked them, so to have Paxton not only dismiss my ass after we were done and then not hit me up afterward was fuckin' with a nigga's head. She treated my ass like I treated females in the past, and that shit wasn't cool. Chuckling, I pulled into the gym's parking lot and got out. Paxton wasn't about to play me like a weak nigga.

Fuck her.

CHAPTER 9

Paxton

"CADE, YOU ARE PISSING ME OFF," I said to my brother without looking up from the report I was working on. This was the first time he'd stepped into the office since being in town, and he was getting on my damn nerves. From the moment he walked in here, he'd been trying to give orders and change shit around that wasn't needed.

"You always got a damn attitude," Cade replied. "Get a nigga and get some dick to handle that shit."

At the mention of getting some dick, my pussy started to throb, and my mind went to Exodus. He had worked me over so damn good a few days ago, and I was still thinking about him. "The fuck is your problem, Cade?" I asked him instead of responding to his comment. "You have been trippin' since you got in town, and now you come in here with your punk-ass attitude as if I owe you something."

"These books are a fuckin' mess, is my problem," he said, then threw the report he was looking at on the table. I looked up, saw the name on it, and went back to reading mine. That was a legit business report he was looking at, and I knew for a fact wasn't shit wrong with it. "Ain't no way we are moving all their supply and barely making ends meet."

"What the fuck are you talking about?" I asked with a laugh. "We made over a quarter of a million last quarter alone. So, explain to me how we are just making ends meet?"

"You know what the fuck I mean, Paxton." He grunted and shook his head. "We got money coming in, but we could be making more. We gotta add more trucks and routes."

"That ain't happening right now," I replied, and Cade sucked his teeth. "We have stuff moving like it's supposed to, and I won't start changing things because you have an itch in your ass you can't scratch."

"Watch how you talkin' to me, Paxton." Cade growled like that shit was supposed to scare me. "I'm not one of those weak-ass niggas you used to dealin' wit; I'll knock yo' ass smooth the fuck out."

"Before you even move out of that seat, I'll put a bullet in your ass, and you know it," I smoothly replied to my brother. Cade knew it wasn't an empty threat because I'd shot him in the past. Usually, I'd just give him a little flesh wound, but the glare my brother was giving me had me thinking of which part of the body I could shoot and not worry about seriously injuring him. My parents were still stressing over Naeem, and I had no reason to add to their stress by seriously harming their other son. I picked up my purse and set it on my desk.

"Fuck you, Paxton," Cade sneered, then got up. He stormed out of my office, and I shook my head. Even though I was my parent's only daughter, my brothers were the most emotional damn niggas I had ever dealt with. Instead of chasing after him like I knew he wanted me to do, I put my purse back down and finished working.

"Yes, gorgeous," I said a few hours later as I answered the phone.

"What are you doing?" Mahogany laughed.

"Leaving work," I answered as I drove down the street. "Why, what's up?"

"Just wanted to see if you wanted to come by, eat, and be a bum with me," Mahogany replied, and I looked at my dash at the time. It was close to seven, and I knew she was home because Focus never let her work past six anymore. "Tobias is at the studio, and I'm lonely."

"Where's Kitten?" I asked as I turned. I was floored when Mahogany mentioned that she had talked her fiancé into naming their dog Kitten. I wasn't big on dogs or pets at all, for that matter, but Mahogany loved that damn dog.

"Sitting right here." She giggled. "So, are you coming?"

"You better feed me well, too," I agreed, shaking my head. Her spoiled ass knew I would come over when she called and asked me what I was doing.

"Seafood boil water already going," she replied, and I groaned. I loved a good seafood boil, and my girl knew that. "By the time you get here, everything should be ready."

"See you in a minute," I replied, then hung up.

The drive to Mahogany's was smooth, with a few spots of traffic, but I made it in more than enough time. I grabbed my purse and got out of the car.

"Where are you?" I called out as I pushed the door open. I loved Mahogany and Focus's house. It probably had to be one of the prettiest places I'd ever been, with floor-to-ceiling windows, wood floors, and bright colors. I went through the living room and into the kitchen to find her stirring a pot. "Oh, look at your belly!"

"It's getting so big," Mahogany said with a roll of her eyes. I nodded and chuckled. At almost six months pregnant, Mahogany looked beautiful. "I told Tobias this would be the last baby he ever put inside me."

"The lies you tell." I laughed as I washed my hands at the sink. "That man already said he would have you pregnant again before your six weeks checkup."

"I would kill him." She laughed and shook her head.

"You better keep your legs closed then," I replied.

"I'm gonna be pregnant again cuz that isn't going to happen," she replied with a serious look on her face. I laughed, then grabbed a small bag under the sink to throw away our trash. "Food is already on the table."

"What's in the pot?" I asked, glancing over at it and heading to the dining room.

"Tobias wanted red beans and rice instead of a boil," she answered, and I nodded.

We sat down, said a quick prayer, and then ate.

"Cade finally showed up to the office," I said after we ate and lounged on the couch.

"Why do I have the feeling it didn't go well?" Mahogany asked from her spot next to me. We'd decided to binge Scandal for what felt like the millionth time. There was nothing like watching Olivia talk crazy to a muthafucka and then stroll away like a boss bitch.

"Because it didn't," I answered with a shrug. "Cade has been acting funny since Naeem was shot."

"Maybe he's just stressed," Mahogany suggested, and I shrugged. "I mean, I would be stressed the hell out if you, Shaka, or Ex were shot and in a medically induced coma."

"No, you wouldn't." I chuckled. "You must've forgotten I saw how you reacted when Focus got shot. You were on your boss bitch shit."

"That was after I damn near passed out, cried into my cousin's chest, and then screamed at him not to die like that was going to get him to stand up and shake it off," she said with a serious look on her face.

"Oh yeah, that's right." I nodded, and we laughed. "But afterward, you were on your shit."

She was about to respond when the back door closing grabbed our attention. As Focus approached, I watched my friend struggle to get out of the couch. "Man, sit yo' ass down, One," he said, watching her. Their sofa was overstuffed and extra-large, so it would cause anyone pregnant or not to struggle to get out of it. "What's up, Paxton?"

"Hey, Focus," I replied to his greeting.

He leaned over the back of the couch, kissed the top of Mahogany's head, and then palmed her belly. "What's good with you?"

"Hi, Tobias," she said, then pulled him down so she could kiss his lips. "Your food is on the stove."

"Y'all had a seafood boil?" he asked, even though he knew the answer. We nodded our heads, and he sucked his teeth. "Y'all gonna turn into a damn seafood boil."

"Whatever." She laughed and pushed him away. Focus stood up and chuckled. "How did the session go?" I loved how much he loved my friend and had no problem showing it. I always knew how they felt about each other; it was apparent by how they moved, but it wasn't until recently that they'd moved their relationship into something permanent. Not even a year later, they were expecting their first child, engaged, and Focus had recently brought her this house as a pre-wedding gift.

"It went good," he replied, leaving the living room and heading toward the kitchen. We both knew that he was going to come right back and sit under Mahogany. A few minutes later, with a bowl of food in his hand, he did exactly what I knew he would and sat under my friend. "So what y'all watching?"

"Scandal," we said at the same time.

"That show with the white dude and black lady?" he asked between bites. "That shit corny."

"You being a hater, Focus, and I don't like that for you." I laughed.

"Nah, for real, it's legit corny." He wiped his mouth with his napkin. "He a cheater, and she a clown."

"Lord Tobias." Mahogany laughed. "They were in love."

"And he had a wife."

"He couldn't just divorce her, though," I said, and he sucked his teeth. "He was the President."

"I don't give a fuck if that nigga was the damn President!" He laughed. "If anything, that nigga was the most powerful person in the world, yet he was treating the woman he was supposedly in love with like she wasn't shit. He was corny."

"You'll never understand how complicated their situation was." I laughed. "He loved her, but she loved him enough not to make his choose."

"Then she stupid." He shrugged. "A man in love will do whatever for his woman."

"Oh, is that why you have a dog named Kitten?" I asked, and Focus stared at me for a few seconds before sucking his teeth and then pushed off the couch. He left the living room, and Mahogany and I busted out laughing. "That man gonna kill me one day if I keep fuckin' with him like I do."

"Nah, I'll just do that thing with my tongue that he likes, and he'll be fine," Mahogany said with a shrug.

"That's how your ass got into the position you're in now." I laughed and got up from the couch. "Go tend to your man and enjoy your night. I'll call you later this week."

"Help me up before you leave." I did what she asked, then yelled to Focus that I was leaving.

"Ay," he said, coming back into the living room.

"What's up?"

"You comin' through Khrisen's new spot?"

"This weekend, right?" I confirmed, and he nodded. "I'll be there."

"Bet," he replied. "I'll have Ex pick you up; you don't gotta fight the traffic."

It wasn't abnormal for Exodus to pick me up when we were all out celebrating. Even though I wanted to tell him I could drive myself more, I had to play it cool and go with the flow. I bit into my bottom lip as I walked to my car. The thought of seeing Exodus in a few days had me hot and horny, and I prayed I could keep it cool when we did see each other.

CHAPTER 10

Exodus

"STOP CRYING and man the fuck up," I said as I sliced through Riley's torso. Bleed spilled from his wound, and I watched it drip to the floor.

"Please, man," Riley cried, and I shook my head. I hated criers. "I'll pay you whatever you want."

"It ain't even about the money, Riley." I patted him on his swollen cheek before pushing up from my seat. I'd been at the warehouse for nearly two hours and had been torturing Riley more than half of that time.

"What's it about then?" he asked. "Because I know that I ain't did shit."

"Yeah, you did." I laughed as I looked through the knives sitting on the table. The warehouse was like my playground. I could imagine everything in one of the many rooms around the building. I usually was a gun type of nigga. Without a second thought, I'd pop you right between the eyes and go on about my life. But sometimes I like to use a knife. It was more personal, left more damage, and inflicted the most pain. I picked up the ten-blade and returned to sit before him. "The day you walked your punk ass on the block, you decided it would be a good idea to shoot at my cousin."

"Who is your cousin?" Riley's head swayed from side to side, and his eyes barely focused on anything before he continued to look around.

"Corinthian, she owns the barber shop off Main."

"Man, I didn't do shit to that girl," Riley sneered. The look on his face let me know he plans to, though. "I just wanted to say hello and welcome to the neighborhood."

"How are you welcoming her to the neighborhood when she has been there for damn near four years, Riley?" I asked.

"Just being friendly." He shrugged. "That's all."

"Nah, that isn't all," I said, shaking my head. "I saw the footage of you stepping to my cousin and then coming back and busting out her windows that night." I stood up and walked around Riley, and shook my head. "The worst part of it all is the shit you did sounded like a scorn bitch move. My cousin told me you tried to talk to her, and she let you down gently, but you didn't like that shit. She said you got loud with her and then threatened to come back and beat her ass. That's why I broke your hands." I patted his severely broken right hand. "You gotta learn not to touch what's not yours."

"I'm sorry, man," he groaned. "I won't do it again."

"Oh, I know." I chuckled. "But I still have one more lesson to teach you. And that's about looking since you know not to touch." I stepped behind Riley and pulled his head back so he could look up at me. I intentionally left one side of his face untouched. "You're allowed to look all you want, just as long as it's not at my family." I flipped the ten-blade between my fingers and stabbed Riley in the eye.

"Ahhhh!" he screamed and thrashed around. I pulled the knife out, stuck my index finger into his cut eyeball, and pulled it out of his socket. "Ahhhhh!"

"Next time, you know better," I said, dropping the eyeball into his lap and leaving the room. His screams were silenced as soon as the door closed behind me.

"You're done in there?" my cousin Cross asked, coming out of the room she was working in.

"Yeah," I replied, looking at the clock on the wall above her door. "What time is your flight out?"

"Not until the morning," she replied with a shrug. "Why, what's up?"

"Want to roll with me to this party?" I asked, knowing that she would say no. Cross wasn't a party girl; she didn't even like being around people the majority of the time. The only time I saw her deal with them was when she was working, and if you saw Cross's little ass coming your way, then it wasn't a good thing. I had no problem admitting that Cross was likely the most dangerous of us all in a family of killers.

"Who is it for?" she questioned.

"Khrisen's opening a new club," I replied. We headed down the hallway toward the back, where the changing rooms were. "I don't plan on being there too long."

"Okay." She nodded. "Pick me up from my hotel in like two hours."

"Bet," I replied, then headed to change my clothes to head home and get ready.

———

"Subtle isn't in his vocabulary, is it?" Cross asked as we moved through the thick crowd. I shook my head as I looked around. I'd been here before tonight, so I knew my way around and guided Cross up the stairs and across the large room until we got to the VIP area. Without having to give my name, the security opened the door and let us in. Unlike the rest of the club, this section wasn't loud.

"What's good, Ex?" Focus said, walking over to me. He stopped mid-stride when he noticed Cross standing next to me. A big-ass smile spread across his face before he started walking again. When he was close enough, he pulled Cross into a big hug and spun her around. "What's good, girl?"

"Hey, Focus." Cross laughed as he sat her down.

"Nah, don't do no hey bullshit with me, man." He laughed and pulled her into another hug. "Yo' ass has been MIA for the last few years, and you just popping up like it's nothing. Where the fuck have you been at?"

"Around." She shrugged. "I heard you're about to have a baby and are engaged. Congratulations!"

"Appreciate it," he said, nodding. "As a matter of fact, you gotta meet her. I know y'all would hit off." Focus turned around and looked around the room before spotting Mahogany. Her back was to us, but there was no doubt it was her because of her big-ass ginger ponytail. "Ay, One." Mahogany looked over her shoulder at the sound of her nickname. "Come here real quick, baby. I want you to meet some-body." She got up from her seat and stepped around the table. I hadn't seen her in a few weeks, so seeing her slightly bigger stomach made me chuckle. "Stop laughing at my woman, Ex."

"Man, you know I love my best friend," I replied.

"One, this is Cross, Ex's little cousin," Focus said as soon as she was next to him. "Cross, this is my woman, Mahogany."

"Hey, Mahogany," Cross said, pulling before they hugged each other. Focus's face twisted like he was confused, and I shook my head. This nigga was so damn slow at times. I'd been friends with Mahogany for damn near ten years and considered her my best friend, so why wouldn't I have introduced her to my cousin.

"Y'all know each other?" Focus asked once they let each other go.

"Met years ago, baby." Mahogany laughed and shook her head. "You weren't watching then?"

"Nah, if you were with Ex, I knew you were cool." He laughed. "But we are about to head out. We just popped in to show support."

"He finally locked her down, huh?" Cross asked after the couple left. I nodded my head as I checked my phone. The payment for Pauly had come through, but it was short. I shook my head; playing with my money was a dangerous game that no one lived to talk about. "Oh, is that the girl Krude swears he's going to marry?"

"Who?" I asked, looking up from my phone.

"Her over there in the yellow." Cross nodded. I looked at the corner to see Krude laughing and smiling in Paxton's face. Immediately, my body got hot, and all I saw was red. Krude bent down to whisper something in her ear, and Paxton bit into her bottom lip and shook her head. This fool was flirting with my girl like I wouldn't kill him. It didn't matter if we were family; he was the opp right now. "They look cute together."

I made my way over to the pair in ten long strides. Without thinking, I grabbed Paxton by her arm and pulled her toward the exit.

"What the fuck are you doing, Exodus?" Paxton fussed as she tried to pull her arm from my grasp. I knew that private bathrooms off the VIP section were only accessible with keycards or if you knew the code. I walked to the one furthest from the room and entered the code to unlock the door.

"You got me completely fucked up," I told Paxton as I pushed her into the bathroom. I locked the door behind me and then leaned against it. "You're serious right now?"

"What the fuck are you talking about, Exodus?" she questioned with an attitude. "And why the fuck did you drag me out of there like you are crazy."

"Check your fuckin' attitude right now, Paxton," I replied with a humorless laugh. I pinched the bridge of my nose as I tried to control my temper. Why the fuck was I so upset was beyond me, but I know for a fact that seeing her smiling in Krude's face did something to me.

"No, you check your fuckin' attitude!" she yelled. "Matter of fact, move the fuck outta my way so I can go back to the party." She tried to push me out of the way, but I wasn't budging from my spot until I was ready. "Move!"

"Ay, you funny as fuck." I shook my head. Up close, the halter-top yellow dress that she had on had me ready to rip it the fuck off her. Her sexy ass was standing in front of me, pissed the fuck off and looking fine as fuck as my dick bricking up.

"What the fuck are you trippin' off, Exodus?"

"Stop talkin' to me." I stepped into her face. I wanted so damn bad to kiss her ass right now that it was crazy.

"Are you serious?" She laughed and shook her head. "Get the fuck outta my way."

I picked her ass up easily, sat her on the countertop, and crashed my mouth into hers. As we fought for control, I stepped in between her legs. I could feel the warmth of her pussy through my pants. Using my left hand,

I reached between her thighs and touched her bare pussy, causing her to groan. I pushed inside her, loving the warmth that welcomed my fingers, yet hating that it was just my fingers simultaneously. I pressed my thumb against her clit, and Paxton dropped her head back against the glass.

"Shit!" she moaned as I worked her over. The look of pleasure that swept across her face almost had me about to bust in my damn pants. I buried my face into her neck, kissing and biting on her as I worked my fingers inside her. "Ohhhhh!"

"Scream my fuckin' name," I said into her ear before I bit into her lobe. "Yell that shit!" Her body started shaking, and I knew her orgasm was close. I lifted my head and looked down at her. "Say my fuckin' name, Paxton." I wanted her to say that shit, scream it at the top of her lungs as I made her cum, but she refused. I wrapped my free hand around her neck. "Be a good girl and tell me what I wanna hear, Paxton."

"Nooooo," she moaned, and I chuckled.

Cool, she wanted to play games, then I'd show her who the fuck she was dealing with. Just as her orgasm started to peak and her body started to shake uncontrollably, I pulled my hand from her pussy and stepped back.

"What are you doing?"

"Heading out," I replied as I stepped to the side and washed my hands in the sink. Without looking at her, I cut off the water, dried my hands, and unlocked the bathroom door.

"Exodus!" she yelled as I stepped out. "Are you fucking serious!"

I was serious as fuck. She put me out after fuckin' talking about how she didn't do sleepovers. Then had the nerve to sit in this mutha-fucka and smile up in my cousin's face like that shit was cool. When I pulled her into the bathroom, I didn't intend to finger her, but she looked too damn good, and I was heated, but the only thing I wanted to see was her face as she came again. I had every intention of doing that, but she wouldn't say my name, which pissed me off. Now her ass could sit in this damn club and be horny and know that her pussy would be calling out to me for the rest of the night. And I'm not gonna lie; if she walked out this bitch and found another nigga to handle that shit, I would kill his ass.

CHAPTER 11

Paxton

"I'M GONNA KILL HIS ASS," I mumbled as I returned to the VIP section. When Exodus pulled me into the bathroom earlier, I knew I would hear his mouth about how I put him out a few nights ago. I was prepared for the hostility of tossing a man to the side after sex. I wasn't prepared for him touching me, nor how my body would respond. His putting me on that countertop, kissing and biting my neck while fingering me, was my peace of heaven on earth. Exodus snatched his hand out of my panties just as I was about to cum and smiled over at me. My mouth hung open as I watched him wash his hands and stroll out of the bathroom as if I was sitting here, ready to tear up this entire club.

I pushed open the door and looked around. Khrisen, Six, and December stood near the bar, talking and laughing. Baby, Monica, Macole, and Langston Eaton sat together, talking. My eyes landed on Krude, seated beside the woman I'd seen walk in with Ex and the man himself. Krude leaned over and whispered something into the woman's ear, and she looked at me and then back at Exodus with a blank expression. I wanted to go off, needed to go off, but something inside of me told me not to. Instead, I headed over to the bar and ordered a drink.

"You look like you're plotting to take over the world," Six said, standing beside me. I thanked the bartender and then turned to face her.

"Nah, just get some revenge," I replied, then sipped my drink.

"Anything you need help with?" Six asked.

"Nope." I laughed. "This one is personal."

"Let me know if you change your mind," Six said, and I nodded.

My eyes found Exodus again, and he lifted his drink in acknowledgment, and I found myself doing the same. This nigga had just taunted the wrong damn one. For the rest of the night, I kicked it with Six and December; finding out they had been secretly married for the last two years had blown my mind. But I understood why they kept it to themselves. December, just like Focus, never wanted his past to catch up with him and put the woman he loved in danger. Unlike Focus, though, that didn't stop December from claiming her. If anything, it made him want her more, and he'd locked her down the second he got the chance.

I kicked it with Six and December for the rest of the night. Every so often, my eyes would find Exodus, and like the first time, he would lift his drink in acknowledgment, but that was it. My poor little pussy was still throbbing, and no matter what I did or how I moved, the feeling didn't go away. Instead of letting frustration get the best of me, I decided to get up and dance. The VIP had its dance floor, but I wanted to get out from the watchful flare of Exodus, so I decided to go out on the dance floor. I let Six know where I was heading, grabbed my drink from the bar, and headed out.

The music was loud but not overbearing to the point that it would give someone a headache. Once downstairs, I finished my drink and set the empty glass on a table as I passed it. Latto's "Big Dick Energy" was playing, and the crowd loved it. I grabbed the first man to approach me and threw my ass back on him. Between the music and the liquor, I was enjoying myself, and the man I was dancing with could keep up. I looked over my shoulder to get a better look at him and was pleasantly surprised.

"Yo, let me holla at you real quick," he whispered, and I nodded.

We stepped to the side into one of the small VIP suites that encased the dance floor. "What's yo' name, Mama?"

"Paxton," I answered, looking him up and down. He stood tall, probably pushing six-two, skinny but built enough that he looked like he could handle the ride I wanted to put on him. Dark but beautiful skin, plump lips, goatee, thick flared nose, dark eyes, and thick eyebrows. His hair was cut short into a tapered fade, and he had waves for days. He was dressed in a chocolate suit with a stark white button-down, and his shoes were the same color as his suit. A gold cross hung around his neck, and when he flashed me a quick smile, I could see a few gold teeth. "You?"

"Qumar," he replied with a deep voice. Now that we were close and the music wasn't as loud, I could hear a slight accent coming through. "My boys call me Mari, though."

"Oh really?" I replied with a smirk of my own. "And what's our woman call you?"

"Daddy," he replied and flashed another smile. "But I don't have a woman." He looked me up and down and licked his plump lips. "Just yet." He pulled his phone out of his pocket, scrolled through it, and handed it to me. "Put your number in here so you can hit me when you are ready to go, and I can get you home."

"I have a ride," I said, then took his phone. "But I'll hit you up sometime this week."

"That's a promise?" he asked, looking me up and down again. I didn't miss his hungry look, and it was well appreciated.

"It's the best I can do," I answered, and Qumar nodded. "Now, let's get back to the dance floor. I have some frustration to work off."

"Something I can help you with?" he asked, and I shook my head. Just because I was annoyed with Exodus didn't mean I had to put Qumar's life in jeopardy. Mahogany wasn't here to calm him down if he snapped.

We went back out to the dance floor and continued dancing. We danced to a few more songs, laughed, and enjoyed ourselves. Qumar had a small crew with him, none I'd ever seen before, but that wasn't my business. We were good as long as he didn't show his ass with anyone I knew.

"Looks like we have an audience," Qumar said when I turned around to face him. I looked up at him, slightly confused, and he nodded toward the other side of the dance floor. I turned around to see Exodus standing with a mug on his face. I threw him a little wave, then crossed my arms over my chest. He stepped toward us, but the woman I'd seen him and Krude talking to stepped around him and blocked his path. She said something to him; he nodded his head and turned to walk away. She turned to look at me again; a slight smirk played on her lips before she threw me a wave and followed behind him. "You know them?"

"Him," I answered with a nod of my head. I turned back to Qumar to see him staring at me, then he licked his lips. "You asked me about a woman, but I never asked about a man."

"I know," I said, nodding my head. Qumar stared down at me briefly before chuckling and shaking his head. The next song started, and the crowd began to rock to the beat. "Are we dancing, or are you gonna stare me down?"

"I got all kinds of plans for you, just know that," Qumar said, then started moving to the beat. I turned around, giving him my ass to grind on, and shook my head. I didn't give a damn about Exodus and how pissed he looked as I enjoyed my time with Qumar.

CHAPTER 12

Exodus

"TWO DAMN MINUTES," Focus fussed as he moved around the damn kitchen. This fool was so damn stressed that I could only laugh. "That's what the fuck I asked for. Two. Minutes."

"That was fifteen minutes ago!" Krude yelled from the other side of the kitchen. He had a big-ass spoon in one hand and a plate in the other. "I told you I wasn't patient! You know that! Why the fuck do you keep having me wait!"

"The food wasn't ready!" Focus fussed. He ran his hand down his face and shook his head. I kept rolling my blunt, letting these fools go back and forth because it's what they did anytime they were together. "I told you it wasn't ready!"

"Why doesn't he just shoot him at this point?" Monica asked from her spot next to Baby. I looked up and shrugged before trying to hold back my laughter. Monica's ass was always trying to shoot some-damn-body and being pregnant wasn't helping her trigger finger not to itch. "Like just give him a flesh wound, nothing too serious."

"Been there. Did that shit," Focus replied as he moved around the kitchen, trying to see what exactly Krude fucked up because knowing my cousin, he was going to fuck up a lot of shit. "At least three times at this point."

"You aren't hitting anything vital then," Monica said, and I had to look over at Baby to make sure that he didn't have any new wounds. "Pop his kneecaps or elbows, and I bet he stops with his shit."

"Let me go find my woman cuz you not about to threaten shit on my ass," Krude said, looking Monica up and down. He threw the plate and spoon on the counter, stormed his tall ass to the door frame, and looked around without walking about the kitchen. "Megan, that dread head girl in here talkin' about shooting me!"

"I'll give her a thousand dollars if she does it!" Megan yelled back, and Monica started to get up from her seat. Baby grabbed her wrist and shook his head no. "Let me come talk to my new best friend!"

"Baby girl, don't get in their shit," he said softly, like he didn't want to start up with Krude. "They crazy as fuck, and we don't need them thinking we agree with their shit, or they'll start coming over."

"What?" Monica said, looking back and forth between Krude and Baby. "Why the fuck would they think that?"

"Cuz he's slow as fuck and doesn't realize we only tolerate him because of Ex," Baby replied with a chuckle.

"Oh damn, she's fine," Megan said, walking into the room. I knew this shit was about to get funny because Megan and Krude fed off each other. While Megan was mainly chill and laid back, something about her being with my cousin pulled out her playful side. When I first met Megan, I was impressed not only with her looks because she was a beautiful woman but also with her attitude and personality. She was an openly bisexual Stem who was comfortable in either look. How Krude had locked her down is still a mystery to me and everyone around him, but he did, and I could honestly say that she brought out the best in him, even though he was dumb as hell.

"Mama, I'll shoot you over that one, and you know it," Baby said, looking at Megan with a smirk.

"I don't want her, but I can appreciate and give props," Megan said, entering the room. She sat down across from Monica and gave her a friendly smile. "Now, about this business arrangement, you were just offering. What's your price?"

"I'm calling my grandma because, Megan, you got me fucked up,"

Krude said, storming out of the kitchen. We all laughed, and Megan stood with a big smile from the table.

"Thank you for your services," Megan said, then dropped a stack on the table.

"You paid for something I didn't do?" Monica said, looking at the money and then back at Megan.

"You stressed him out; that was all I needed," Megan said, leaving the room.

"You pick that money up, and she'll call you later for drinks," Baby said, and Monica shrugged her shoulders.

"Shit, I'm gonna order something cuz this fool fucked up everything," Focus fussed from the other side of the kitchen. "Muthafucka had to use one fuckin' spoon to look through it all. I hate yo' cousin."

"Get in line." I laughed, then lit my blunt and took a pull. "Why the fuck do you think that clown isn't invited to shit? He is going to be on time, probably early, fuck shit up and then get mad when ain't nothing right. The fact that Megan is with his ass is a blessing because she keeps him under control."

"That's under control?" Monica questioned, and everyone in the room nodded.

"That's the best we gonna get." I laughed.

"One gonna come in here fussing, and if she starts crying, I swear I'ma hang his ass off the balcony by his ankles," Focus said as he started to clean up.

"Where she at anyway?" I asked, looking around for her. I'd been here long enough to know that if Mahogany were in the house, she would've come out of whatever corner she was hiding in to bother me.

"Took Kitten to the vet," he answered. The fact that she had talked that nigga into naming the dog Kitten was still comical to me. But niggas did what their girl wanted when they were in love. "She and Paxton should be pulling up in the next few minutes. Lennox texted me saying they were less than five minutes away."

The mention of Paxton's name had my dick bricking up. She was still in my system after a few days, and that shit kind of pissed me off. I went back to smoking while Focus ordered food to feed everyone, and Baby and Monica sat at the table talking. She was reviewing a website, showing him how she had fixed stuff and improved the overall look. My phone rang, and seeing Nine's name on my screen pulled me from my seat. I threw Focus a quick nod toward the backyard to let him know where I was going and stepped out.

"What's good?" I answered as I closed the door behind me.

"I got that information you asked me to find," he said. "The shooting happened close to midtown, off Linwood and thirty-first."

"Any idea who it was?" I asked.

"Nah," Nine answered. I shook my head. My nigga was good, but he wasn't a miracle worker. "It looks like it's some security cameras in that area that I'm trying to get into, but that shit ain't making sense."

"What do you mean?"

"The shit too high-tech for a pawnshop," he said, and I nodded. "But that makes it more interesting for me. I like a good challenge."

"Hold off on getting too far into it," I said. I knew that area, knew a bitch that worked at the pawnshop, and would let me see the footage without thinking twice about it.

"You sure?" he questioned, and I could hear the disappointment in his voice. Nine liked shit like this, so he was always behind some computer. Nigga could probably work for the government with how good he was at hacking shit, but the money from the streets was always better. Plus, he liked outsmarting the government too damn much to work for them. "Cuz I'll have the information for you in less than ten minutes."

"Positive," I replied. I looked up to see Paxton walk into the kitchen. She wore stone-washed jeans ripped at the knee, a loose white tee tucked in the front, and some sandals. Her hair was pulled into a big-ass ponytail on the top of her head, and dark sunglasses on her face. Somebody said something, and her glossy lips broke into a big smile, and she threw her head back, exposing her neck that had my mouth watering.

"Did you hear me?" Nine shouted, pulling me out of the trance Paxton had me in.

"Nah, what you say?" I wiped my hand over my mouth and beard and shook my head.

"Nothing." He laughed like he knew something I didn't. "Hit me up if you change your mind."

"Bet," I said, then hung up. After stuffing my phone in my pocket, I stepped back through the house's back door and looked around. Mahogany looked up from her phone and smiled at me. "What's good?"

"I didn't know you were here," she said, coming around the island to hug me. I quickly kissed her forehead and hugged her before she returned to stand next to Focus, looking over his phone and shaking his head. "How long have you been here?"

"Long enough to know my cousin won't be invited again," I answered with a laugh. I looked over at Paxton, who looked at her phone with a sly smile. That shit pissed me off because who the fuck had her smiling and shit. But instead of saying anything, I ran my tongue over my teeth and turned my attention back to Mahogany, who was looking at me through narrowed eyes. I flashed her a quick smile, but she smirked before giving me her back. I couldn't hear her, but I could tell from the way Focus's head popped up, and he looked at me and then back at her that she'd said something.

I didn't want to give her shit else to talk about, so I sat back down at the island and rolled another blunt. We wouldn't smoke now that she was home, but it gave me something to do while we waited to eat.

"I'm about to head out," Paxton said from behind me.

"Where are you going?" Focus asked her. They had a cool relationship; he treated her like a little sister, and she bothered him like she was.

"On a date," Paxton answered, and my face twisted up like I smelled something funky. Who the fuck did she think she was going on a date with? I looked up from the blunt I was rolling and smirked. That shit wasn't about to happen.

"With whom?" Focus asked with a laugh. "That nigga you were dancing with at the club?" That was another thing that pissed me the fuck off. Seeing her throwing her ass on another nigga had me ready to end his ass. If it weren't for Cross telling me she needed help with something, I would've ended Khrisen's club on opening night and not give a fuck.

"Maybe." She laughed. "But that's not your business now, is it?"

"Get that nigga killed." Focus laughed, then knocked twice on the island. "Two to the dome without a second thought."

"Leave her alone." Mahogany laughed as she jumped into the conversation. "Enjoy yourself, Paxton, and call me later."

"Will do," she said. They exchanged quick hugs, and then Paxton was gone. I grabbed my phone and texted Nine, letting him know I needed a location for Paxton for the rest of the night. He replied with a question mark, but I ignored that shit. I didn't need that nigga questioning me. I sent him the fee he changed for work and put my phone away.

I looked up to see Focus staring at me with a smirk. My nigga may not have opened his mouth to ask me what the fuck I was up to, but his facial expression did. I shrugged my shoulders, then went back to rolling blunts. I didn't know what the fuck I was up to, nor did I have a plan, but that date shit was out the window.

CHAPTER 13
Paxton

THREE HOURS LATER, I stepped out of my house dressed in a fitted red maxi dress and heels, ready to enjoy my night. Qumar and I had been texting each other throughout the past few days. I explained to him I wasn't always available because my brother was in the hospital and running a company, and he seemed to understand and accepted the time I could give him. When he'd asked me on a date for this evening, I had hesitated to accept, but I thought it over and decided a night out wouldn't hurt me.

"How are you doing?" I asked my mama as I drove to the restaurant. I knew she was tired; she was running on fumes between running back and forth to the hospital and trying to take her off her and Daddy. "You need me to bring you back anything when I come up there?"

"No, Paxton," she sighed, and I rolled my eyes. Mama wouldn't let anyone else take care of her, but that didn't stop me from trying. "Where are you headed?"

"On a date," I answered, and I felt slightly guilty. My brother was laid up in the hospital, and I was going to live my life. I knew Naeem would want nothing but the best for me and wouldn't want me sitting at the hospital all day and night, but that didn't take away from the guilt.

"Oh good," she said. "Please enjoy yourself."

"I'm going to try," I said as I approached the restaurant. I'd never been to Indigo, and while I'd heard nothing but good reviews about the food, I had no desire to go either. Even though I was hood, raised in it, and enjoyed it, I didn't particularly appreciate being placed in situations I couldn't control. Indigo was known around the city for its wild nights and unruly crowds. It was the place you went to when you needed to drop a nigga or bitch without worrying about who saw you. "I'll call you when I leave here."

"All right. Love you."

"Love you more, Mama." I hung up and parked my car. Without thinking twice, I patted my thigh to ensure my gun was there since I still hadn't gotten my other one back from Exodus and got out. When I pulled open the heavy wood door to Indigo, I instantly knew I fucked up, and this wasn't a place for me. I looked around the whole area, not seeing Qumar, and decided to walk back out.

"Damn, you just gonna roll like that?" Qumar called out. I saw him walking out of the building from my door. Today, he wore black slacks with a matching vest and tie. His gray button-up sleeves were rolled up to his elbow, and just like the first night I'd met him, he wore a gold cross around his neck. "You couldn't wait for me to step to you?"

"I looked around but didn't see you," I said, shrugging.

"I was in the back working," he said, and it took me a few seconds to realize what he meant. He owned this place, which would explain why he was dressed the way he was. "We were swamped for a little while, so I lent a hand to help. I was in my office when I saw you pull up."

"How did you know it was me?" I asked.

"I didn't know at first, and then I saw you get out of the car, and even though I didn't see your face at first, I'd know that body from anywhere." He looked me up and down from over the hood of my car, and goosebumps appeared on my arms when he smiled at me. "You hungry?"

"I can eat." I nodded. I rounded my car, and he took my hand in his. We walked back to the door, and he pulled it open. This time, the small crowd that was initially by the door was seated. He gave a quick nod to the hostesses, and we made our way through the dining room. People called out his name, and Qumar gave a few head nods or waves, but we didn't stop moving until we were in the back. He pulled open the frosted glass door, and we entered a small dining room. The glass table was set, and a bouquet of roses was placed in front of one of the chairs. "You did all this?"

"Yeah," he said, letting go of my hand and walking over to the table. I expected him to pull out his chair and sit down, but instead, he pulled the chair behind the roses. "Have a seat."

"You're a gentleman," I said, laughing slightly, and he nodded. "I like that."

"For real?" he asked after sitting down. He shook his head and smiled. "If I knew that, I would've pulled out all the stops."

"What do you mean?" I asked.

"I would've picked you up, drove us somewhere that didn't have my name attached to the deeded, bought you flowers, had a candle-lit dinner, then wined and dined you." Qumar smiled, and I waited for the bomb to drop. He was almost too smooth, and I'd dealt with enough smooth men to know one when I saw one. "So, tell me about yourself."

"What do you want to know?" I countered. Giving my personal information wasn't something I often did. I'd been scorned one too many times in the past. Our server arrived, set a few appetizers and plates, and quickly left the room.

"Whatever you want to tell me." He shrugged, and I playfully rolled my eyes.

"Sir!" one of Qumar's employees said, entering the dining room. He was young, no older than eighteen, and looked scared. His eyes looked like they were about to pop out of his head, and he kept pointing to the door. Surprisingly, he looked exactly like Qumar, which made me wonder if they were brothers or cousins because their relationship was apparent. "It's an umm, an ummm."

"A what, Quinn?" Qumar stood up on full alert.

"A fire!" he yelled. "In your office, and the bathrooms, and storage room!"

"Shit!" Qumar took off toward what I assumed was where the fire was, and I sat back in my seat. Even though I was interested in what was happening, it wasn't my business, and I had to let that man take care of his building. A few minutes later, I looked up at the sound of the door opening. I expected to see Qumar returning, but it was Exodus with a mug on his face, a gasoline jug in one hand, and a blow-torch in the other.

"What's up?" he asked casually as he set everything on the table and sat in Qumar's seat. Without a care, he picked up the menu off the table and looked it over. "What are you thinking about getting?"

"What?" I question, dumbfounded because what the entire fuck?

"Food wise." He peeked over the menu at me and shook his head like I was the slow one here. "I'm thinking of getting some ribs, they sound good as fuck, but then again, the seafood alfredo sounds good as fuck too. I'on eat crawfish, though, so I pick them out; you gonna eat them?"

"What?"

"Ay." He sucked his teeth and set the menu down. "You're not slow, so stop acting like it. I asked what you were getting to eat. I know you ain't ate yet because Mahogany told Focus that y'all didn't eat while y'all was out. So, pick what you want to eat. If you aren't sure, say that, and I'll order something for you."

"Ex-o-dus," I said, breaking his name into syllables to know he was listening to me. "What the entire fuck did you do?"

"Nothing." He shrugged. "I'm just waiting for you to pick out what you want to eat so we can order."

"Did you set some of his business on fire?" I questioned, and all he did was stare at me. Every few seconds, he would blink, but no words came out of his mouth. "Why the fuck did you do that?"

"Why are you out on a date with him?" he countered, and now it was my turn to be stuck and stare at him. "Hello? I know you hear me talking."

"What is your problem?" I jumped up from the table, and Exodus had the nerve to stare at me like he was bored with the entire conversa-tion. I started to laugh and shake my head. "You set his damn building on fire for what reason?"

"I'on share Paxton," he said with a shrug. "Like at all. I haven't ever been a nigga that liked to share, which is probably why I'm an only child. Them niggas must've looked at me and was like, nope, this is it. One and done."

"What does that have to do with me?"

"You," he said as he grabbed an egg roll off one of the plates in the middle of the table. He took a bite of it and nodded his head in appreciation. "You were just on my dick the other day; my face was in your pussy. My fingers had yo' ass ready to scream for your life, but you were being stubborn as fuck. I got plans to repeat that shit later but I'on share." He shrugged his large shoulders like what he said didn't already have my pussy tingling at the thought of what he'd done to my body. "The minute I decided you were mine, the rest of these niggas were supposed to be dismissed."

"Yours?" I laughed and shook my head. "Exodus, we fucked, one time, and that's it. I am not yours. You are not mine."

"We go together." He reared back in his seat and mugged me.

"No, we don't!" I laughed again. "We. Fucked. One. Time."

"Oh, for real?" he questioned and nodded. I expected him to start showing his ass, but instead, he took a few more bites of his egg roll, finished it, then stood up from the table. He dropped two hundred dollars on the table, grabbed his blow torch and gas jug from the table, and walked out of the room. I dropped in the seat and ran my hand over my face, confused as hell as to what he was talking about and why he thought we were together. We'd done a quick fuck, well, it wasn't fast, but it wasn't anything permanent. We were grown. I thought he could handle something with no strings, but obviously, he couldn't.

"All right, so look," Exodus said, barging back into the dining room. Qumar stood in front of him, looking pissed the fuck off. I'd seen niggas be so scared they were pissing themselves when a gun was pulled, but Qumar didn't. If anything, he looked like he would get Exodus back if he didn't kill his ass for doing this shit. The fact that Qumar wasn't afraid was a plus in my book. "You got two options. You can either tell this nigga you are taken, and we go home, I eat your pussy until you aren't mad at me. Or you don't; I kill this nigga, and then we go home, and I fuck you till you forgive me."

"Or option three, you leave us be," I said, shaking my head. "We are not together, Exodus."

"Yes, we are, Paxton," he argued with me. Exodus was calm as hell, which I knew meant he didn't give a fuck about what I was talking about. He had his mind set on me leaving with him, and my dumb ass was thinking about it. "Now, if you don't want me to merk this nigga, get yo' fine ass up, and let's go." I could see from where I sat that his safety was off.

"Fine." I sighed and stood. Qumar looked ready to blow, but I wasn't worried about him being upset. I saved his life; he could live to be mad another day. "Now, let's go."

"Walk ahead of me so I know you not gonna change your mind once I let this nigga go," Exodus said, shaking his head. I moved from the table, grabbed my purse, keys, and phone, and headed toward the door. "Give me a kiss real quick."

"What?" I cut my eyes at him.

"A kiss." He smirked, and I kept walking. This nigga was crazy as fuck.

CHAPTER 14

Exodus

"MY NIGGA, LISTEN," I said once Paxton closed the door to the room. Through the frosted glass, I watched her fine ass walk through the larger dining hall and out the door. "This shit wasn't personal at all. She endangered your life because she was stubborn." I pushed him away from me and shook my head. "But Paxton's taken, like for real, taken no bullshit."

"Do you know who I am?" he said, turning around to face me. I looked him up and down, not giving a fuck about what he was talking about. I hated when niggas did that whole 'do you know who I am' shit. Like nigga, I don't give a fuck who you are, obviously, or I'd know your damn name. "By the time you walk about this fuckin' building, your entire family will be dead."

"Oh really?" I chuckled and shook my head. "You want their names, or you gonna have somebody go and find them?"

"Don't worry about it," he said, pulling down his vest to straighten it. "Just know that I'm coming for you, them, and then making Paxton mine."

"Oh, word?" I laughed and shook my head. "Bet." I took my phone out of my pocket and dialed a number.

"Yeah?" Kino, my cleaner, greeted me. "What you got for me?"

"Entire building clean up," I said, mugging the shit out of this weak-ass nigga. He stood across from me, running his tongue over his teeth and mugging me. I took the phone from my ear so Kino didn't think I was talking to him. "Ay, nigga, what's your name?"

"Qumar," he replied with a smirk as if that shit meant something to me. I waved my hand to show him I needed more information than that. "Moore. Qumar Moore."

"Bet." I nodded, then returned the phone to my ear. "And after the cleanup, get me everybody in Qumar Moore's family. I want this nigga to have a family reunion." I hung up with Kino without needing to give him any further instructions and turned my attention back to Qumar. "You Muslim?"

"What?" He twisted his face up like he smelled something bad. "Nigga, what the fuck does that have to do with anything?"

"Just like making small talk sometimes." I shrugged, then stuffed my phone back in my pocket. "I don't want to disrespect anybody's faith and shit."

"Yeah, nigga, I'm Muslim." He chuckled. "Why?"

"No prayer for you is all." I shot him twice in the head. His body hit the ground, and I shrugged. My granddaddy always said to respect a man's faith because that's all he has sometimes. Qumar didn't have his life, but he could have his faith in death.

I made my way out of the room. The restaurant had cleared out when I set fire to his office. Initially, I did that shit just in there, but then I had to pee and thought, why the fuck not? Let me add a little razzle-dazzle to my shit and set the bathroom on fire too. The little nigga that found the fire was panicking and shit like it was a big-ass fire, and it wasn't. All he would have had to do was get the fire extinguisher and put them out, but he was running around like a damn chicken with its head cut off. Before I grabbed Qumar, I popped his ass to shut him up.

When I got outside, Paxton was sitting in her car, on the phone, yelling at somebody. I shook my head and made my way over to her. I tapped lightly on her window with my gun and stared at her. "Open the window."

"What?" she fussed as soon as the window was down. I could hear

Mahogany and Focus laughing through the speakers. "What do you want now?"

"Yo' spot or mine?" I casually asked, smirking at her. The sight of her pissed the fuck off turned me on. If she was mad, then that meant her ass cared. "I'm kind of hungry though, so if you have food at your house, then we can go there cuz ain't shit at mine." Focus and Mahogany laughed harder, which seemed to piss her off more.

"You can starve for all I care," she snarled, and I was legit taken aback because why the fuck did she have an attitude with me for? I was trying to be a good nigga and make sure she ate after being out with this fuck nigga, and she was mad.

"Ay, chill with that shit, Hitta." I chuckled and shook my head. "Get out so we can go. We can decide where we are going on the way." I reached over and grabbed her door handle and tried to pull it open, but the door was locked. "Unlock the door."

"Get away from my car." She sighed and shook her head. "I'm not doing this with you today."

"I'on think you understand how this relationship shit works," I said, shaking my head. "We go together." I waved my gun between us, and Paxton rolled her eyes. "You like my girlfriend, and I'm yo' nigga. We spend time together. We go on dates. Spend the night at each other house. Cook and eat together, and we fuck." I shook my head. "We don't make love or have sex cuz that shit isn't what we do. We fuck. Like straight nasty, sweaty, you'll probably end up pregnant with the type of fuckin, but it's cool cuz we both fine as fuck, and our kids will be fine too."

"Oh shit." Mahogany's voice rang out through the speakers. I'd completely forgotten about her being on the phone, but I didn't give a fuck. Mahogany was both our best friends. She was going to be our baby's godmama. "Tobias, go get Exodus!"

"Hang up on her ass." I waved off Mahogany's dramatic ass. "Matter of fact, I'll do it." I reached through the window and pressed the end button on the steering wheel to hang up on her. "Now, back to us." I sighed and shook my head. "Get out of the car. I'll drive and have one of Kino's people bring your car."

"Who the hell is Kino?" she asked, and I sucked my teeth. She didn't know Qumar was dead, and now I had to tell her. I wiped my hand over my mouth and then smiled at her. "Oh no, don't give me that damn smile. Who the hell is Kino, and why will he be here?"

"I killed Qumar," I mumbled, causing her to throw her hands in the air. "Shit wasn't my fault, though."

"Whose fault was it then, Exodus?" she yelled, and I took a step back because I didn't like that shit. She wasn't about to yell at me and think I would take it. I unlocked my truck doors, but the sound of her car door slamming made me turn around. Paxton was headed back to Indigo's, and I let her stubborn ass. She opened the door, stomped inside, and I walked to her car. Without shame or care, I pulled my knife out of my pocket and stabbed three of her four tires. Since we were in a relationship now, I knew I would have to replace them, but oh damn well.

"You find what you were looking for?" I asked once she was back outside. Her face was void of all emotion, but I could see a little spark in her eyes. Her ass liked the crazy side of me that would just do what the fuck I wanted. I leaned out of my driver's window and smirked at her. "You ready to go?"

"I'm not going with you!" she shook her head. Paxton stopped dead at the sight of her car sitting on three flats. She cut her eyes at me, and I shrugged. I exited my truck, rounded it, and opened the passenger door.

"Get yo' shit so we can go," I told her. I watched her shoulders drop just slightly before she went to get the car. A part of me wondered if she'd tried to drive it on flats, and while that shit would be funny as fuck, it would piss me off. Why the fuck she was being so stubborn was beyond me, but she was. Paxton started up her car, and I sucked my teeth. Instead of being crazy, she rolled up her window, cut the car off, snatched her purse and shit out of it, and slammed the door.

"You're replacing all my tires!" she fussed as she stomped to my truck. I tried to help her inside, but she snatched her hand from me, and I shook my head. She quickly put on her seatbelt, put her purse in her lap, and crossed her arms over her chest. She wouldn't look at me, but I didn't give a fuck; I stepped closer and buried my face into her neck. I felt her shiver when I kissed and bit her neck. "Get off me."

"Hitta." I chuckled as I pulled back from her. "You are too fuckin' fine; you know that?" I kissed her cheek, then stepped back and closed the door. I returned behind the wheel and pulled off just as Kino and his people pulled up. We exchanged a quick nod as we passed each other. "You like chocolate?"

"No," she mumbled with an attitude. I shrugged and kept driving. My left hand on the wheel and my right on her thigh. I made lazy circles on her thigh with my index finger as I drove. I didn't have a destination in mind, but it didn't matter because I had Paxton by my side.

CHAPTER 15

Paxton

"SO, you just gonna sit over there with an attitude?" Exodus asked me for what felt like the millionth time. We'd been riding around the city for damn near an hour just listening to music. He'd stopped a little bit ago and grabbed some wings from a small hole in the wall off Main. They smelled so damn good, but I wasn't about to budge and eat because I knew it wouldn't do anything but encourage his behavior. "Cool with me." I could see him shrug and bite a fry out of the corner of my eye. "We gotta make a quick stop."

"Just take me home, Exodus," I sighed and shook my head. "I'm not in the mood for your crazy shit."

"Later," he replied as he kept driving. We ended up stopping at a preschool, and he parked the truck. I cut my eyes at him but didn't say anything. "I gotta pick up somebody." He turned the truck off, removed the ignition's keys, and hopped out. With ease, he walked his bowlegged ass to the school's front door and rang the bell. Even though I was in the truck, I could hear the buzzer that unlocked the door sound, and a few seconds later, Exodus pulled the door open and walked in. Once he was out of sight, I pulled my phone out of my purse and called Mahogany.

"Hello?" she answered, sounding like she was sleeping.

"You're sleeping while your best friend fuckin' kidnapped me?" I fussed. I kept my eyes on the door to ensure I didn't get caught on the phone. I wasn't kidnapped, but Mahogany didn't know that. She knew Exodus was crazy and had even warned me a few times, but I didn't believe her.

"What?" She giggled like the shit was funny. "That man did not kidnap you."

"I'm sitting in his truck in front of a daycare because he killed my damn date and flattened my tires."

"How did he flatten your tires?" she said, concerned.

"Mahogany!" I yelled. "How the hell are you worried about him flatting my tires and not that we are in front of a damn preschool or that he killed someone?"

"Because he's probably just picking up Judah," she sighed. "And we both know we are used to him killing people. Let's not act brand new to the kind of man he is."

"Mahogany," I groaned, dropped back in my seat, and covered my eyes. "This man is a psycho, and you are just chatting it up like this is normal."

"Because it is." She laughed again. "Wasn't it you that said not too long ago that you wished you fell in love with a man like Exodus? Well, before you fall in love, you have to date him."

"I'm not dating him!"

"Girl, yes, you are," she replied. "If he is picking up Judah from school, then you are dating him because nobody meets Judah unless it's serious."

"Who is Judah?" I fussed because I was tired of not knowing who it was. "He has a kid or something?"

"No," Mahogany answered. I moved my hand from my eyes just as Exodus walked out of the building with a cute little boy. Instantly, my ovaries began to cry, and I knew I had to keep my legs closed. It didn't matter how fine he was or how cute the little boy was. Exodus was crazy; I knew that before I opened my legs to him, but that didn't detract from the fact that he was. And he had the type of dick that would have me telling him I would have his baby.

"Mahogany, this little boy looks just like him!"

"Judah is not his son," she explained, but I wasn't trying to hear it. I hung up the phone just as he opened the back door.

Exodus lifted him into the truck, helped him snap his seatbelt, and then looked at me curiously. "Ay, Judah, you see that pretty lady in my front seat?"

"Yeah," Judah said in a little voice. He was adorable with his dark chocolate eyes, thick eyebrows, golden skin tone, and sharp little haircut. He wore blue cargo pants, a white tee, and a cookie monster varsity jacket. "What about her Ex?"

"That's cousin's future wife," he said, smirking. "She's being mean to me, though, and I'on like that."

"What you do, Ex?" Judah asked, slightly surprised. He looked at me and then back at Exodus with a suspicious look. "You didn't share your candy?"

"Nah, man, I shared!" Exodus said, trying to pretend like he was sad. "I gave her all my candy, man. I mean, had her so happy that she got some that she cried." My mouth dropped open at his words because Exodus wasn't talking about candy, and we both knew it. "And you know she put me out of her house after that man?"

"You did?" Judah said, turning to look at me. I immediately felt guilty and shook my head. "That's not nice of you."

"You're right." I nodded because a child was reprimanding me for putting his family out after we had sex. He didn't know that, but I still felt terrible.

"Tell Ex you're sorry," Judah said, crossing his arms over his little chest. "And mean it. Mommy always says if you say sorry, then mean it, or it doesn't count because don't nobody want a sorry ass man or woman who can't admit when they're wrong."

"I'm sorry, Exodus," I apologized.

"It's cool," Exodus said, trying not to laugh. He turned his attention back to Judah, who looked pleased with himself. "But ay, little man, don't be saying ass. Yo' mama will fuck me up if she knows you are out here cussin'."

"Okay." Judah nodded. Exodus put his hand out, they dapped to each other, and then he closed the door and got in the front seat. "Ex, you got some chicken up there?" Exodus grabbed the small box on the dash without words and handed it to Judah, who took it. He dropped his head and said a quick prayer, then started eating.

"Judah is my cousin, Corinthian's kid," Exodus explained as we drove from the preschool. "He's the youngest of the Bible Thumpers, but he runs this shit."

"Bible Thumper?" I asked him. Even though I didn't want to talk, I loved hearing Exodus's voice. It was deep, almost had a rumble to it, but soothing at the same time.

"Yeah, it's what Krude's homeboy Domo calls us." He nodded with a smirk. "He started calling us that after meeting the numbers."

"Ohh," I said, understanding. People were always confused about how or why Mahogany and her cousins were referred to as numbers instead of their names. Everyone's respective nickname was also their birth month and date. Except for Zero, he was born on October tenth but hated the name Ten, so they called him Zero instead. "So, you all are the Bible Thumpers, and they are the Numbers."

"Yeah." He took his eyes off the road to glance at me for a second. "What are we gonna call you then?"

"Hitta, I guess," I replied with a shrug.

"Nah, that's my nickname for you," he said, shaking his head. "They gotta call you something else." The possessiveness in his voice had me squeezing my legs together to try to stop the thumping my pussy was doing. He must've known what his words did to me because he smirked, reached over, and rested his hand on my thigh as he drove.

"Where are we going?" I asked to change the subject and try to control my hormones.

"We about to head to the park," he answered, looking through the rearview mirror to look at Judah. "Right, Judah? We kickin' it at the park for a little bit?"

"Right," Judah answered. I turned in my seat to see him with a big smile. He turned his attention from Exodus to me and held out his plate of food. "You want some?"

"No, thank you." I shook my head and smiled. Judah stared at me for a few seconds, then pushed the plate toward me again.

"Eat a piece of chicken," he said, sounding like Exodus.

"You might as well do it." Exodus chuckled. I looked over at him and shrugged. "Little dude bossy as fuck, and if he thinks you need to eat, then you're supposed to eat."

"Right," Judah agreed. "Ex always tells me you never let a woman go without. If you do, it makes you a sorry ass nigga."

"And we ain't sorry ass niggas, right, Judah?"

"Right, Ex," Judah said, nodding. "So here, get a little piece of chicken. It's good."

I reached over, took a small wing off his plate, and ate it. I couldn't front it was good as hell, and I would be returning to get more later. By the time we reached the park, Judah had finished his food and cleaned his hands with the baby wipes Exodus had stashed in the back. As soon as Exodus shut off his truck, Judah unbuckled his seatbelt so that he could get out.

"You takin' too long, Ex," Judah fussed as he climbed from the backseat to the front after Exodus helped me out. "I wanna get on the slide."

"My bad, man." Exodus laughed. He helped him out of the truck, and Judah took off. This had to be normal for them because they started calling out his name as soon as the other kids saw him. "Impatient ass, dude."

"He's ready to have fun," I replied, and Exodus shook his head. We walked to the back of the truck, and Exodus dropped the hatch, and we leaned against it. "Y'all do this a lot?"

"Yeah," Exodus replied with a nod. The sun was bright, so I had to shield my eyes to see him. "If the weather is nice, then we are out here. He burns off all his energy before I take him home." He crossed his arms over his chest. "Corinthian probably gonna be pissed at me though when we drop him off."

"Why?" The sound of Judah laughing pulled my attention from Exodus to him. Judah was swinging from the monkey bars, having the time of his life.

"I pulled him out of school early." Exodus laughed. "I've been doing it since she put him in that punk ass school, but she gets mad every damn time like that's going to stop me."

"You don't like his school?"

"Oh, nah, it's cool as hell," he replied. The sound of a lighter flicking and the smell of weed hit my nose. "I just don't like my boy away from me that long. We have been locked at the hip since my raggedy cousin pushed him out."

We sat watching Judah play for the next three hours. Exodus promised him they would hang out this weekend before he agreed to leave. Seeing him with Judah, not showing his ass or killing someone, made me look at Exodus differently. There was no doubt that he was crazy as hell, nor did it take away from the fact that he'd killed my date earlier today, but I was starting to see a different side of him.

CHAPTER 16

Exodus

I TURNED my truck off and turned to look at Paxton. She was on her phone, more than likely texting Mahogany. Judah was knocked out in the backseat, but I knew he would be by the time we left the park. We hung out every few days, sometimes, we didn't do shit but eat and watch sports, and other times I ran that little nigga ragged because I knew his mama had a long day. I grabbed Paxton's phone from her hand, and she cut her eyes at me. "Come on."

"Where?" she asked with a little attitude. That shit was too fucking cute; I mean, I knew I was going to have to fuck her until she realized I wasn't the nigga to play with, but at least the shit would be enjoyable.

"This Corinthian house," I said, then exited the truck. I rounded it and then opened her door to help her out. After she was out, I kissed her lips and got Judah out the back. I usually wasn't a touchy-feely kind of nigga, but I liked touching Paxton. We walked to the front door, and Corinthian pulled it open, and I knew she would cuss my ass out. "Before you start, he ate, ran around the park, and will be asleep for the rest of the night."

"Yet you didn't call and tell me you were picking him up," she replied with an attitude, and I shrugged. "I went to pick him up, and the lady at the front desk said that you picked him up hours before."

Corinthian stepped back, and we walked into the house. "Corinthian, this is Paxton, my girlfriend; Hitta, this is my cousin, Corinthian," I said, introducing them. Paxton cut her eyes at me while Corinthian looked at me with a confused look. I'd never brought a woman around any of my family and claimed her as my woman, so I knew that Corinthian would have questions. "Y'all can chop it up while I get my boy ready for bed."

"Exodus, I am not your girlfriend!" Paxton fussed, and I waved her off.

"We already discussed this; yes, the fuck you are," I threw over my shoulder. I could hear Paxton fussing, but I didn't give a fuck. I laid Judah on his bed and started getting his stuff together so he could shower. Corinthian wasn't about to let him go to bed without showering. It took me a minute to get everything together, but once I woke him up. Judah wasn't a crybaby for a four-year-old, so it wasn't shit to get him in the shower. His mama ensured he was growing up to be independent, so I checked my phone while he showered and got ready for bed. Kino had hit me up a couple of hours ago, saying that Qumar was taken care of, as well as his people. He made it look like a murder-suicide since he had to knock off a few family members, and I was good with that. I sent him payment for his work.

"We are still going to the park this weekend, right, Ex?" Judah asked, coming out of his bathroom with his durag and brush.

"Yeah," I said, standing up. I took the durag and brush from him and started brushing his hair. His mama kept his line sharp, and I stayed on his waves. He was swimming at four, and I loved that shit.

"You bringin' yo' girlfriend?" He yawned.

"You want me to?"

"Yeah, Ex, she's fine." He nodded, and I chuckled. "Bring her."

"I'll see what I can do." I chuckled. Judah got into bed after I was done. "Say yo' prayer, little homie." Judah nodded and then said a quick prayer. I shut off his light as I left the room. He would be asleep in no time. "He good for the night."

"Thank you, Ex," Corinthian mumbled, and I hugged her quickly. "But next time, call."

"I'm not promising you shit I know I can't do," I said, shaking my head. Corinthian pushed me off her, and I laughed. "He wanna hang out this weekend."

"His daddy asked to get him this weekend," she said, and I sucked my teeth. "Don't start Ex."

"Fuck that nigga," I said, then dropped on the couch beside Paxton. She was on her phone again, but I could see she was texting her mama this time. "What time you want me here to pick up Judah cuz he not going with Isaac bitch ass."

"That's his daddy's Ex," Corinthian argued, and I waved her off. I couldn't stand Isaac, and she knew that. He was a damn deadbeat who only came around when he thought Corinthian would let his bitch ass come back home. He didn't give a fuck about Judah and didn't fake that shit. The only reason Corinthian even let him around Judah was because our granddaddy was cool with his people. If it were up to me, Isaac and his entire family would be dead.

"What time?" I asked again. "And if you try that bullshit about him being his daddy, then his daddy gonna end up in a body bag."

"I'll have Judah call when he's ready." She sighed, and I nodded. Her eyes cut to Paxton, and I smirked. Instead of answering her unspoken questions, I stood up.

"We about to head out," I announced, and Corinthian nodded. I helped Paxton from her spot and hugged my cousin. Paxton and Corinthian spoke, and then we headed out.

"You taking me home yet?" Paxton asked as I drove. I looked over at her and shook my head, and she sighed. "I want to go home."

"Why?" I asked as I drove through the city. "You ain't having a good time? I thought this is what folks in relationships did."

"We aren't together." She sighed, and I grunted. "We had sex once! Nothing more, nothing less."

"You think I slang dick to just anybody?" I asked. When I got to a red light, I turned and faced her. "I don't give free dick out." I grabbed my dick through my pants, and Paxton's eyes dropped to my bulge. "Stop looking at my shit if we're not together."

"It's not that serious, Exodus." She laughed and shook her head. Her eyes slowly moved from my dick and back to my face. "I thought this is what niggas wanted. A woman that was okay with a fuck and then went about their business."

"Who the fuck told you that shit?" I yelled, and she started to laugh harder. "Like legit, who said that so I can kill that nigga. I am not with that shit. You have been dealing with whores, and I ain't one."

"What is wrong with you?" She questioned, and I turned my attention back to the road. "I always knew Krude was crazy as fuck, but I didn't know y'all were just alike!"

"I'm nothing like that nigga."

"Yes, you are," she said after getting herself together. "It's a family thing. I bet y'all act the same way."

"No, we don't," I grunted. When I looked over and saw the tears running from her eyes, I ran my hand over her face to fuck with her. "Stop being childish and tell me what you like to do."

"Exodus," she sighed. "We don't have to do this like for real. I'm good with the sex we had. You don't have to pretend like it's more than that."

"Hitta, you kind of slow, you know that?" I asked, shaking my head.

"I'm slow?" she questioned, and I nodded. "How?"

"If you gotta ask, that's another reason you're not the brightest bulb in the box." I shrugged. "But it's cool; I ain't trippin' off it. Our kids are going to have to take after me."

"Kids?" Paxton started shaking her head. "We are not having kids! We aren't even together! You are trippin'."

"If you say so," I replied with a shrug. We rode in silence for a little while. Paxton would look over at me and shake her head occasionally, but I didn't give a damn. We were together, in a whole relationship. If I had to kill every nigga that she went on a date with until she realized that, then I was cool with that, too. I wasn't even going to hide that shit, either. I'd kill them in front of her if need be.

CHAPTER 17

Paxton

"THAT MAN DID NOT KIDNAP YOU!" Mahogany laughed as she walked back into the living room. She had a bowl of popcorn in one hand and a taco in the other. My poor friend had some of the most fucked-up cravings I'd ever witnessed. "Stop saying that."

"He took me against my will," I argued and rolled my eyes. Shaka waddled her fat ass back into the living room and shook her head. "Y'all don't understand my problem."

"What's the problem?" Shaka questioned with a laugh. It took her a few tries, but she successfully sat on the couch and got comfortable. "It's not like he's a bad guy. If anything, Exodus is probably the most normal out of all of them."

"And that's not saying a lot." I laughed.

"Okay, so what did he do that was so bad?" Shaka asked. I broke down everything that happened with Qumar, and Shaka sat there with a big-ass smile on her face by the time I was done. "Y'all got such a cute ghetto love story!"

"What?" I laughed.

"You and Exodus!" she said, and I rolled my eyes. "Like, for real, it's chaotic as fuck, and y'all probably will need therapy, but it's cute.

He even gave you a cute little nickname! If that isn't love, I don't know what is."

"It's drama and chaos," I said, shaking my head. "And more importantly, it's not a love story."

"The man said y'all go together!" Mahogany interjected.

"And?" I threw my hands up. "Niggas say shit all the time."

"You know she gonna be in denial," Shaka told Mahogany, ignoring me. They shared another look of skepticism. "Ever since her ex-Darryl, she's been jaded. I like her and Exodus together. They make a cute couple."

"A bit crazy, and I'm not going to lie, that makes me nervous, but if anyone were going to handle it, it would be them. Ex isn't going to back down when she's going off, and she's going to ignore his crazy moments," Mahogany said to Shaka. I watched them converse like I wasn't even in the room.

"Y'all know I can hear y'all, right?" I asked, and they turned to look at me with bored expressions. "Like I'm right here."

"Anyway," Shaka sighed, then turned back to Mahogany. "I get the hesitation, but I can't wait to see where this goes. You think she'll be pregnant before we give birth?"

"I hope so," Mahogany said, smiling. "Can you imagine all three of our kids growing up together?"

"We aren't having a kid," I said, knowing they didn't give a damn about what I was saying.

"Y'all fucking?" Shaka asked, glancing over at me.

"One time," I said, holding up my index finger. "Just once."

"One time," Mahogany said, pointing to her stomach. "Matter of fact, the first damn time." My eyes dropped to her stomach, and I shook my head because there was no way I was pregnant.

"Y'all probably didn't even use a condom." Shaka laughed. "Miss ma'am, y'all fucking, going on dates, he's killing niggas for you, you've met some of his family, and he gave you a nickname. This is a ghetto love story." She waved me off and shook her head.

"We fucked, never been on a date, and that man kills for a living," I argued. "It won't happen again."

"Yeah, okay," they said in unison. I could tell from the twisted expression on their faces that they didn't believe me, but it didn't matter. I knew the only way to prove it to them would be to stay true to my word.

———

"Morning," Exodus said, walking into my office the following day. I looked up from my report to see him shut the door with his foot. He had a small brown bag in his left hand and a small bottle of orange juice in the other. He'd been calling me since seven this morning, but I'd refused to answer the phone. Seeing him standing in my office now made me wish I'd stayed home in my bed.

"What are you doing here?" I asked as I leaned back in my seat. I crossed my arms over my chest to hide how hard my nipples were. The smell of his cologne hit my nose, and my panties started to water. He was fine, probably too fine for his own good. Exodus set the food bag on my desk and sat in one of the chairs in front of my desk.

"Brought you breakfast," he said, like it was normal for us. "I guessed the type of breakfast burrito you wanted." When I didn't move, he shook his head, leaned across my desk, and grabbed the bag. "One is a sausage, egg, and cheese, and the other is steak, egg, and peppers. Which one do you want?" He lifted his brow in question and waited. "Speak up, or I'm going to pick for you."

I was hungry. I won't lie and say I wasn't, but I didn't want to encourage Exodus's behavior. I meant what I said to Shaka and Mahogany about us not being together. Exodus was not good for my system, but I knew he wouldn't give up if I kept fighting him. Exodus liked a challenge, and my telling him no would only make him more interested. "What are you doing here?" I asked again because bringing me breakfast wasn't a good enough answer.

"Pick a burrito," he repeated, shaking his head. "I'm not talking about shit until after you pick a sandwich and start eating."

"The sausage one," I chose, and he handed it to me. I opened the wrapper, and my mouth started to water. Without shame, I took a bit and moaned as the flavors hit my tongue.

"Shit good, ain't it?" he questioned, and I nodded. "Next time, don't be so fuckin' stubborn and just pick."

"Whatever." I covered my mouth with my hand and rolled my eyes. "Now, back to you, answer my question."

"Came to have breakfast with you." He shrugged like the shit was usual for us. "I called you a couple of times this morning, but you didn't answer."

"I've been busy working," I replied, and he nodded.

"Understandable. I've been going since five and am just now eating." He shook his head and smirked. "I had to fix some stuff at one of my laundry mats before it opened."

"Nothing too serious, was it?"

"Nah," he said, shaking his head. "I handled it and then rolled out. I won't have any problems anytime soon."

"Good," I said, nodding. I went back to eating my burrito, and so did he.

"What's your favorite color?" he asked randomly.

"As a kid, I would've said green or pink," I answered. "But now I would go with Lapis; it's a shade of blue. Why?"

"Just asking," he replied. "Favorite flower?"

"Lily's."

"Food?"

"Steak." I smiled.

"Why didn't you take the steak burrito then?" he asked, looking down at his food and then up at me. "I would've given it to you."

"I didn't want to." I shrugged.

"Yeah, okay," he grunted. "Who is your favorite singer?"

"Erykah Badu," I answered without thinking.

"It fits," he said, nodding. His phone started ringing, and he pulled it out of his pocket. His face twisted up, then he shook his head. "I gotta head out." He took another big bite of his burrito and wiped his mouth with his napkin. After he stood up, he cleaned his mess without me having to ask. "What time are you getting off?"

"I plan to leave around six to head to the hospital."

"Cool." He nodded. "I'll hit you up in a little." He rounded the desk and dropped a kiss on my lips that had me moaning and wanting to do more, but he pulled back with a smirk. "This was a good little date." He nodded his head like he was proud of himself. "Have a good day." Exodus strolled out of my office just as quickly as he appeared.

I sat there confused because did this nigga just say date? Breakfast at my office was not considered a date. I shook my head, returned to eating my burrito, and reviewed the reports. He was crazy; there was no doubt about it.

CHAPTER 18

Exodus

"JUST KILL ME, MAN!" Jaymie yelled at the top of his lungs. I was in a good mood. I'd had breakfast with Paxton, picked up a few things for dinner, and then headed here to get back to work. "Please, Ex!"

"Oh man, stop crying," I said without looking at him. The table in front of me was stacked with different knives. Big, small, straight, curved, hooked, long, short. I had a plethora of options, but the essential fact of it all was that they were all sharp as fuck. "I haven't even started doing anything yet."

"But I heard of you, man," Jaymie cried.

"Oh, for real?" I looked up at him then. I wasn't surprised that he knew my name. I just wanted to know what he knew. I took the reverse S-curve knife off the table and looked it over. It was one of my favorites. "What have you heard about me, Jaymie?"

"That you're ruthless." He cried louder. I chuckled as I walked around the table. "I ain't did to end up here, man."

"How do you know?" I asked, looking down at him. I had him strapped to a metal table, naked as the day he was born. It was a rule when it came to the warehouse. Any nigga or bitch that came in here was stripped. It was a mental thing that I knew fucked with them big time. I'd come into rooms to find niggas crying with piss running down their legs before I even had the chance to open my mouth.

"Because I'm a small-time drug dealer, man," he sobbed, and I shook my head. Yeah, he was small, typically not even close to being on my radar, but Nine said his name was connected to Naeem's baby mama. They linked every time Naeem left town. "I serve to make money for my girl and kids."

"Yeah, so about that," I said, looking at Jaymie. "Tell me about her."

"I have been with Star for years! She a good woman; I'm the one that does the fucked-up shit."

"Star?"

"That's my girl's name." He nodded. "Her real name is Starletta, but I call her Star." His eyes bugged out of his head, and he started to cry more. "Did she send you? Does she know I been fuckin' around and is tired of it? I swear, man, I'll leave all the other bitches alone; you ain't gotta kill me."

"Man, Star can't afford me." I chuckled. I moved around the table so that he could see me and not strain by looking up. "I want to know about Yalonda."

"What about her?" he asked.

"You fuckin' her?" I knew the answer to the question by the way his eyes got big again. Yeah, they were fuckin' probably had been for a minute.

"She paid you?" Jaymie shook his head from side to side and sniffed hard as hell. "That bitch playin' you, man. Yalonda is looking for her next paycheck! She tried to pin her youngest kid on me a few months back, but I got a DNA test done on the low. It turns out she wasn't mine. I showed her the paperwork, and she was pissed. Crazy ass girl tried to run me over with her car, talkin' about I invaded her privacy."

"How long y'all be fuckin' around?"

"Years, man."

"Where is she hiding at?" I asked.

"I don't know." Yalonda must've pissed him off for real because the fear that he had been displaying was now gone, and anger radiated off him like a heat wave. "When I catch that bitch, just know it's like that on sight of her."

"Ah yeah?"

"Yeah, man." Jaymie sucked his teeth. "She had one of her niggas jack me for a few blocks of weed a couple of weeks ago. Bitch ain't shit."

"Damn, man," I said, pretending to understand his struggle. "That's fucked up."

"I know!" he fussed. "She acts like a nigga don't know it's her, but she knows I'm not stupid. I had to double my payment to my plug for that shit."

"Who is your plug?" I didn't give a damn who it was, but the more information I had, the better. Niggas missed little details a lot of times because they didn't think that shit mattered. His plug might not mean shit now, but I may need the information later for another reason.

"Xavi," he answered. "Nigga charged me way too much for the blocks in the first place."

"Shit, crazy," I said, shaking my head. "But you not gonna have to worry about that shit."

"Why not?"

"Oh, cuz you gonna be dead," I answered with a shrug. "You want a verse for your soul?"

"Come on, man!" Jaymie yelled, and I chuckled. "I don't want a verse!"

The door busted open, and Krude walked in with a mug on his face. He looked down at Jaymie, sucked his teeth, and shook his head. Without blinking for the second time since walking into the room, he pulled his gun from the waist of his pants and shot Jaymie twice in the chest.

"Nigga, what the fuck?" I spat.

"You were taking too damn long, and I need help." He shrugged, then put his gun away.

"I didn't get a chance to say my verse." I grunted, then walked back over to the table where I had all my knives and set the one in my hand down.

"Say two when you kill the next nigga," he said, waving me off. "You act that shit matters. They dead, going to hell, and that's it."

"How do you know they are going to hell?" I asked with a laugh.

"Cuz we the last person they see before they die," he replied, and I grunted. "Since you finished here, you can help me."

"With what nigga?" I mugged the shit out of him. "Because if it's some bullshit, then I ain't helping."

"It's a surprise, nigga!" Krude said, smiling big as hell. "It's going to be fun as fuck, though. Watch what I tell you!"

"This shit better be quick too cuz I got plans later," I said, shaking my head.

"It won't take long," he said, then left the room. I grabbed my phone off the table, sent December a text reminding him of the information I needed, and followed behind my crazy ass cousin.

CHAPTER 19

Paxton

I QUICKLY WALKED through the hospital garage to get to my car. I was tired and ready to sleep in bed until noon. After work, I came straight here and sat with Naeem. My parents needed a night in their beds, and I had no problem allowing that to happen. I knew Mama wouldn't stay gone long, so her walking back into his room at six this morning wasn't a shocker. I unlocked my car and stopped dead at the sight of Exodus sitting in the driver's seat.

"Hey, Hitta," he said when I opened the door. The blunt that he was rolling sat in his lap as he smiled at me. "You look tired, baby."

"What are you doing here?" I asked, confused as hell. "As a matter of fact, how did you get in my car?"

"I unlocked the door." He shrugged, then got out. "Here, give me your bag." He took my purse out of my hand and my small backpack off my shoulder and put it in the backseat. "Did you get any sleep while you were sitting with Naeem?"

"Exodus?" I sighed and shook my head. "What are you doing here?" I felt like that was all I was asking him since he kept popping up. I'd seen him more in the last two weeks than in the years I'd known him.

"You already asked me that," he replied with a small laugh.

"Because you didn't answer me the first time," I replied.

"You spent the night at the hospital with my brother-in-law; I knew when you were ready to go, you would be tired, so I came and waited for you so I could drive you home."

"Where is your truck?" I looked around, not seeing his black F250 anywhere.

"Krude dropped me off," he said like it was no big deal. This man had no clue how crazy he sounded, and I was too tired to argue with him. "Now, come on." He took my hand and walked me to the car's passenger side. After I was in the car, I put on my seat belt and got comfortable.

"Don't speed in my car," I said once he pulled off.

"Girl, I'm about to be a damn NASCAR racer in this little mutha-fucka." He chuckled, and I shook my head. "Just close yo' eyes. I'll wake you when we get there."

"Don't kill me, Exodus." I yawned, then closed my eyes. He may have been talking shit, but I knew he wouldn't jeopardize my life.

The next time I opened my eyes, I was lying in a bed. Confused, I looked around to ensure I was seeing what I was seeing correctly. I knew I was in Exodus's bed, but how I got there was beyond me. I looked down at my clothes again, confused because I wasn't dressed in the red sweats and black tee I was in earlier. Instead, I was in a pair of green boxer briefs, a black wife beater, and some tall socks that were too big. I climbed out of bed and walked into the bathroom to pee and get myself together. Once I was done, I went to the living room to find Exodus sitting on the couch.

"How long have I been asleep?" I asked.

"Since we got on the highway." He shrugged without taking his eyes off the TV. He looked comfortable as hell in a pair of ball shorts, socks, and slides. "When I pulled up, I tried to wake you, but you were knocked, so I brought you in."

"You carried me?" I asked with a laugh, and Exodus nodded. "Why?"

"How else were you supposed to get in the house, Hitta?" He glanced over at me, then went back to playing the game. "I didn't want to keep sitting in that little ass car, so I brought your fine ass in."

"And my clothes?"

"Oh shit, I gave you a little wash-up." He smirked, then licked his lips. "I stripped you, spread you out, and washed you." He looked over at me. "And I can't even lie. I was hard as fuck the entire time. Yo' pretty ass pussy was just sitting there looking good as fuck. I kissed it a few times to show her appreciation."

"Oh goodness." I groaned and shook my head.

"That's the same damn thing I said." He chuckled. "Yo' food in the microwave."

"What did you order?" I asked, heading toward the kitchen.

"I cooked," he replied, and I stopped dead. Exodus looked over at me and lifted his brow. "What?"

"Can you cook?" I asked.

"Fuck yeah," he answered. I stood there waiting for him to start laughing or say something to show that he was joking, but he didn't. Exodus sucked his teeth, shook his head, and stood up. My eyes dropped to the bulge in his shorts before meeting his eyes. "Hitta, stop looking at me like that and go eat."

Instead of arguing with him, I headed to the kitchen. The most amazing smells hit my nose, and my mouth started to water. I went to the microwave and opened it. A plate of steak, mashed potatoes, and broccoli awaited me. I warmed it up, returned to the living room, and sat beside Exodus.

"Give thanks first," he said without looking up at me. I opened my mouth to say something, but Exodus shook his head. "Lord, we thank you for the skills to nourish our bodies. Thank you for all that you do. Thank you for this meal and any activity that follows. In your name, I pray. Amen."

"Any activities?" I asked with a laugh.

"Yeah." He nodded. "Now eat and watch me dog this nigga."

Exodus relaxed on the couch, propped his legs up on the coffee table, and returned to playing his game. I hesitantly cut into my steak, then took a bite. The flavors hit my tongue, and I moaned out loud in pleasure.

"Shit, good, ain't it?" He smirked.

"It is," I covered my mouth and answered. "I didn't know you could cook."

"You ever ask?" He glanced at me quickly, then looked back at the TV. "Cuz I know you can cook. Like to read all the damn time and love to swim."

"How do you know all that?"

"I'm an observant nigga." He shrugged. "Plus, I like seeing you in a swimsuit, so I was real observant then."

"Whatever." I laughed, not believing him.

"Oh, you don't believe me?" he questioned.

"Nope," I said in between bites of my food.

"Yo' favorite one is that purple and gold one Mahogany designed a few years back for her exclusive line. It has a deep cut down the middle and only has straps on one shoulder." I knew the exact swimming suit he was talking about because it was my favorite. I'd fallen in love with it as soon as Mahogany had shown me the design. It was one of three owned by Mahogany, Shaka, and me. Each of us had a different color, but I wore mine more often than they did.

"All right, what else have you noticed?" I finished eating and set the plate on the side table beside the couch.

"You care more about your comfort than the fashion trends, even though you are best friends with one of the dopest fashion designers. You like to color; your backpack contains coloring books and shit. You don't drink often, but when you do, it's always some fruity shit that gets you lit. You love to dance, and anytime music is playing, you are moving." He sat up, excited about something on the screen, then dropped back. "Oh, and you dated that fuck nigga for far too damn long. I'ono why y'all broke up, but that shit is my blessing."

"He cheated." I shrugged, and Exodus turned to look at me with a confused look.

"What?"

"Yeah, it was wild." I laughed and shook my head.

"What happened?"

"I caught him having a threesome," I said, and he smirked. I knew the next sentence would have him dropping that smirk. "With two other men."

"Get the fuck outta here." Exodus completely ignored his game and turned to face me. "Like you caught that nigga fuckin' two niggas?" I nodded my head. "And he lived?"

"I wanted to kill him, don't think I didn't. I don't know why I didn't, but I regret making that decision every damn day."

"It was that nigga from a few months ago at the restaurant?" Exodus asked with a twisted expression on his face. "The one that I beat up?"

"Yeah," I answered. "That's him."

"Oh, that nigga looks gay." He laughed and returned to his game. "But don't trip off it. It'll be handled."

"It doesn't need to be handled," I replied, shaking my head. "I'm not worried about him. He can live his life, and I will continue living mine."

"Right, cuz you got a new nigga now," he agreed, and I rolled my eyes.

I wasn't about to keep having this conversation with Exodus. We weren't in a relationship; he knew that. Yet he kept saying it as if it would magically come true. I got up from the couch and took my plate into the kitchen. I only washed my dishes by hand. I had a dishwasher, but I hated to use it. Even after being in the house for over three years, I had not used it once. It was just something about filling the sink, making soapy water, and washing dishes that relaxed me.

"I would've washed that," Exodus said, sneaking up on me. He wrapped his arms around my waist and buried his face. I continued to wash my dish, even though I could feel my pussy start to throb. In the past, my body had never responded to a man's touch like it did his.

"It's just a plate and my silverware. You cleaned up everything else already."

"It's my house; you are the guest. It's my job to handle all that, at least the first few times you are here."

"I've been here plenty of times." I laughed and shook my head. "This is Mahogany house, remember?"

"No, it's not," he said, kissing my neck several times. "I bought it from her the day Focus showed her the house he bought for her."

"Really?"

"Yeah," he said. His big hand slid into my boxer briefs, and I bit my lip. "She wasn't going to do shit with it, and I needed a place to lay my head while I'm here. It's a win-win situation." Exodus cupped my pussy, then applied pressure to my clit with his middle finger. Instantly, my legs started to shake, and I had to hold on to the counter to keep from falling. Exodus bit into my neck, and I moaned. "You ain't notice none of her furniture is here? I had everything redecorated a few months back. This my shit." The fact that he was trying to hold a conversation while he was playing with my clit was beyond me. I didn't give a fuck about this house, the decorations, or even anything else at this point but my orgasm that I felt building. "You ain't notice Hitta?"

"Noooo." I moaned as he pushed his fingers into me. I shook my head, and he chuckled. "I mean, I did, but shit!"

"That's so damn fucked up," he said as he dropped kisses on my neck. "I'm here trying to make a good impression, and you don't even notice. I gotta do better." His fingers moved inside of me faster, and I moaned louder. This shit felt too damn good. His middle and ring fingers were working my insides while his thumb was working over my clit. My pussy was spazzing, and I could feel my juices running down my legs. "I gotta work on my hosting skills. Can you help me with that?"

"Yyyyeeesss." I cried as my orgasm pushed to the top. My body got hot, and I grabbed his wrist so he could pull his hand away at the last second like he'd done at the club. "Ohhh shit, Exodus! I'm cumming!"

"Cum them, Hitta." He chuckled. His hand moved faster, and my eyes rolled into the back of my head as I came. "Pretty ass." He kissed the back of my neck. I let out a small sigh and then let go of his hand. My heart was beating out of my chest, and I was out of breath, but I felt amazing. I usually wasn't one for a quick nut, but the way that Exodus had taken control of my body and had me cumming within minutes had me ready to change my mind. "You want to play the game with me?"

"What?" I questioned because this nigga seriously didn't ask me if I wanted to play the game like he didn't just have me cumming not even a minute ago from just his fucking hand.

"You want to play the game?" he asked again and stepped back. I instantly missed the warmth of his hand on pussy when he pulled it away. I turned around and looked at him. "I was playing when you came down."

"I don't know how to play," I answered.

"Cool, I can teach you," Exodus said, then nodded. "Come on."

We returned to the living room, and Exodus handed me one of the remote controls from the TV stand. He sat on the couch, grabbed me, pulled me down between his legs, and showed me how to play Call of Duty for the next three hours. It was probably the most stressful ass thing I'd done in a long time, but I enjoyed myself.

CHAPTER 20

Exodus

"WHY THE HELL is the studio door locked, nigga?" I asked after Focus opened the door. He mugged the shit out of me and shook his head before returning to the soundboard. I dropped down on the couch beside Mahogany and pulled her into a quick side hug before letting her go. Even though Focus and I had been boys for years, he knew I didn't look at Mahogany as anything more than a little sister that nigga didn't like for nobody to touch her for too long. How he would handle having a kid under her was beyond me. She was sitting there eating a big-ass salad, so I was mindful not to move too much.

"I was in here fuckin' on my woman nigga," he joked, and I started to laugh. Even though that shit was said jokingly, I knew it was a good chance he was telling the truth. Especially since Mahogany sat next to me with a mug on her face. "Now, what the fuck are you doing here?"

"Came to run some shit by you." I shrugged.

"About what?" he questioned. "If it's about what the hell to do about Paxton, then you talkin' to the wrong person. Talk to your best friend over there."

"I wasn't coming to talk about her." I laughed, then turned to Mahogany. "But since you are here, why you ain't tell me her bitch ass ex cheated on her with two niggas?"

"She told you?" Mahogany asked with a laugh, and I nodded.

"Nigga what?" Focus said, turning from what he was doing to look at us confusedly. "How the fuck y'all find that shit out?"

"She caught him." Mahogany shrugged between bites of her food.

"When One?"

"The day it happened," she replied. I grunted to stop myself from laughing. Mahogany was the only person who would answer Focus like that and live to talk about it.

"One, make me fuck you up," he grunted, and she giggled because she didn't give a damn about his attitude. "Now answer the question. When did this happen, and why didn't anybody tell me?"

"What were you going to do, Tobias?" she questioned, then rolled her eyes. "Kill him?"

"Yeah." He nodded, and she sucked her teeth.

"That's why no one told you."

"Well, y'all could've told me," I said, and Mahogany cut her eyes at me. "What?"

"Why would we do that? You're as bad as he is!"

"How?"

"Did you not burn down her date restaurant not too long ago?"

"No." I shook my head.

"The lies!" Mahogany fussed.

"I didn't burn it down!" I said, and Mahogany rolled her eyes again. "I just set a few places on fire, is all."

"Nigga, are you serious?" Focus laughed, and I shrugged. "Why the fuck did you do that?"

"She was on a date," I answered as if the shit made sense. "It was the logical thing to do."

"You can't even spell logical," Mahogany said as I mugged her. "But Tobias, it gets worse. He then killed the man she was on a date with."

"It wasn't just because." I sucked my teeth and shook my head. "When Hitta left, he was talking shit, talkin' about he would take her out again like I didn't let him know she was off limits. It was disrespectful, and I handled it accordingly."

"By killing him?" Mahogany questioned.

"The man said she was on a date, baby," Focus replied, and I knew that nigga understood what the fuck I was thinking. I'd seen him step way too many times over Mahogany without a second thought, and that was before they were in a relationship. Now that they were engaged and had a baby on the way, I knew my nigga would destroy the entire world of her ass. "Sometimes you gotta handle things a little differently."

"Right," I agreed, and Mahogany stared at both of us before pushing herself off the couch. She set her salad on the table in front of us and walked away. "Where are you going?"

"To pee," she threw over her shoulder as she headed toward the back. "Y'all continue with y'all conversation because, obviously, a voice of reason isn't going to be appreciated right now."

"Man, she crazy." I laughed once Mahogany was gone. Focus shrugged and went back to work. "But back to the reason I'm here."

"Speak on it."

"I need some date ideas," I said, and Focus turned around to look at me like I was crazy. "Look, I know I said I wasn't here for no help with Hitta, but shit, I was lying."

"You call that girl Hitta?" he asked with a smirk.

"Yeah." I nodded. "That's her nickname and shit."

"Nigga, I'on even wanna know why." He smirked and leaned back in his chair. "But I ain't got no date ideas for you. You legit going to have to ask One."

"I'm not trying to hear her damn mouth," I groaned, rubbing my hands over my face. Hanging out with Paxton a few times over the last week or so had been dope. We clicked, and shit was easy. When I got up the other morning to an empty bed and my truck missing, I wasn't even pissed. She'd been riding around in it for the last day, but I also knew her every move because of GPS. Any other woman would've gotten a bullet to the head by one of my cousins without a second thought.

"Then who you gonna ask?" Focus laughed. "It ain't like you can call her mama and ask her."

I stopped rubbing my hands over my face and thought about it. I didn't have her mama's number, but I knew where she was. Paxton had mentioned that her parents, mainly her mama, sat at the hospital with her brother daily. I pulled my phone out of my pocket and checked the time; it was close to three. I could make it over to the hospital to chop it up with her mama before she left her office.

"Where are you going now, nigga?" Focus asked as I stood.

"To introduce myself to my future mother-in-law," I answered, then dapped him up. "I'ma grab her something to eat before I get there, though. You know, show her the kind of son-in-law she will have."

"Nigga, you a fuckin' fool," Focus said, and I shrugged.

"Just doing what I gotta do." I laughed and headed to the door. "Tell Mahogany I'll hit her up later this week."

———

"Excuse me, Mrs. Littlejohn," I said, pushing Naeem's room door open. Paxton's mama lifted her head from her book and stared at me curiously. "My name is Ex. I'm Paxton's boyfriend, and I brought you lunch."

"Boyfriend?" Mrs. Littlejohn replied with a laugh, and I nodded. "Honey, my daughter doesn't have a boyfriend."

"We are fairly new," I said with a shrug as I stepped further into the room. I glanced at Naeem, connected to a few machines in the bed. He looked like he was asleep instead of in a medically induced coma. "Paxon mentioned you are up here when she's at work, and I thought bringing something to eat would be a good idea. Have you eaten?" I held up the game from Karter's BBQ as proof.

"Not yet," she said, smiling.

"Well, here you go." I sat the food bag on the small rolling table and then pushed it to her. Mrs. Littlejohn watched me for a few seconds before nodding her head.

"Have a seat," she said, pointing to the chair beside her. I walked over to the seat and sat, ensuring I wasn't in her view of Naeem. "Now tell me how you met my daughter."

"I've known Paxton for a few years now," I answered, and she lifted her brow. "I'm best friends with Mahogany and Focus."

"Oh, wait, you're Ex?" she asked, and I nodded. "What's your real name, love?"

"Exodus DeCorte," I answered, and Mrs. Littlejohn nodded.

"Any relation to that big-time pastor, Dr. DeCorte?"

"He's my granddaddy," I answered, and she looked surprised, which caused me to laugh a little.

"You think you can get your granddaddy to pray for my baby here?"

Instead of answering her, I pulled my phone out of my pocket and sent my granddaddy a text asking him to send a special prayer for Naeem. When he stated it was done, I showed Mrs. Littlejohn his response; it seemed like a small weight was lifted off her shoulder. "You know I was just joking, right?" she asked as she opened her food container. Since I didn't know what she ate, I had them through a little of everything, and from the look on Mrs. Littlejohn, I had made the right decision.

"Naeem's life matters, so I know every little thing counts," I answered with a shrug. "If my granddaddy can use his connections to the man above and ask him for Naeem to have a little bit more time on this side healthy, then so be it."

"You are a sweet one," she said with a nod. "Now tell me what made you come to see me today."

"Two reasons," I said, and she took a bit of the small beef slices. Just like her daughter, Mrs. Littlejohn danced in her seat as she ate. A small smile pulled at my lips as I watched her. If I ever wondered what Paxton would look like forty years from now, I was looking at it. "First, so that I could meet you. I plan to lock our daughter down, and I know that as a man, I gotta talk to you and her daddy first. I plan to speak with him soon."

"And the second reason?"

"I'm trying to figure out some date ideas for Paxton," I shyly said. It felt weird asking her mama for help, but I knew that if anyone could tell me what Paxton would like to do, it would be her mama. "As I said, we are fairly new, and Paxton is so worried about Naeem that she isn't doing anything but coming here and going to work. I have to show up at her house to spend time together, and while I'm not complaining, I want to do something special for her, too."

"Didn't you all go on a date not too long ago?" she questioned, and my face twisted. Mrs. Littlejohn's face went blank, and she looked away.

"That wasn't me, but he has been taken care of and isn't in the picture now," I said, and she looked at me with a smirk.

"Okay then." She nodded. "Now, let me think."

"Price doesn't matter either," I said, not thinking. "She could want to go anywhere, do anything, whenever, and I would make it happen. No questions asked."

"Take her swimming," her mama said. I looked at her like she was crazy. "Paxton loves to swim. Cook for her. Or a concert, she loves music. Paxton isn't a materialistic girl; she likes authenticity, and it'll come naturally if you're authentic in your pursuit of her."

"Cool," I said, nodding my head. I understood what she was saying and respected her for not just offering her daughter up on a plate for me to take. I had to work for her daughter, and I was cool with that.

"Now, Mr. Exodus DeCorte, tell me about yourself," she said after a few minutes of silence.

"What you wanna know?" I asked with a chuckle.

"Are you a killer?" she asked, getting straight to the point. I wanted to lie to her and say no, but I wasn't raised to lie to anyone. If Mrs. Littlejohn was asking, then that meant she wanted to know. "I only ask because I know how my daughter is, and if you are serious about her, then I need to know if you can hold your own. I don't condone my children's choices in life, but I can't and don't try to change them. Paxton is a beautiful woman, but quick to anger and doesn't always think before reacting. Even as a child, I always told her to stop and think before reacting." She let out a small laugh. "She never did, though, especially when it came to Naeem. She protected him with everything in her."

"Mrs. Littlejohn, I'm just the kind of nigga you would want to stand in front of Hitta," I said, smirking. "That tough shit she into doesn't scare me. She has only been tough because she's never had a nigga let her be soft."

"And you're the one that can?" she asked with a smirk, and I nodded. "We'll see."

"You know my granddaddy taught me to pray, right?" I asked her with a shrug. "Well, let me tell you, I have been praying for a woman like your daughter for a long time. She's my prayer manifested."

CHAPTER 21

Paxton

"I SEE why you like these big-ass trucks," I said, smirking from Exodus's truck. I'd expected him to call me going off once he realized it was gone, but he hadn't. I hadn't heard from him for almost a full day, and when I did, he told me to meet him at the range. Because of my day, going to the range sounded like a good idea.

"Why do you think that?" he asked, closing the truck door. Like any other time we were together, he stepped into my personal space and stared down at me with a little smirk.

"You tower over people; they move out your way when they see you coming, and any time I hit a curb, I knew I didn't fuck anything up," I answered with a smile. Exodus looked at his rims and then back at me thoughtfully. "I only hit one."

"You fuck my shit up; that's your ass," he said, and I shrugged. "Bring yo' ass, Hitta." He grabbed my hand and pulled me toward the front entrance.

Inside the gun range was quiet, soft music played through hidden speakers, and rows of glass display cases with guns inside. Even though I knew how to shoot and had done it plenty of times, this was my first time stepping into a range. I walked around looking for anything that called my name, and when my eyes landed on a yellow and black Glock, I fell in love.

"You know the point of coming here is to shoot what you normally can't get a hold of, right?" Exodus said, coming to stand behind me. He wrapped his arms around my waist and buried his face into my neck. "That Glock isn't abnormal."

"I know, but it doesn't take away from the fact that I like it." I shrugged. "I don't have a fascination with guns. I go with what I know and like, and that's it."

"I get it," he replied with a nod, then dropped two quick kisses on my neck. "But that doesn't change the fact that you're here to change shit up. Go shoot one of those 338 Sniper rifle or something."

"I'll stick to what I know." I laughed.

"Oh, damn, I ain't know you were scared," Exodus said, lifting his face from my neck. I turned and looked at him, confused about what he was talking about.

"What?"

"You heard me, Hitta." He chuckled. "You scared, but don't worry; I won't tell anyone. It'll be our secret."

"I'm not scared," I replied with a smirk.

"Oh yeah?" he questioned, then nodded. "Bet. So, if you aren't scared, let's put a wager on it."

"Money?" I was surprised, but it didn't sound like a bad idea. "How much are you talking?"

"Nah," Exodus said, shaking his head. "No money."

"Then what?" I asked suspiciously.

"Twenty-four hours," Exodus answered. "Winner gets the other person no questions asked for twenty-four hours."

I thought it over for a second. I knew Exodus was a killer; I had seen him do it plenty of times, but I couldn't back down from a challenge. Against my better judgment, I stuck out my hand. I could handle that with no problem for twenty-four hours, win or lose. "Deal."

Exodus walked away from me with a smirk and spoke with one of the men behind the counter. After a few minutes, he returned and led me toward the back of the building; as soon as I stepped through the back door, the loud bang of guns being shot hit my ears. Exodus dapped up the man, grabbed my hand, and led me through the main room into a small one.

"This is where we are going to shoot," he said after closing the door. Every so often, the sound of a gun being shot was heard, but for the most part, it was quiet. "Everything is already set up."

"You had this all planned?" I asked, looking around. The room was small but long and brightly lit.

"Kind of," he answered with a shrug. A big-ass gun sat on a table that was along the wall. "I knew we would have a private room, but not the kind of guns we would be shooting. That came to me at the last minute." Exodus skillfully set up the gun and then turned to me with a pair of glasses in his hand. "It's certain rules that they don't play about. Using eye protection is one of them, so you gotta wear'em."

"I'm good with that," I said, taking the glasses from him and putting them on. "Now, what are the rules for our competition?"

"Shit, simple," he said with a shrug. "You get fifteen shots; whatever points hit on the target are yours. Whoever has the most at the end wins."

"How many shots are you taking?" I asked, looking over the target. It was a standard outline of a person's upper body, like you always saw on TV. There were numbers in each outlined section. The closer you got to what I thought were probably kill shots, the higher the count compared to those closer to the outside of the body.

"I'm gonna take six," he answered. I looked at him, confused about why he took a lower amount. "You ready?"

"Yeah." I nodded.

Exodus showed me the basics and even let me shoot a few times to get in some practice. When it was time for them to count and I started trying, I hit most of what I wanted. My aim was off, but I didn't trip off it because I'd never shot a gun this damn big. After cleaning up and helping Exodus set up, I stepped back and watched him. I didn't expect him to hit his target in the brain and then the heart. With those two shots, he was close to my score, and he looked over his shoulder at me with a smirk I knew I'd been had. Thinking quickly, I got down on the floor with him, on the opposite side of where the Sniper rifle was, and got close to his face.

"What are you doing, Hitta?" he asked with a chuckle.

"Trying to see how you handle a little pressure," I answered. I got close to his face and licked his cheek without thinking. Exodus chuckled and shook his head. "You taste like chocolate."

"Yo' pussy tastes good too, so I guess we have that in common," he said, then shot the rifle. I glanced over to see he'd missed, and I smiled. "Stop smiling." He cut his eyes at me and smirked. "All I gotta do is hit another heart shot, and I win."

"Oh yeah?" I laughed. I got up from the floor and slowly started to pull my shirt out of my pants. I'd come here straight from work, and while my work clothes consisted of a green fitted V-neck tee shirt and a pair of black high-waisted jeans, I was cute. "What happens if I take my top off? Will you be able to concentrate, then?"

"Try it and see," he said, looking at me with a hungry expression. I pulled my top off, loving that I'd decided to wear a cute lace black bra this morning. Exodus looked me up and down, licked his lips, and returned to the rifle. He adjusted the scope and then turned back to look at me. "The shot still looks good." I kicked off my black Jordans and slowly started taking off my pants. Exodus's eyes never left me as I pushed them down my legs and stepped out of them. Even though I had done this as a joke to get his attention off winning, the look Exodus gave me had me ready to let him win. "I like those panties."

"Thank you," I replied with a smirk. Exodus's nose flared, and he licked his lips before returning to the rifle. He glanced up at me one more time before firing twice. Neither shot hit the spot that would be needed for him to win. "You missed, so that means I won!"

"Oh yeah?" he said, getting up. He was wearing a pair of gray joggers, and I could see his print on proud display.

"Yep." I nodded, then reached down to pick up my clothes to put them on.

"Check again, Hitta," he said, leaning against the wall and crossing his arms over his chest. I pulled on my shirt and pants, walked over to where he was standing, and pressed the button to call over the target.

"Ain't no fuckin' way," I mumbled as I counted up his points in my head. I snatched the target paper off the rack and turned to look at Exodus, who had a big-ass smile. "You still won?"

"Yeah." He shrugged. "Those two shots put me up by one." He tapped the target and then kissed my cheek. "This shit is about to be fun."

"I was played," I fussed, and he shrugged. "You cheated!"

"Probably, but you'll never be able to prove it." He laughed. "Now, let's go."

"Where are we going?"

"To eat, I'm hungry as fuck."

CHAPTER 22

Exodus

"AIN'T THAT SOME SHIT," I said, shaking my head as I looked over the security footage that my connect Toni let me see. Even though it was a reasonable distance from Naeem's baby mama's apartment, I could see enough to know that it wasn't Yalonda who shot him. The small pawnshop on the corner shared a parking lot with them, which was the only reason I could see her spot. A green Tahoe pulled up on Naeem's car and opened fire from Yalonda's side. Now whether she set that shit up or not was another story, and that was only something she could explain.

"You got everything you need?" Toni, the security guard, asked me, and I nodded. I pulled three hundred out of my pocket and dropped it on the desk. "We running it back?" She looked me up and down like I was a fresh piece of meat. Back in the day, I would knock Toni off when I was in town, but that shit was never anything else, and we both knew it. She had an on-again-off-again boyfriend, and I wasn't the kind of nigga that was worried about her ass enough to care.

"Shorty, my girl would kill you and me both if I gave you some dick." I chuckled as I stood up.

"You got a girl, Ex?" Toni asked, and I nodded. "Since when?"

"A couple of days," I answered with a shrug.

"Oh, that shit new then," Toni said, waving me off. "We can still get a quick one in." She reached for the waistband of my ball shorts, and I grabbed her wrist. Paxton and I may not have been officially in shit, but the moment she swallowed my dick and nut that other day changed everything. If she thought for one damn second, I was about to let her ass do that to anybody else; she had lost her damn mind. I can't even front it was a part of me that wanted to look for her exes and kill them niggas because I wanted to be the only nigga in the world that knew what her insides felt like.

"I'm good," I told her, and she stood there shocked.

"Oh, it's serious like that?" she asked with a laugh, and I nodded. "Damn, what did she do to get you to lock her down? Because I swear, I have been trying for a few years now with no luck."

"Girl, stop playing." I chuckled and stepped back. "But I appreciate you letting me see the video."

"No problem." Toni nodded. "Let me know what else you need, and if I can help you, I will."

"I appreciate it," I replied, then left the back room. A few niggas were standing around the front desk, one that I locked eyes with, but he turned his head before I could place where I knew his face from. I ran my tongue over my teeth as I tried to figure out if I would show my ass. I was trying to turn over a new leaf, so I decided not to. That was until I knew where I had seen that nigga before. It would come to me eventually, and I knew I could walk my ass back in here and get the information I needed from Toni.

"Have a good night," Toni called out as she stepped out the back. I looked up at the mirror above the door to see her adjusting her pants, then wiped her mouth like we'd been back there fucking. I shook my head because her ass didn't even realize she looked like a straight hoe.

I stepped into the house an hour later and immediately went to shower. I'd been on the move all day, and the second the hot water hit my body, I was in a zone. After a few washes, I got out, dried off, put lotion on, and threw on a pair of boxer briefs and ball shorts. I didn't plan to leave the house for the rest of the night.

"What's good?" I answered the phone as I flipped through the different apps on the TV.

"Nigga, she cut me!" Krude's overdramatic ass yelled into my ear. "I can't believe this shit! I mean, I can cuz she crazy, but then again, I can't!"

"Who cut you, Krude?" I lazily asked because I already knew the answer to the question.

"Megan!" he yelled, and I chuckled. "I thought she loved me, nigga! She can't love me if she is trying to kill me!"

"What happened?"

"We were on a date, right," he faked sobbed. "We came back to the house, was chillin', and I was preparing to eat her pussy because shit, her pussy is good as fuck."

"Too much detail, Krude."

"Ain't no such thing," he argued, then sucked his teeth. "Anyway, like I was saying, I was about to get down cuz, nigga, unlike you, I keep my woman satisfied."

"Krude, I swear I'm gonna hang up on your ass," I replied.

"Whatever, back to the story," he huffed. "So, we were kissing and shit, and the next thing I hear is somebody banging on the door. I'm trying to ignore that shit, but she wasn't having it. I got up and checked it, and when I opened the door, some woman walked in wearing nothing but bootie shorts and a tank top. Immediately she starts rubbing on a nigga, and shit, we both know my woman is a little freaky, so I let her. The next thing I know, she's on her knees trying to pull my dick out of my shorts."

"Who was the woman?"

"I don't fuckin' know, nigga!" he yelled again. "I was at her house!"

"Wait nigga, you let some random feel on you and try to pull your dick out?" I questioned with a laugh. "You better be happy that all she did was cut you."

"The bitch was her old bitch!" Krude fussed. "Megan came around the corner, called out the girl's name, and started swinging. I mean, I didn't ask any fuckin' questions at all. I was turned on and scared for my fuckin' life at the same damn time. She beat the girl's ass, dragged her out of the house, then turned her rage on me. Talkin' about shouldn't no other bitch feel comfortable touching on me and how I was disrespecting her by allowing it."

"How did you end up cut, though?"

"She was fussing, and I followed her into the kitchen."

"Big fuckin' mistake," I interjected.

"Hell yeah! I wasn't thinkin' that at the time, though! She was fussing, and I'm trying to explain myself, and I told her she was acting crazy, and you know that's Megan's fuckin' trigger word. Next fuckin' thing I know, my fuckin' chest out cut up."

"You need to go to the hospital, Krude?" I asked and stood up from the couch. This nigga stayed with drama when it came to this woman.

"Yeah," he groaned. "I feel like I'm getting lightheaded."

"All right, give me a little bit, and I'll be there," I said, then hung up. I wasn't rushing to this nigga side because if it were that damn serious, he would've called 911. After throwing on a shirt, socks, and slides, I grabbed my keys and wallet off the dresser to leave.

When I pulled up to Megan's house and exited the car, Megan and her best friend Nyla stood on the front porch, talking. "What's good?" I greeted them. Nyla was a cute girl, short as hell, but most women were compared to me. I knew she was married, and from the look of her stomach, she was expecting her baby any time now. I looked around expecting to see her husband lurking in the background, since that nigga rarely let her out his sight.

I gave them both a quick hug. "What are you doing here, Ex?" Megan asked.

"Came to check on Krude," I answered with a shrug. "He talkin' about he's lightheaded."

"He is the house," Megan said, shaking her head. "I don't know why he called you, though."

"Cuz you cut him." I chuckled, and both women turned and smirked at each other.

"That's what he told you?" She laughed, and I nodded. "Go on and see him then."

I pushed open the door and looked around. Megan's house was gold and white with hints of green. "Yo, Krude!" I called out.

"In here, nigga," he said from the living room. I stepped over the two dogs' sleep at the door and headed to the living room. Like the dramatic nigga he was, Krude was laid out on the couch with an icepack on his chest. His arm was thrown over his face, and every time he moved, he winced in pain. "Took you long enough to get here."

"Nigga, you not even hurt!" I grabbed the icepack off his chest and stared down at him. He had three minor ass scratches on his chest, and that was it. The shit wasn't even bleeding. "You got me driving over here, and you not hurt!"

"You don't see these wounds?" He stood up and pointed to the three minor cuts. "Megan tried to end me!"

"She barely scratched you!" I threw my hands in the air. "I swear on the phone, you said you were hurt! You even said you felt lightheaded!"

"Because I did!" he yelled, and, at this moment, I wished Megan had fucked this nigga up. "I had to put some cold water on it to stop the bleeding and everything."

"Grandma was right about your ass," I said, shaking my head. "When you were little, your mama swore you were sane, but Madea said your ass was off. I can see right now that she was right."

"Nigga, she said the same thing about you!" he argued, and I shrugged. "If I'm off, then so are you." Paxton's words from the other day replied in my head. Wasn't no way Krude and I were alike. This nigga was slow as fuck; I wasn't.

I smacked his three little scratches, and this nigga had the nerve to cringe and then rub them as if they hurt. "Ain't shit but a fuckin' love tap."

"Nigga, you know I got sensitive skin!"

I stared at my cousin for a few seconds, then walked out of the house just as quickly as I walked in. Megan and Nyla were still on the porch talking, when I walked out. They looked at me and busted out laughing. "Why do you call him every time he calls?" Megan asked.

"Cuz I always have a feeling that the one time I don't, he's seriously gonna be hurt," I replied with a shrug.

"By me?" Megan asked, and I nodded. The smile that was on her face dropped, and she looked at me seriously. "Krude is dramatic as hell. Did I go off on him for Whitney rubbing up on him? Absolutely, but those scratches he got on his chest were from him pulling me off her. Krude put his body between her and me, and I reached across him to grab her and accidentally scratched him. We didn't even realize it until after we were arguing in the kitchen. I never touched him, intending to hurt him. I would never touch him while angry."

"I can't stand this nigga," I said, shaking my head. The fact that Krude left those little details out had me wanting to go back in there and pop his ass. "Y'all have a good night."

"You too," they said, laughing. I gave them another quick hug, then got back in my car. Krude called me repeatedly, but I didn't answer his ass. He knew I was annoyed, and when I answered, I would cuss his dumb ass out.

Without thinking, I went to Paxton's house and pulled into her driveway. I got out, walked to the front door, and knocked. When Paxton opened the door, I looked her up and down. Immediately I felt my dick start to brick up, and my mouth started to water. I wanted her ass and bad. This girl was becoming an addiction I never wanted to get rid of.

CHAPTER 23

Paxton

"I'M CASHING in on a few hours," Exodus said as soon as I opened the door. I stared at him, completely surprised that he was there and how much my body reacted to him.

"What?" I questioned. He looked me up and down again before pushing past me and walking into the house. The scent of two different perfumes hit my nose, and I immediately reared back. Chuckling, I shook my head and slammed the door. Exodus didn't stop moving until he was in the living room and dropped on the couch. I ignored him, sat back in my spot, grabbed the remote off the table, and pressed play to finish watching my show. "You said twenty-four hours."

"Right." He nodded. "I didn't say how they had to be paid out. I just said twenty-four to be in control. I'm cashing in on some of them now."

"That wasn't the deal, Exodus!" I laughed and shook my head. I expected him to take an entire day when I had no clue but a whole day to drive me crazy. After we left the shooting range the other day, we went to eat and then went our separate ways. Exodus phone rang, and against my better judgment, I looked down at the screen. Instead of a contact name, there was a yellow heart. Exodus swore he had something to do out of the blue once he was off the phone, and I wasn't one to argue with him. I told him I was going home to shower and then relieve my mama from the hospital. He nodded his head, and then we parted ways.

"What are you watching?" he questioned from his spot. I didn't turn my attention from the TV, but I could feel his eyes on me. "Yo, you don't hear me?"

The doorbell rang, and I got up to get the food I had ordered earlier. That's who I thought it was when I answered the door for Exodus. I greeted the delivery guy; I gave him a cash tip even though I'd tipped him through the delivery service and walked back to the living room. Exodus had taken the remote and switched to a basketball game. I sat down and opened up my food, not caring that he was still expecting me to move because he said so.

"What are we eating?" he asked without looking up from the TV.

"I'm eating sushi," I replied, sitting back in my seat. "How are you watching the game?"

"ESPN," he answered.

"I don't have ESPN," I said, not believing this fool had the nerve to download and sign me up for a subscription without my permission. Shaka had a bad habit of doing that, and I kept saying I was going to a password on my TV and never got a chance to do it. That shit would be changing tonight.

"I signed into my account." He shrugged. "What do I look like spending your money?"

"Oh." I bit into my first bite and danced happily in my seat. I loved sushi but didn't eat it as often anymore.

"Yeah, oh." He cut his eyes at me. "Throw me one of those plates."

"You eat sushi?" I asked, surprised. I knew most men, especially black men, couldn't stand it.

"Yeah," he answered, reaching over and taking a container off the table. The entire time, he didn't take his eyes off the TV. Another thing I was surprised by was that we were watching a WNBA game.

"You got money on the game or something?" I questioned, and Exodos shook his head no. "Then why are we watching the WNBA?"

"My little cousin plays for LA," he answered, pointing to the TV. "Number twelve, the one with the ball."

"Really?" I asked, surprised, and he nodded.

"Yeah."

"One of the few Bible Thumpers?" I asked in between bites of food. Exodus chuckled, then nodded his head. "Where does she fall into the lineup?"

"Next to the last," he answered. I watched as he chewed his food; for the first time in my life, I was even turned on by that. "I'm the oldest; then it's Krude, Corinthian, Cross, Psalms, Judge, and Mercy. Oh, and Judah."

"All of you are named after the Bible in some kind of way?" I noted, and he nodded. "Is there a reason?"

"My granddaddy wanted all of us to be named after some part of the Bible. I think he thought our parents would name us normal names. The only two slightly normal are Krude and Judah," he replied, and I nodded. His grandfather was a big-time pastor. He had one of the biggest congregations in Vegas and was plastered all over the TV and internet. "It's a family tradition at this point. All their kids are named after the Bible, so, in turn, they followed suit and named all of us after things associated with the Bible."

"Any of y'all follow in their footsteps?"

"Completely the opposite." He laughed. "Everyone is in the same business as I am except for Corinthian and Mercy."

"They know what y'all do?"

"Yep." He nodded. "Mercy steers clear of anything related to either family businesses, and Corinthian just asks me not to kill anyone that means something to her." He smirked, and I knew he hadn't listened even though she had asked. "Now, enough about me; tell me about you."

"Nothing to tell." I shrugged. "Middle child to older parents. Big brother is a dick; younger brother can't think without using his."

"How'd y'all end up running a trucking business?"

"We took over our father's company. When he was running, it was a fully legit trucking business. After a while, we started including not-so-legal businesses in our routes. We all have a hand doing certain things; I run the office here."

"Yo' parents know what y'all do?"

"Yo' grandparents know what y'all do?" I countered.

"Yeah." He laughed, and I was surprised. "Who the hell you think taught us to shoot?"

"Get the fuck outta here," I replied, waving him off. "You're telling me that the big-time pastor knows he got killers in his family?"

"Shit, the big-time pastor will send us after someone if need be. He always warns folks that they never know when the devil will knock at their door. He doesn't tell them that sometimes the devil is one of us, and he sent us."

"That's crazy." I laughed and shook my head.

"That's life." He shrugged.

The game came back on, and we settled into our respective spots and watched it. Mercy was good, damn good, and Exodus was proud of her. The way he cheered her on like we were sitting on the sidelines had me laughing the entire time we watched her play. When I became sleepy, I cuddled up with him on the couch and let sleep take over. When I woke up the following day, Exodus was gone.

———

I walked into Yalonda's apartment and looked around. Coming to her house was my last option. There wasn't any way she would be here, but I hoped I could find some information she'd left behind. I let myself in using Naeem's extra key I had taken the last time I was at the hospital. Her three-bedroom apartment was clean and neat, like she'd just stepped out, but I knew she hadn't returned since Naeem had been shot. I lucked up, found her iPad under her bed, and returned it to the living room. Surprisingly, it wasn't dead, so I looked through it. There wasn't much on it because I knew my niece used it to watch YouTube. At the last minute, something told me to check the emails. Yalonda had an appointment at the clinic coming up. This bitch had something to do with my brother being shot, but was going to the clinic? I hope whatever she had, she couldn't get rid of. I stood and dropped the iPad in my purse just as the front door opened and Cade entered.

"The fuck are you doing here?" I asked, looking him up and down.

He looked like he hadn't slept in a day or two, which was the opposite of how he looked when I saw him at the office.

"Same thing as you, I'm guessing," he replied with a shrug. He pushed the door closed behind him and looked around. "You find anything?"

"No," I said, shaking my head. It was something in my brothers' eyes that made me lie. The appointment at the clinic could be a dead end, but I wouldn't know that until I went to check. I looked at my watch, realizing I had to get across town in less than fifteen minutes to catch Yalonda.

"You got somewhere to be?" Cade questioned as I moved past him. I nodded and grabbed the door handle so that I could leave. "You sure you didn't find anything?"

"Didn't I say no, Cade?" I answered with an attitude. "If you don't believe me, go look yourself."

"Check that attitude, Paxton." He chuckled and ran his hands over his beard. "If I keep telling you that shit, I'm going to forget you're my sister."

"Please do," I said, looking Cade up and down. "I have been wanting to forget you're my brother too." I patted my purse, and Cade ran his tongue over his teeth. He didn't know that Exodus had my gun, but he didn't need to know. I loved my brother, but I wasn't a fool. If he told me, he would forget I was his sister; I believed him. I'd seen Cade snatch up a girlfriend without a second thought, so I'd shot at him a time or two in the past when he'd come at me.

Cade stepped to the side and allowed me to walk out the door. He watched me walk to my car and pull off. I thought about my brothers' attitude the entire drive to the clinic, and I couldn't shake it. Cade was hiding something, and as soon as I figured out what the fuck went down with Naeem and Yalonda, I was going to figure out why Cade was acting the way he was.

Once I was near my destination, I grabbed my phone and dialed Exodus's number.

"Yeah?" he said after the third ring. He was breathless, and I could hear a woman in the background. Instantly I wanted to hang up and find him to see what bitch he was around. But I didn't, mainly because he wasn't my nigga, so I didn't have a right to be jealous, and also because I had other shit to worry about.

"You have my gun," I said as I switched lanes. "I need it back."

"No," he replied, and I found myself getting agitated.

"What do you mean, no?"

"I'm pretty sure the answer is self-explanatory." He chuckled. "But to make sure we are on the same page, what part of it didn't you understand?"

"Exodus! Give me my damn gun back!"

"Ay, yo, chill with the yellin', Hitta," he growled.

"No!" I stopped at a red light. "Give me my damn gun!"

"What the fuck do you need it for?" he growled. "I told you that you don't need that shit if I'm around you!"

"You're not around Exodus!" I fussed. "I'm by myself! In my damn car alone! So, I need my gun!"

"Where are you going, Hitta?" he questioned, and I shook my head, not wanting to answer him. "Huh, where you going?"

"To the clinic on thirty-fifth," I answered.

"Why?" he asked, then sucked his teeth. "You know what? It doesn't matter. I'll meet you there." He hung up before I could reply. Frustrated, I hit my steering wheel a few times. I sped for the rest of the drive, hoping to get to the clinic before Exodus.

I exited the car, went to the front door, and opened it. The last thing I expected to see was him standing in front of the receptionist's desk with his gun pointed at her. "The fuck took you so long?" he asked without looking at me.

"What are you doing?" I asked, surprised as hell.

"Why did you need to come to the clinic?" he asked me.

"To look for Yalonda," I said, looking around. The waiting room was empty except for the girl at the front desk who looked like she would piss herself if she hadn't.

"Yo' brother's girl?" He turned to look at me with a surprised look, and I nodded. "Oh."

"What did you think I was doing here?" I couldn't help but ask. Exodus bit into his bottom lip and shrugged. "That's not an answer."

"It doesn't matter," he said, then returned to the receptionist. "You heard her; check the system for Yalonda."

"I need a last name," the poor girl weakly answered.

"Mathews," I said when Exodus turned and looked at me. "DOB 7-5-98"

The receptionist nodded her head and then started typing. Her face twisted up in confusion for a second, then she nodded to herself. "She had an appointment yesterday; she came."

"What was it for?" I asked.

"An abortion," she quickly answered.

Exodus looked over at me and lifted his brow in question. I nodded my head, and he put his gun away. "Look, lil mama, I didn't mean to have to pull my gun on you, but sometimes niggas don't think shit all the way through. I apologize." He dug into his pocket with his empty hand and pulled out a small wad of money. He sat it on the desk, turned, and walked out of the clinic, dragging me behind him.

CHAPTER 24
Exodus

I WAS TRIPPIN', like majorly trippin', to the point that I was acting out of character, and I knew that shit wasn't cool. When Paxton called me talking about she needed her gun and then was on her way to the clinic, my mind started racing with all kinds of shit. At first, I thought she was hurt; all I saw was red. But then she said she was going to the clinic. I was ready to blast her ass. When I walked into the clinic and didn't see her, I politely asked the receptionist if she was there. She didn't even check the computer before telling me no, and that shit annoyed the hell out of me. Me pulling my gun was just instinct. Most of the problems I dealt with could be solved with a bullet. And at that moment, she felt like a damn problem.

"What is your issue?" Paxton yelled as I dragged her to her car. I looked at her and then shook my head; no words needed to be said. I took her keys out of her hand and unlocked her car doors. She'd dropped my truck off to me this morning on her way to work and was pushing her shit. She didn't even look right behind the wheel of her tiny ass Audi, now that I'd seen her drive my truck. "Umm, hello! I know you hear me talking to you right now."

"Shut up," I replied and opened her car door. Paxton stared at me with a confused look, and it took everything in me not to kiss her ass.

Even though I was pissed, I still wanted to kiss her, and that shit rocked me to my core. "Get in the car. Drive home, and I'll meet you there later."

"What?" She reared back and looked at me. "Exodus, who the fuck do you think you're talking to?"

"You!" I took her bag from her arm, threw it across her seat, and turned to look at her. "Now, get your stubborn ass in the car before I shake the shit out of you."

"I will not," she said, crossing her arms over her chest.

I bit into my fist and shook my head. I wasn't a woman beater and would never put my hands on one, but right now, I wanted to shake the shit out of Paxton. Like, have her damn head looking like a bobble-head that set in the window of the corny-ass white women's cars. Against my better judgment, I pulled my phone out of my pocket and dialed my grandmother.

"Hello?" she answered on the third ring.

"Madea tell this stubborn ass girl to get in the car before I lose the little bit of patience I have left," I told my grandmother. Even though I'd never mentioned Paxton to her and knew she would have questions later, I didn't care. I called her because no one ever told her no. It didn't matter if she'd known you for two seconds or your entire life when she asked you to do something; you did it.

"Give her the phone, Exodus," she sighed, and I shoved the phone to Paxton. "Oh well, hello."

"Hi," Paxton shyly responded, and I sucked my teeth. In all the years of being around Paxton, I had never seen her act shy with anyone.

"You aren't Mahogany," Madea said with a laugh. Over the years, there had been plenty of times I'd called Mary DeCorte on Mahogany. "What's your name, honey?"

"Paxton Littlejohn," she replied.

"Oh, I've heard of you!" Madea replied. "Well, it's good to put a name to a face. You are gorgeous."

"Thank you."

"You're welcome." She sighed, and I knew without having to see her because I knew my grandma well, she shook her head and rolled her eyes. "Now answer this for me, will you, sweetie?"

"Yes, ma'am."

"Is my grandson rubbing his beard with a blank expression?" she asked, and Paxton looked up at me. A small smile tugged her at plump lips, and then she nodded. "Okay, and is his nose doing that little flare thing that it does?" Again, a nod. "And does he keep flexing his hand like it hurts?" Nod. "Well, baby girl, get your ass in that car and do what he says because I am not there to stop him from going upside your head."

"He wouldn't hit me," Paxton replied with a laugh.

"No?" Madea questioned with her own laugh. She knew I wouldn't, but the fact that Paxton was comfortable enough to tell her that also had to come as a surprise.

"No, ma'am, he wouldn't," Paxton said as if she knew something no one else would. "But because you asked so nicely, I'll get in the car and go home."

"Thank you," Madea said. "Can you give Exodus the phone back, please?"

"Yes, ma'am," she said, then handed me the phone back.

"Yes, Madea," I said through clenched teeth as I watched Paxton get in the car and shut the door.

"I like her, Exodus," she said with a big-ass smile. "Call me later so we can talk." She hung up the phone simultaneously as Paxton rolled her window down.

"Your grandmother is beautiful," she said as if we were having the best conversation in the world, and I didn't want to shake the hell out of her. "You favor her a lot." I ran my tongue over my teeth and stared at her. "Can I have my gun now, please?" She stuck her hand out the window and wiggled her fingers.

Without a word, I walked back to my car. This girl was driving me fucking crazy, and she had no clue. She treated me like a fuck nigga when I wasn't a nigga to play with. I would have to show her that shit because I wasn't about to waste my breath talking when I knew she would never listen.

"So that's a no to my gun?" she yelled.

"Hell no!" I barked as I climbed into my truck. Paxton laughed as she rolled the window up, then pulled off.

———

"You gotta stop just pulling your gun and not thinkin' that shit through," Corinthian fussed after I told her everything that happened. Krude lay across the floor with a big-ass smile on his face. Why I'd decided to talk to my cousins was beyond me, but here I was, sitting in Corinthian's living room, still pissed off about dealing with Paxton yesterday.

"Fuck the gun shit," Krude said, still laughing. "You called Madea on her ass? Like legit snitched because she wouldn't do what you wanted her to?"

"And I'll do that shit again," I answered, looking between them. Corinthian and Krude shared a look before they busted out laughing.

"Big cousin, you like this girl," she said after catching her breath.

"You wouldn't say?" I questioned, confused as to how she figured that out. I was fascinated with Paxton at this point. Whenever we weren't hanging out, I wanted to be with her. I legit called her out of the blue to hear her voice and showed up at the spot to see her face. My days included Paxton, spending time with her mama and daddy at the hospital while they sat with Naeem and checking in on my businesses. I hadn't been to the warehouse since killing that nigga for stepping to Corinthian wrong, and I was cool with that.

"You do," she said, nodding her. Besides Mahogany, Corinthian was the only woman I had ever seen in person who rocked a short haircut and looked good on them. Since she was a tiny woman, maybe standing close to five feet, and was shapely, Corinthian tried to downplay her looks. Cutting her hair was one of the ways she tried, but unknowingly, it added to her appeal. There had been plenty of niggas in the past that one of us had to body because of her. She didn't know, and we planned to keep it that way. "It's the only reason you reacted the way you did."

"She ain't lying," Krude interjected, and I pushed his bowl of grapes that he had sitting next to him across the room with my foot. "Nigga!"

"Shut up," I grunted. "Nobody asked your ass shit."

"Yes, the fuck you did!" he argued. "When you brought your grumpy ass in here, fussing about how she doesn't listen, then started explaining what the fuck happened."

"I hope Megan beats your ass next time you do something stupid," I said, and he shrugged.

"That's so fucked up." Corinthian laughed, and it was my turn to shrug. "But back to you, Exodus. You like her." I opened my mouth to agree, but she held up her hand. "You do, and I know you do because if you didn't, her being at the clinic wouldn't have mattered to you. Nor would you be trying to find out who shot her brother. If you're not invested, or it doesn't make you money, you don't care. You already said she wasn't paying you even though she offered, so you have to care, which means you like her. Plus, you brought her around Judah, which has never happened before."

"Right, but as you said, she is treating you like a sneaky link, which I think is your other problem," Krude said. He'd gotten up while Corinthian was talking, grabbed his fruit, and sat beside her. "You said y'all fucked, and she put you out the first night, right? Well, nigga, she is treating you like a nigga would treat a female, and that shit is bothering you. Especially cuz you find yourself liking her."

"Okay, so I kinda am feeling her."

"You introduced her to me and Judah as your girlfriend!" Corinthian fussed, and I smirked.

"I did that shit so that nigga knew not to flirt with her," I said. "You know yo' son be having women in the palm of his hands without even trying."

"Oh, so you jealous?" Krude laughed, and I mugged the shit out of him. "You jealous of your younger cousin and getting used for your dick, and now you are in your feelings. You gotta fix that."

"How is he going to fix it, Krude?" Corinthian asked with a laugh.

"Kidnap her." He shrugged.

"What?" Corinthian and I yelled in unison.

"You heard me," Krude said, like the shit was normal. "I know she got that shit going on with her brother, but you can still snatch her ass up for a day or two. Show her you ain't a no punk nigga, dick her down real good, and then she'll act right."

I sat back in my seat and thought over what he was saying. I could snatch her up, take her home with me for a few days, then bring her back. I wiped my hand over my face and shook my head. I had to be trippin' if Krude's suggestion sounded good.

"Don't listen to him, Ex," Corinthian said, shaking her head. "He doesn't know what he is talking about regarding women."

"It works!" Krude fussed. "I did that shit with Megan, and look at us."

"You did it with Megan?" I asked because I'd never heard that shit before.

"I tried, but she tased me in the nuts when I jumped out at her." He shrugged like that shit was normal. "But Paxton, don't give me the violent vibe." He stopped and thought it over. "But just in case she is, I'd used chloroform on her ass."

"Where the fuck is he going to get chloroform from Krude?"

"Nigga, do you niggas know how to do anything for yourself?" he asked, looking at the two of us as if it was a normal thing to have. "I got some if you want to borrow it."

Me and Corinthian shared a look, then I shook my head. I wasn't surprised by the shit my cousin came up with or that he readily had chloroform available. Instead of questioning him and knowing I would get a headache, I rubbed my hands over my face and relaxed back into my seat.

CHAPTER 25

Paxton

"THEY ARE THINKING about lowering his medicine and trying to pull him out of the coma," Mama said as soon as I walked into Naeem's room. I sat down next to her and rested my head on her shoulder. My eyes wandered over the food on the small tray beside her. She had eaten, which was one less thing on my plate that I had to worry about. Just like Mama thought I wouldn't take care of myself because I was stressing over Naeem's condition, I had the same worries as her. "He's been fighting it, anyway."

"I figured he had been," I replied with a slight nod. "You know Naeem has never been on anybody else's schedule but his own."

"Even in the womb." Mama laughed. "He came a month early, kicking and screaming, mad at the world. Even being so little, he knew what he wanted and did what he wanted."

"Which is why him fighting that medicine isn't a surprise to anyone of us."

"I know," she sighed. "I just don't know what state he will be in when he wakes up. The doctors are concerned about it, just like I am." She looked down at me and smirked. "I know you, and I know him. If the Naeem that wakes up isn't the Naeem, we know you'll never stop hunting Yalonda." I lifted my head and looked at Mama. "There's no reason to deny it."

"I haven't been since the first couple of days," I said, then turned back to look at my Naeem. Guilt instantly washed over me, and I shook my head. My free time was spent with Exodus. We weren't going out, but he was either at my house or I was at his when I wasn't here. "I plan to change that, though."

"How does that song go?" she said, giving me a sad smile.

"What song?"

"Oh, you know, that one that goes, 'Mama, don't worry, you raised a gangsta.' Or something like that."

"Mama, what the hell have you been listening to?" I laughed.

"That's my ringtone on Naeem's phone." She laughed. "It's kind of catchy."

"Girl, you're too old to be listening to that," I said, shaking my head. "Stay with what you know. Don't go do that dark path."

"I could say the same to you, but I know you won't listen," she said, and I nodded. "Just promise me you'll be smart. Don't go out there working on just emotion. Listen, when people talk and pay attention to what they aren't saying. And if you can have someone in your corner. I know you and your brother don't trust easily, but having someone watch your back would help me sleep at night."

"All right, mama," I agreed. Mama didn't usually talk to me about me and my brother's illegal activities. She looked the other way because she knew she couldn't and wouldn't change our minds. But I considered her words. And as for having someone in my corner, the only person I could think of was Exodus. And as if he knew I was thinking of him, Exodus texted my phone.

Exodus: Meet me at the corner of Benton and Twenty-second.

Me: When?

Exodus: Now

"You're leaving?" Mama asked, and I stood up. I nodded and dropped a kiss on her cheek. "Well, be careful."

"Always," I said as I left. "Love you; call me if anything changes."

I pulled up next to Exodus's truck and watched him get out. He looked good in blue jeans, a green tee, and Jordans. "Who you know that owns a green Tahoe?" Exodus asked after he pulled my door open. I shut my car off and unbuckled my seatbelt. He let out an annoyed sigh, and I cut my eyes at him. "Who?"

"Just Xavi," I answered. A quick look of confusion swept across his face before it went blank. "Why?" I exited the car, stepped aside to stand in front of the back door, and slammed the door shut. My body was wedged between him and the car, and even though I didn't want to, I loved the feeling of him being close to me.

"That truck, his truck?" He nodded toward something over my head. Quickly, I glanced back and saw Xavi's truck. I knew it was his because of the black streak from the front to the back with his name on it.

"That's Xavi's." I nodded after turning around. "Why?"

"Cuz that truck pulled up next to your brothers' car and started shooting," he answered.

"It wasn't Xavi, though," I said, shaking my head. Exodus's face twisted up like he didn't believe me. "Xavi was in the passenger seat of Naeem's car when he was shot. Whoever was driving his truck was the shooter."

"Then let's go find out who it was." Exodus shrugged. He started walking, but stopped when he noticed I wasn't beside him. "Why are you not coming?"

"My gun?" I said, putting my hand out. Exodus smirked and shook his head. "You're not going to give me my gun back, knowing we could enter a dangerous situation?"

"What happened to the one you had strapped to your thigh?"

"I left it at home." I shrugged, and he sucked his teeth in disbelief. "I did." I didn't even try to stop my laughter when Exodus wiped his hand over his face. "Just give me my gun, Exodus."

"I swear I should give your ass like a dessert eagle or something big as fuck for no reason," he replied as he walked back to his truck. He yanked the driver's door open and grabbed my gun from the panel. I didn't have any doubt that it had been there since he took it from me. Why didn't I check for it when I had his truck was beyond me. Exodus slammed his truck door, walked over to me, and stared me down. "You do some stupid shit in there, and I swear on everything I love, I'll make you regret that shit."

"Is that a promise?" I teased with a smirk on my face. "Cuz I'll probably be reckless no matter what." For no reason other than I wanted to, I lifted to the tip of my toes and kissed his lips quickly. Exodus's shocked expression mirrored the enteral panic I felt once I realized what I'd done. I stepped back, checked over my gun, flipped the safety off, and headed to the house. "You not gonna say a verse?" I glanced over at Exodus as we stepped on the porch.

"Nah," he said, shaking his head.

"Why not?"

"Who said we were going to kill anybody?" he asked with a laugh.

I expected to hear him laugh or even crack a smile, but he didn't. Instead, he wore a serious look on his face. If, for one minute, he thought I would let anyone in this house walk out alive was comical. I didn't believe in forgiveness; if he did, then that was on him. With no words, I banged on the door with the butt of my gun and waited for someone to answer.

CHAPTER 26
Exodus

SHE WAS GOING to kill any and everyone we came in contact with. I knew that the moment I called her after Nine got me the address connected with the truck. The thought didn't do anything but turn me on. The image of Paxton with a gun in her hand, staring down a nigga or a bitch, was the sexiest thing I could think of. It was probably why I was so damn fascinated. I knew my mindset wasn't normal, but it didn't stop me from wanting her ass. I also knew that if one nigga stepped to her wrong, I would spazz the fuck out.

Jaymie's bitch ass voice echoed through my mind. He said that Yalonda had set him up with connecting Xavi. What were the chances that this was the same nigga? I texted Nine, asking him to look more into Xavi and Naeem. I wouldn't bring it up to Paxton until I knew it was more to the situation.

Paxton lifted her hand and used the butt of her gun to beat on the door. There were a few minutes of silence, then we heard someone yelling that they were coming. Paxton's impatient ass pounded on the door again, and I chuckled.

"Man, who the fuck is beating on my damn door?" Xavi yelled as he pulled the door open. His eyes got big when he realized it was

Paxton and tried to shut up. I put my foot in the door to stop him from slamming it and shook my head.

"You smash his foot again. I'm going to put three bullets in your balls, Xavi!" she yelled, pushing against the door. "Open this mutha-fucka up so we can talk!"

"Nah, Paxton," Xavi said, pushing against the door. He was a little nigga, both height and weight-wise. He had to be no more than five-three and weighed no more than a buck ten soaking wet. To see his little ass struggling to try to close the door was funny as fuck. "You don't know how to fuckin' talk!"

"Fuck it," she said, then looked over at me. "Move your foot and let him slam it close. I'll shoot this muthafucka down." I did what she said, and the door slammed closed. "You got two fuckin' seconds! One!" she flipped her safety off and aimed it at the door.

"No!" he yelled, then snatched it open. Paxton aimed her gun right between his eyes and backed him into the house. "Look, Paxton, I don't know shit."

"You know something, or you wouldn't be hiding from me," she said, shaking her head. We stepped into the house and looked around. Xavi lived like a fuckin' slob. Clothes, shoes, and food containers were everywhere. Instantly my skin started to crawl, and I was ready to fucking go. Out of the corner of my eye, I watched a roach crawl up the wall, and I knew I was going home to shower after this.

"I don't know shit, Paxton."

"All right." She nodded. Her hand holding her gun quickly dropped, and she shot two bullets into his right thigh. Xavi fell to the ground, screaming and holding his leg. A woman came from the back dressed in a t-shirt and panties. I'd seen her around the hood a few times, but didn't know her name. Without thinking twice, Paxton shot her in the chest and then turned her attention back to Xavi. "Now, let's try this again, shall we? Who shot my brother?"

"I don't know," Xavi groaned. His leg was bleeding badly. She'd more than likely nicked an artery, and he would soon bleed to death. "I swear I don't know."

"Who pulled up on y'all at Yalonda's house?" she asked. When

Xavi said nothing, Paxton stepped on his leg, making him scream. "Tell me what I want to know, Xavi, and this will all be over."

"It was Cade," he finally answered. Paxton's face went from twisted to hurt to anger in seconds. I didn't know who Cade was, but I damn sure planned to find out. "Cade borrowed my truck the day before. He said he wanted to surprise you and Naeem. When he pulled up on us, I thought he would do that. I ducked down on the floor when he pulled his gun out and started blasting. I didn't know shit about that nigga doing that shit!"

"Then why did you run?" Paxton asked, shaking her head. "If my brother shot Naeem, why did you run?"

"Because what the fuck do you think he would do to me if he shot his own brother?" Xavi yelled. "Y'all got the same blood flowing through y'all veins, and he didn't hesitate to pull the trigger. I know my life doesn't mean shit to him!"

"Why did Cade call and borrow your truck from you?"

"He does it all the time," Naeem whined like a fucking baby, and that shit annoyed me. "Whenever he comes into town, and he doesn't want y'all to know for whatever reason, he will hit me up and ask to borrow my truck. It's usually only for a few hours; he moves in and out quickly. He has for a couple of months."

"And you never mentioned that shit?" Paxton kicked Xavi in the stomach.

"I didn't think about it! Naeem and Cade always drop in on each other without mentioning it."

"Why?" Paxton yelled.

"I don't know!" Xavi moaned and swayed from side to side, still holding his leg. "Naeem always said he was just checking in on Cade and the company, but the last few months, he said he didn't trust Cade. The morning he was shot, he said he would talk to you later that day. I'm just the middleman here, Paxton! Naeem is my nigga, we get money together, but I don't clock his moves like that!"

"Well then, you aren't needed then, huh?" she asked, then shot him in the chest. I called Kino, letting him know I needed a cleanup, and dropped him off at my location. Paxton looked down at Xavi and shook her head.

"You ready?" I asked, and she nodded. Cade being responsible for Naeem being shot was fucking with her heavily, I could tell. But shit, I didn't blame her; if I found out my brother was responsible for my other brother being shot, I would be lost too.

I followed behind her, wondering where she was headed. Paxton's house was on the other side of town, but I knew I wouldn't let her move without me being by her side. We would do that if she needed to ride around and get her mind right. When we started heading south, I realized the only place she could probably be going was my house. I hit the garage door opener when she pulled into my driveway. My garage was big enough to park at least six cars in, but my trucks were big, so they took up more space. Paxton parked her Audi in my spot, and I left my truck in the driveway. As if on autopilot, she exited her car, grabbed a bag from her trunk, and headed into the house with me on her heels.

"I need to shower," she said, and I nodded. I would give her some space, so I whipped up some burgers and fries while she showered. When she didn't come back down by the time I was done, I headed upstairs to look for her. I didn't hear the shower going when I entered my room, but I could hear the water moving.

I pushed the bathroom door open to find Paxton in the bathtub, relaxed, laying back with her eyes closed. She had the lights low, but I could still see the tears slowly rolling down her face. The sight of her being hurt broke something in me, yeah, Cade was her brother, but that nigga was going to die for hurting her like this. Plus, I wouldn't ever want to put some shit on her soul; killing her brother would be too heavy of a burden.

"Slide up," I said after stripping off my clothes. Paxton did as I asked, and I climbed into the tub behind her. The water was hot, but I wasn't surprised because most women loved scalding hot water. "Chill, man." I pulled her back so she rested against me, and we stayed like that for a while. I let her cry out because I knew her pain was deep. Paxton loved her brothers, yeah, she said that her oldest brother got her damn nerves, but she never mentioned that there was bad blood between them.

"This is going to break my parents," Paxton mumbled softly and sighed. "I don't want to tell them, but I have to." She angrily swiped away her face. "I hate Cade for doing this! He didn't have to try to kill him over his and Naeem's beef."

"You had no clue he was in town?" I asked, trying to piece shit together with the bit of information Xavi told us. Something was telling me there was more to the story, but with Naeem still in a coma and Cade missing, there was no way we would get more information.

"No," she answered, shaking her head. "And Naeem never mentioned going to check in on Cade, which makes none of this shit make sense. I gotta find Cade." She tried to get out of the tub, but I grabbed her wrist. "Let me go, Exodus."

"Nah, Hitta," I said, shaking my head. She cut her eyes at me, and I saw her hurt. Paxton carried this shit like it was her fault. "Chill out and stay in the tub. It ain't shit you can do right now, anyway."

"You don't know what I can do!" she hissed and tried to snatch from me again, but I held on tight. "Let. Me. Go."

"No can do, baby." I chuckled. I wasn't just talking about physically, either. The short time we'd spent together over the last few weeks showed me she was it for me. "Now sit down and finish your bath."

"No," she stubbornly refused.

I jerked her arm and made her fall into me. Water slashed over the edge of the tub and onto the floor. Paxton stared down at me with fire shooting from her eyes, but I didn't give a damn. "Chill the fuck out," I said, then crashed my mouth into her. Paxton tried to fight against kissing me, but I pushed my tongue into her mouth, not giving a fuck that she was pissed at me. I let go of her wrist when she started kissing me back, and she wrapped her arms around my neck. Right before Mahogany sold me her house, she had the bathroom remodeled, so the tub was big as fuck. We had more than enough space length and width wise. Paxton unwrapped one of her arms from around my neck and started stroking my dick. My shit was already hard, but feeling her touch made it harder.

Without instruction, Paxton let me go and adjusted herself over my dick. The water was warm, but I could still feel her hot ass pussy as she hovered over my dick. She lowered herself slowly, giving her time to adjust to my size without hurting herself. "Shit," she moaned once she was seated. Paxton started to rock her hips, and I grabbed onto her waist. I started to fuck her from below, but she shook her head. "Don't move." I stopped and let her take control of the entire situation. This had to be the shit Krude was talking about when he said that Megan fucked him because the way that Paxton was controlling my dick had my toes curling and me biting into my lip to keep from moving. She planted her feet on the side of my body and smirked at me before she rocked faster. Her pussy felt so good that I had to let go of her and hold on to the tub's edge to keep from cumming. She was using my dick to let out her frustrations.

"Shit, baby," I groaned and dropped my head back. Her pussy started clinging down to my dick, and I bucked up. "Fuck!"

"I'm cumming," she moaned, and I could feel her start to lose control. "Shit, Exodus!" I opened my legs more and let go of the tub to grab her waist. She started buckling faster as she chased her nut, and I fucked from her below. "Shit!"

"Cum for me, Hitta," I groaned as I wrapped one of my hands around her neck and pulled her to me. I latched onto her mouth and kissed the fuck out of her as she came on my dick. Her pussy clamped down on my dick, and I nutted. There was no way I was pulling out as she slammed down on my dick, nor did I want to. Paxton lay against my chest. I could feel her heart beating against my chest, and I wrapped my arms around her waist. Her pussy was still spazzing around my dick, but I wasn't trying to pull out. I ran my fingers up and down her spine, and we sat in the tub, quiet as fuck. I knew Paxton was thinking about everything, and while that shit seemed too much for her to bear, I wasn't worried about it. I'd kill her brother myself; that was already decided.

CHAPTER 27
Paxton

THIS WAS the second time I'd woken up in Exodus's bed. I did not know what was happening the first time because I was knocked out; I'd willingly gone this time. After having sex last night, we shared a shower, ate the burger and french fries he'd made, then went to bed. In my mind, I'd decided that he'd cashed in more of his hours from our bet, but I knew the real reason was. I wanted to spend the night. I only wanted to be alone after discovering that Cade was responsible for shooting Naeem and killing Xavi and his girlfriend, Sheena. Exodus wasn't having it, though; I don't think I was either because I'd driven to his house last night without even realizing it.

I pushed myself out of bed and looked around; I was alone. Exodus's phone had rung an hour ago, and he'd jumped out of bed. He got dressed, kissed my forehead, and left without a word. Granted, he thought I was asleep, but that was beside the point. After peeing and handling my hygiene, I stepped out of the bathroom wrapped in a towel. The other overnight bag I pulled from my trunk when I got here sat in the corner of the room. I grabbed it and dropped it on the bed. The clock on the wall said it was close to eight, and I needed to get to the hospital to relieve my mama. She had stayed the night, and I wanted her to get home and rest. I put on lotion and then on my clothes. I didn't feel like putting on any make-up, so I pulled off my bonnet, fluffed my curls with water and leave-in conditioner, and called it a day. My phone was dead on the table next to the bed, but I had a charger in my car, so I wasn't worried about it.

Once on the road and my phone had come back to life, I scrolled through my text messages while sitting at a light. I replied to a few of them but ignored the rest. I stopped and grabbed Mama something to eat before getting to the hospital. I waved to the receptionist as I passed her and got to Naeem's room.

"Hey, baby girl," Daddy greeted me as I entered the room. I looked around for Mama but didn't see her.

"Hey, Daddy," I replied, then kissed his cheek. "Where, Mommy?"

"Already at the house," he responded. "She's running on fumes and not resting, so I got here early to let her get home and rest."

"You already ate, I see." I nodded toward the food bags in the trash beside him.

"Nah, yo' mama did," he said, shaking his head. I put the food bag on the small rolling table and pushed it toward him. "Why thank you, baby."

"No problem, Daddy," I replied, then pulled everything out of the bag. My mama was a picky eater, but Daddy would eat just about anything you put in front of him. I handed him a breakfast burrito, and I sat down next to him.

"So, what have you found out?" Daddy asked in between bites of his food. I looked over at him and sighed because I didn't want to tell my daddy his oldest was responsible for all this, but I knew I had to. "Oh, I know that sigh." He let out a small laugh and shook his head. "Whatever you know must be bad, and you don't want to tell us." I shook my head, and he nodded his. "Okay, so how about this." He took another bite, chewed, then swallowed it. "Don't tell me what you don't want me to know. Just promise me you'll be careful."

"Okay," I said, nodding.

"You know you never told me about that date you went on not too long ago," Daddy said after we finished our food. The nurse checked on Naeem while we ate and informed us that the doctor had decided to lower his medication. They were slowly weaning him from the medication. He hadn't woken up yet, but we had faith that he would and would be okay.

"It was a shit show," I said, laughing, and Daddy looked at me, confused. "Qumar."

"Qumar?" Daddy's face twisted up. "The guy you went on a date with name was Qumar?"

"Yes." I nodded.

"That's a dumb ass name," he replied with a chuckle.

"It's what his parents named him." I laughed and shook my head. Daddy grunted and shrugged. "Anyway, he just wasn't it for me."

"Why not?" He leaned back in his seat and got comfortable. Daddy was a tall man, standing close to six-five and still in decent shape for a man his age.

"He just didn't do it for me." I didn't want to tell him it wouldn't have mattered, even if I was interested because Exodus had killed him. Daddy was an understandable man, but I doubt he would understand a man like Exodus. Shit, it was times I didn't understand him or why he acted the way he did, but the more time I spent with him, the more I enjoyed it.

"So, you're back on the market?"

"I wouldn't say that," I answered with a smirk.

"Why not?"

"There's this man." I shrugged. "I don't know what we are doing, but I'm enjoying the crazy ass ride."

"Okay, now baby, let me ask you this," he sighed, and I knew I would get a long lecture in the form of a question. I rolled my eyes and then sat back in my seat. "Don't settle for a man because you think me and yo' mama wanna see you with somebody. Qumar may not have been the one for you, but don't just jump to the next one because you think you should. Don't waste your time if he doesn't treat you right, make you smile, and feel protected and loved. These new-age niggas don't know anything about loving a woman. So, find someone that does."

"Daddy, you never asked me a question, you know that?" I asked, and he smirked at me.

"I didn't have to." He shrugged. "As soon as I started talking, the look on your face told me what I needed to know."

"Which was?"

"That his crazy matches yours, so it's fine." He laughed, and I rolled my eyes. "Whenever you're ready to bring him around, just let me know. I gotta feel your brother will be awake sooner rather than later, and our lives will be good."

I glanced over at Naeem and sighed. He would wake up, but what happened afterward was in the air.

CHAPTER 28

Exodus

"I'MA KILL HER BROTHER." I pushed down on the drill, cutting into Hampton's leg. He screamed as the drill bore into his shin. I hit the reverse button and pulled the drill out of his leg. The blood seeped from the small hole, and I shook my head. "I know it's fucked up because I'm feeling her ass too. I didn't expect it to happen, though. Like our chemistry has always been there, she is fine as fuck, but we have the same best friend, and I never wanted to start anything and end up having to end it, and our best friend be stuck in the middle. But you know how niggas are; I just had to sample it, and her sex is definitely Chef's kiss, but I thought once I got a little sample of it, I would be good." I stepped back, put the drill on the table beside me, and pulled my goggles off my face. "I was wrong as fuck, Hampton. Like seriously wrong."

"Kill me, man," Hampton cried, and I shook my head. This nigga wasn't dying that easily; he had to suffer. Instead of responding to him, I walked around the table and stared at my work. I'd been here for nearly two hours. After waking up to Paxton still in my bed and having breakfast with Mrs. Littlejohn, I headed straight here. Hampton had been dropped off last night, stripped like everyone is, dunked in an ice bath, and only pulled out once I was here. "Please, just kill me."

"I can't do that yet, Hampton," I replied. "See, you have some information that I need, and since you tried to come to me with some bullshit while I was being respectful, this is where we are."

"I didn't know what was happening!" Hampton screamed. "Some niggas came to my spot last night and snatched me up. I was scared, man!"

"You called my mama a bitch as soon as I walked into the room, man." I chuckled and shook my head. "I was just going to come in here, ask a few questions, then that would be it."

"You are lying," he fussed and shook his head. "I heard of you nigga; I know how you roll. If somebody walks in here, ain't no way they are walking back out alive. The shit doesn't happen."

"Who told you that?" I questioned with a laugh.

"The hood talks!" Hampton yelled. "They know if Cross is looking for you, then you a dead nigga!"

"That's fucked up!" I laughed and shook my head. "I ain't even Cross, but I'll be sure to share the information." The fact that my cousin had niggas shaken was always comical to me. Cross didn't even live here, shit really; she was a nomad, in my opinion. But if she liked it, then I loved it.

"You aren't Cross?"

"Nah, man," I said once I got myself together. "I'm Ex."

"The prayer, nigga?" Hampton's eyes bucked out of his head as he looked at me. "Oh shit, no nigga, just ask your questions so I can tell you want you to want to know. There's no reason I'm here because I don't do shit to get on your radar!"

"Tell me about Cade," I said, getting straight to the point. "And understand something, nigga." I stopped talking for dramatic effect. I knew Hampton would talk; there wasn't any question about it. I picked up a sharp-ass knife off the table and looked it over. I always wanted to skin a nigga alive, but no one lived long enough to finish. I looked at Hampton and shook my head; his ass wouldn't survive past the second or third cut, let alone peeling his skin off. "I don't take too well to being lied to, either."

"He's hiding out," Hampton said. "He did some shit; I don't know what, but he's staying low."

"When's the last time you saw him?" I set the knife down.

"Two days ago, he came by my spot to borrow some money, but I told him no. He already owes me a few bands as it is."

"What does he need the money for?"

"I don't know." I picked up a meat cleaver and walked back over to Hampton. There were six straps holding his body down to the table, so I wasn't worried about him getting away. I flatted out his hand and chopped off the tip of his fingers on his right hand. "Ahhhhh!" he screamed, and I moved around the table.

"Think about your answers, Hampton," I said. "Now try again."

"He said he hit a quick lick for his baby mama," Hampton cried. "I didn't ask no questions cuz that bitch stay in the streets. It's rumors that those kids ain't even his, yet he's claiming them."

"Why you niggas always lying about shit?" I asked more to myself than him. "One minute it's I don't know, then the next you're telling it all. You could've had all your fingers intact if you just told the truth."

"I'm sorry!" He cried harder when I lifted the meat cleaver to slice on his other hand. "What else you wanna know, man? I'll tell you!"

"Where is Cade hiding?" I asked again.

"He's with his baby mama," he answered quickly. "When he came by not too long ago, he was boasting about how he was taking over some shit and wasn't nobody going to stop him. His baby mama was with him, hyping him up and talking about it's about time. He been playing second string for too long."

"That's all?" I asked, and he nodded. "You sure?"

"Yeah, man, that's all."

"Who is his baby mama?" In all the conversations about her family, Paxton only mentioned her brother Naeem having kids. Not even Mrs. Littlejohn said anything about more grandkids, so hearing that Cade had kids was a surprise.

"Yalonda," he cried.

"Wait a minute nigga." I chuckled. "Ain't his brother baby mama named Yalonda?"

"They aren't Naeem's kids," Hampton sobbed. "They are Cade's. Yalonda and Cade been fuckin' around for years. Way before she got with Naeem. Those are his kids; everybody knows it." It looked like

Yalonda was playing both of them. She had the brothers thinking they were their kids and telling another nigga that they, well, at least the youngest, was his. It wouldn't surprise me if she were the mastermind behind all this.

"Well, shit," I said, shaking my head. The plot thickens in this whole drama. "And you sure you don't know where they are?"

"Nah, man," Hampton replied. "They are hiding out because they know Cade's sister Paxton is looking for them. Cade said he was going to have to knock her off too."

"What?" I growled. I could feel the vein in my neck throbbing, and my body got hot. There wasn't a chance in hell he was going after Paxton. "He said that shit?"

"Yeah." Hampton nodded. "He said he was going to kill her."

"You did good, Hampton," I said, patting him on the cheek. "Real good."

"You gonna let me live then?" he asked, hopeful. "I answered all your questions. I didn't lie to you anymore! Just let me live, man!" As his punk ass begged for his life, I looked over the knife table. He wasn't going to live; there wasn't any way I was letting him walk up out of here. Since he answered my questions, I would let his death be quick. My phone vibrated, and I checked it to see a message from Paxton.

Paxton: I'm cashing in on more of your time.

Me: How are you cashing in on my time, Hitta?

Paxton: Don't ask questions; just be ready to go in two hours.

Me: Where are we going?

Paxton: Didn't I say don't ask questions?

Me: I'll be at your spot in two hours.

I checked the time, knowing I would probably cut it close. Getting to my house from here would take close to an hour. After showering and getting ready, it would take me another thirty minutes to get to Paxton's spot. I put my phone away and turned back to Hampton, who was still crying and begging for his life. I picked back up the meat cleaver and walked over to him.

"Do not let your hearts be troubled. You believe in God; believe in me as well. John chapter fourteen, verse one." I chopped off Hampton's head before he even knew what was happening.

CHAPTER 29

Paxton

"YOU'RE GOING to bust your damn head open," I said to Exodus as I slowly walked. I stuck my head out every two steps to ensure I wouldn't hit a glass wall. We were at a 'Smoke & Walk,' which was nothing but glass mazes, and people smoked while they tried to figure out how to get out of them without busting their heads open or getting injured. The girls and I went every year, but with them being pregnant, I didn't want to risk them injuring themselves, so I texted Exodus and told him to be ready to go in two hours. I'd had tickets since last year because they sold out so fast, and I didn't want them to go to waste.

"Who fuckin' thought this was a good idea?" he asked, following behind me. He'd already hit his head several times, and I could see a small knot starting to form, but I didn't say anything. "You had me hot box for thirty minutes before we started this shit. I'm too high to try to figure out where I'm supposed to walk."

"That's the point," I said with a laugh.

"That's the point?" he questioned and mugged me. "That sounds crazy as fuck." Exodus took two more steps, then turned slightly. His head hit the wall so loud that I had to turn around and look at him. "These muthafuckas are trying to kill me!"

"No, they aren't." I laughed and made my way over to him. "You are just trying to move too fast. What's the rush?"

"I'm hungry as fuck!" he fussed and rubbed his head. "You smoke me out, put me in a damn glass maze, and then tell me we can't eat until we leave? Hitta, I'm not a damn lab rat looking for a piece of cheese at the end. Stop playin' with me."

I looked over the knot on Exodus's head that he'd hit to make sure he wasn't really fucking himself up. Because he was light skin, it looked a lot worse than it probably felt, but he would still be bruised. I grabbed the collar of his shirt and pulled him down to me.

"You'll survive." I kissed him, ensuring it wasn't too much because we could never stop once we started up. "Now let's go. If you leave here without fuckin' yourself up too bad, I'll feed you."

"You ain't got no damn choice," he fussed, and I shook my head. "I know it's got to be a cheat to this shit."

"It is," I replied, and Exodus sucked his teeth in frustration. "All you have to do is put your hands out. It's a slightly windy day, right?" I looked over my shoulder to see him staring at me with a mug on his face. "Put your hands out."

"For what?" He lifted his brow in question. "You're not about to have me looking stupid so you can laugh.

"Put your hands out, Exodus," I sighed. He stared at me for a few seconds, and I could see the wheels turning in his head. "Please?"

"If you take a picture of me lookin' stupid, you walkin' home," he fussed, then did what I asked. "I'on feel shit."

"Exactly." I nodded. "If it's windy and you don't feel anything, something is blocking the wind. Move your hands around; walk that way if you feel the breeze."

Exodus moved a few steps to determine whether I was telling him the truth. When he realized I was, he looked at me and ran his tongue across his teeth. "You could've told me that shit from the jump."

"Then I wouldn't have gotten to see you bust your head a couple of times," I replied. Exodus mugged the hell out of me, and I laughed.

———

"Okay, so tell me something," I said as we lay in bed a few hours later. We'd eaten, showered, and were relaxing. We ended up finishing three mazes before calling it a night. Once Exodus figured it out, he wanted to keep going, and because we were having so much fun, I didn't object.

"What you wanna know?" Exodus replied. He had his hands behind his head and looked up at the ceiling. I sat up, my back against the headboard, looking through reports. The small lamp next to my bed was the only light on, but it was enough to let me read what I needed to.

"What's the significance of the rosary you always have with you?"

"You know my grandparents raised me, right?" he asked, glancing over at me. I nodded, and he turned back to look at the ceiling. "Well, my daddy killed my mama when I was six. Nigga got drunk, was driving reckless, and hit a pole. My mama died on impact, and he lived, walking away from the wreck with no injuries, not even a damn scratch. I was pissed; even at six, I knew my mama didn't deserve to die, and that nigga did. My daddy didn't even serve any jail time for it. He didn't even plan her funeral; Madea did. She was mourning the death of her daughter-in-law and watching her son drink himself to death."

"Where were your mama's parents?" I asked after I set down my papers.

"Long dead." He shrugged. "They died before I was born."

"I'm sorry," I said. "I know that had to be hard."

"No reason to be sorry, Hitta." He smirked. "I didn't know them, so it's cool. Anyway, on the day of the funeral, Madea gave me this rosary and told me it was my mamas."

"Can I see it?"

Exodus rolled over, grabbed the rosary off the end table next to the bed, and handed it to me. I expected it to be light, but it had a little weight. Rose gold rings connected black, wooden balls, and at the end was a black cross. "Exodus chapter fifteen verse thirteen?" I read out loud the tiny words written on the cross.

"In your unfailing love, you will lead the people you have redeemed," he said, without looking at me. "She used to swear that was meant for me." He let out a small laugh. "Out of all the grandkids, I was supposed to become the preacher. She swore I would lead countless souls to the Lord."

"You do." I slightly laughed, and he looked over at me and smirked.

"I'm pretty sure my mama didn't mean it like you do." He laughed. I handed him back his rosary, then laid down next to him, resting my head on his chest, and traced my index finger over his stomach. His front torso was covered in a large mural of downtown. It was so detailed that I found myself studying it. Some of the buildings had lights in the windows; the streets had lines as well as the sidewalks. Stop lights were colored in, street signs were labeled correctly, and even the sewer covers had lines of steam seeping from them.

"She would still be proud of you, though," I said.

"You think so?" he questioned.

"You're successful, handsome, loyal, and stand on your own two feet. What wouldn't she be proud of?" I asked, looking up at him. I brushed my finger over his thick eyebrows, and he smirked. I touched him increasingly, and Exodus seemed to notice, too. But he didn't seem to mind. If anything, he encouraged it by staying close to me.

"I guess you're right."

"You're a little off, but it's excusable." I laughed, lighting up the mood. Exodus sucked his teeth and shook his head. I laughed and grabbed his chin between my thumb and index finger to make him look down at me. "Your mama would be proud of you. She's watching over you every minute of every day, smiling down at you."

"Oh, you think so?" he questioned, and I nodded. "Well, let's give her something to cheer for then." He moved quickly, grabbing me under my arms and pulling me up, then flipping us over so I was beneath him. I could feel his dick harden as he stared down at me before lifting his head to look at the ceiling. "Mama, if you don't want to see this side of me, you might want to go look at Madea for a few hours."

"Hours?" I questioned with a laugh, and Exodus looked down at me and smiled. The hungry look in his eyes instantly had my pussy soaked and throbbing. He reached down, pushed his shorts off, and settled between my thighs. Since I wasn't wearing any panties, I knew he could feel my wetness. He grabbed my hands and pinned them above my head with one hand, and using the other, he guided his dick inside me, causing me to hiss. "Shit!"

"Yeah, hours," Exodus said, then started moving inside me. I had no objection; if he wanted hours, that's precisely what he would get.

CHAPTER 30

Exodus

"KILL HER BROTHER," Cross said casually as she walked through Krude's living room. I shook my head and returned to looking for the information December had sent me a few days ago. Finding Cade was easy; that shit took a couple of hours once I got his number from Hampton's phone. It was the business plans that had me stressed. If someone with no business experience looked over the files, they would think shit was on the up and up, but I knew what I was looking at. Paxton and Naeem operated their business well, they made damn good money, but Cade was raking it in. He had his hand in everything, taking a more significant cut by adding taxes and fees that weren't originally there. Because they were so damn good and made good times, I'm guessing that no one questioned the prices.

"He can't just kill the brother," Judge said, looking up from the book he was reading. They were in town for the weekend, and while I loved my cousins, I was ready for the weekend to be over, and it was only Friday morning. "He could, but if he likes this girl, he can't just kill the brother."

"He loves her," Corinthian said, jumping into the conversation. I looked up from the report and mugged the hell out of her.

"Why do you say that?" Cross questioned, with a confused look on her face. Out of all of us, she was the only one that had never been in love. Cross didn't believe in emotional attachments, and because of that, she only used niggas for sex when she felt like it.

"Because she's all he ever talks about; he spends all his time with her, and he introduced us to her as his girlfriend," Corinthian answered.

"It could be deep infatuation," Judge said, looking between Cross and Corinthian. "Most people don't understand that love is just a chemical reaction. He could find someone else he's attracted to and forget about her tomorrow."

"You haven't seen how he looks at her, though," Corinthian said, and Judge stared at her with a blank expression. Just like Cross, Judge didn't do personal interactions with others well. If it wasn't science, then he didn't give a damn.

"Then he needs to go blind," he replied, and I tried not to laugh. Judge didn't give a damn about what Corinthian was trying to tell her. We all knew it, as did Corinthian, but it didn't stop her from trying to give our cousin some understanding of connections. "If he looks at her and it alters his mind, he needs to stop looking at her."

"It's not that simple, Judge." Corinthian laughed. "One day, you'll understand it. Something in your big brain will flicker, and those endorphins you hold close to you will start going crazy, and you'll fall in love."

"And God help us all when it doesn't happen," Cross interjected as she sat beside me. She picked up a paper off the table and looked it over before sitting it down. "It's enough crazy DeCorte vibes going off between Ex and Krude. Adding your ass to the mix will only have everybody stressed out."

"These niggas don't have y'all stressed?" Judge questioned.

"Oh, they do, but we can handle them," Cross answered. "Megan is a saint, and Paxton keeps Ex on his toes. Whoever you end up with will probably belong in a straitjacket because no one clinically sane can tolerate you."

"Pot meet kettle," Corinthian said, pointing to them.

"Shut up." Cross laughed. "But back to this one over here who is on hush mode." Cross pointed to me. "You are going to have to kill her brother. It's that simple. If Hampton was telling the truth, do what you gotta do to protect her."

"Would you kill yo' nigga sister to protect him?" I asked Cross, and she nodded. "Legit?"

"Legit," she replied. "But that's why I don't do relationships and all that shit. I loved hard once, and it damn near destroyed me. Doing it again would have me destroying the world, big cousin."

I nodded my head in understanding because Cross was speaking her truth. She'd fallen in love years ago; I mean, loved the nigga hard as hell, only for him to walk away from her. It had taken all of us to pull her out of her depression and even a few years of isolation before Cross had come out of hiding. And when she did, she was different and more closed off.

"So, what do you think he should do?" Judge asked. "Since, surprisingly, you are not for killing him suddenly."

"Oh, he going to have to kill the brother. I completely stand on that." Cross shrugged. "He's just gonna have to do it in a way that makes it look like an accident, so she'll never forgive him."

"What you got in mind, science man?" I asked Judge.

"Burn his ass up in a fire." Judge shrugged. "It's the easiest way. I know you aren't in the mood to plan a crash or anything like that."

"I don't normally do fires, so explain to me how he could do that without someone thinking it was a setup," Crossed asked him. "Because from what I understand, even if his body is charred, certain chemicals can still be trashed through a blood panel if they are lucky enough to get blood. And if you strapped him down, adhesives can still be found."

"Gas leak or carbon monoxide after getting drunk at a club or party, and he falls asleep in the car." Judge shrugged, and I ran my hand over my face.

"Does he need to be found, though?" Corinthian asked, and we all looked over at her. Usually, she was quiet if we were talking about stuff like this, so her asking questions surprised us all. "I mean, I'm just asking."

"To give her and her family closure, he's gotta be found." I nodded.

"Oh yeah, you in love." Judge sighed and shook his head. "You worried about closure and shit." He pushed his six-foot-three frame off the floor and shook his head. "Down goes another one of us. Let me call Madea now and tell her I ain't next in line for this love shit."

"She already told granddaddy she got your wedding colors picked out," Corinthian said, and Judge mugged the hell out of her. "She told me the other day when we talked."

"It ain't happening," he said, pulling his phone out of his pocket and leaving the living room. We all laughed when we heard our grandma's voice when she picked up the phone. Judge talked big shit, but as soon as he got on the phone with Madea, that tough guy act was dropped.

I sat back in my seat and shook my head. These niggas weren't helping the situation at all. A room full of killers, and I included Corinthian in that list as well, since she knew how to kill but chose not to, and none of them were helping.

"Ay, Ex," Krude said from his spot on the other side of the room. I looked over at him and lifted my brow. "Kill that nigga; tell Paxton the truth though, because if you don't, she will resent you. If you want your relationship to work, keep it a buck with her. It's only fair for her and you at the end of the day because if she finds out on her own, she will never forgive you." How this nigga out of everyone else was giving some helpful advice was beyond me.

"I appreciate the advice, Krude." I nodded.

"It's nothing." He shrugged. "And if you decide not to tell her, let me know so I can get you that chloroform so you can kidnap her."

"I'm not gonna kidnap her, bro." I laughed.

"She gonna kill you if you don't," he said, and a big-ass smile spread across his face. "Which could work for me. I'm next in line to Madea's favorite after yo' ass." He shook his head. "Don't call me; let her knock you off so I can start getting the first peach cobblers of the year."

CHAPTER 31
Paxton

"HE'S AWAKE," Mama said as soon as I entered Naeem's room. I dropped my purse, keys, and phone on the chair beside his bed and rushed to my brother. "He's been asking for you since last night, but the doctors thought it would be best for him to rest before having visitors."

"Naeem, open your eyes, baby bro," I said, standing beside him. My hands instantly went to face when his eyes slowly opened, and the tears I'd held back for a little over a month finally started falling. "Hey, Lil man."

"I told you to stop callin' me that shit," Naeem replied. His voice was scratchy and sounded rough, but I didn't care. He was awake, and that's all that mattered. I dropped a few kisses on his forehead before stepping back. "You happy to see a nigga, huh?"

"You have no idea." I laughed as I helped him adjust to the bed. I knew he would still be weak and fatigued, but I didn't care about any of that as long as he was awake and alive.

"I knew your ass was a damn punk under all that rah-rah shit you be doin'." He smirked as I wiped tears from my face. "You cryin' and shit like a nigga was going to stay down for a long ass time."

"I didn't know what to think, honestly," I answered with a shrug.

"All I know was that you were going to wake up, and if you didn't, it would be hell to pay."

"You ain't doing nothing but speaking facts." Naeem nodded. His eyes cut to Mama before turning back to him. "It's some shit I gotta handle when I get outta here."

"Don't rush your recovery," I said, shaking my head. "I need you at a thousand percent before you step outta here."

"Paxton, give me your car keys," Mama said, interrupting the conversation. I knew she didn't want to hear Naeem or me talking the way we were, so her excusing herself was understandable. "I'm gonna grab something to eat and get some fresh air."

"She has been here every day, hasn't she?" Naeem asked once Mama was gone. I nodded my head, and he sighed. "I asked her last night, and she swore she hadn't been. I knew she was lying, though."

"We traded off." I sighed and sat across from him. "But she was here the majority of the time. Daddy, too."

"When I'm outta here, I gotta get them on a cruise or something as a thank you," Naeem said. See, that was the thing about my baby brother. He looked out for our parents and was always thankful for what they did for us.

"How long are they saying you gotta stay?"

"A week or so if all my tests come back normal." Naeem shrugged. "But after that, I got some work to do." The look of hatred that seeped from my brother's glare sent chills down my spine. Naeem usually wasn't the violent one; he did what he needed to do when he had to, but besides that, it wasn't him that was out there popping off. It was me.

"What do you remember from the shooting?" I asked to see what he knew. If he didn't remember Cade shooting him, then I was the one who was going to have to tell him.

"I was chillin' with Xavi, waiting on Yalonda to bring me the kids. She walked up to the car and was trippin' like big time." He shook his head and rubbed between his eyes. "She has been on some bullshit the last few months, talkin' about I ain't dropping enough money for the girls or seeing them enough like they damn near don't live with me. They were only with her because she swore she was missing them, but

I heard from her best friend's cousin that they were with her damn mama the entire weekend she had them. Bitch was being a deadbeat and thought I would be the one to deal with it. She was on her rah-rah shit, and the next thing I know, Xavi's truck pulls up behind her, and somebody starts blasting."

"You see who it was?"

"Yo' fuckin' brother," Naeem angrily answered. "Cade was in Xavi's truck. When he pulled up and dropped the window, I thought that shit was a little off, but before I could speak, he was lightin' my ass up."

"You think it was a setup?"

"Fuck yeah!" Naeem roared. The machine connected to him started going off, and a nurse rushed into the room. She checked Naeem over, reminding him he had to stay as calm as possible, or they would have to ask me to leave. I apologized for my brother's outburst and told her I would keep him calm. She looked me over a few times before finally agreeing and leaving the room.

"You fucked her before you were in here or something?" I asked Naeem after the nurse left.

"Shit, no." He laughed and shook his head. "I ain't ever see that girl before in my life. I mean, she fine as fuck, but I'on know her."

"Well, she looked like she was trying to get to know you." I laughed, and Naeem waved me off.

"I ain't worried about no female until I handle this shit with my baby mama, Cade, and Xavi. The way that nigga was moving that day got me side-eyeing his ass too."

"Only Cade and Yalonda," I said, and Naeem nodded. There wasn't shit else that needed to be said because my brother knew I wasn't about to fuck around. I still had to tell Naeem about Cade fuckin' around with Yalonda and possibly being his girl's biological father. I knew that would break my brother, but he needed to know the truth. What he did with it was up to him, but I wasn't about to hide shit from him. "Tell me why you've been checking in on Cade."

"Money was comin' up short," Naeem answered with a shrug. "I have been looking at the books hard the last year. I was trying to get some of the pressure off you and learn what I can, you know? I told you when this shit started, I wanted to learn everything I could. You have been holding the shit down, and I wanted to step up more."

"Naeem, you know I enjoy my job, right?" I asked him, and he nodded.

"That doesn't matter, Paxton. You could love that shit for the rest of your life, but you are putting your shit on hold to run our company. Yeah, you and that fuck nigga dated for a while, and you might even have thought you loved him, but that shit was weak, in my opinion. Me stepping up allows you to be able to take time for yourself. Find you a nigga, have some damn kids. I can't be the only one giving Mama and Daddy some."

"So, how does that involve Cade?"

"He was skimming money; at first, I thought I was trippin' cuz a few of our connects would say something about a price increase, but when Air hit my line talkin' about his price wasn't what we agreed to, I knew I had to look at it again. I pulled his file and a few more to compare and noticed the price differences from what we were moving. The more I looked, the more I realized that shit was happening and had for a while."

"And you just knew it was Cade?" I asked, trying to wrap my mind around what Naeem told me. Our accounts were broken down by location, and each had a site. We got together quarterly to go over our books. There had been talk of us using an accountant, but nothing had been decided. Now, hearing this had me ready to reach out.

"It was all Cade's accounts," Naeem said with a shrug. "I had Reggie look into it, and she said that Cade was moving wrong. After that, I started doing pop-ups and shit to look into it."

Naeem was dropping names like I was supposed to know who they were. I'd never heard of Air or Reggie, but if Naeem trusted them on their word alone, let me know what kind of people they were. The only person in Naeem's life I ever questioned was Xavi; everyone else proved trustworthy on multiple occasions.

"Why didn't you tell me?" I asked.

"I planned on telling you the day I was shot. I was going to get the girls, have Xavi drop me off with you, and call Reggie so she could break shit down for you."

"Who is Reggie?" I asked, slightly confused.

"The accountant I hired," he sighed. "Shorty a fuckin' lunatic too. She always fussin' at my ass about shit. Talkin' about I gotta step my shit up. Our business could be bringing in triple what it does if I pulled my weight. Her ass be stressin' me the fuck out, and she does that shit with a smile."

"I gotta meet her." I laughed, and Naeem mugged the hell out of me. "Seriously, she sounds like she has a good head on her shoulders."

"She keeps tryin' me. I'm gonna knock that muthafucka off," Naeem replied, and I laughed. "Nah, but seriously, she was right about Cade. After I started popping up on him and checkin' his books, I realized he was legit skimming us both hard. I mean, nigga was walkin' away with damn near half the money."

"So, what was your plan?"

"Kill him." He shrugged. "In the beginning, I was just going to beat his ass, put him out of the company. If I had to work double, then so be it, but that nigga wasn't about to let us look bad. I'd already reached out to all the people he had gotten money from, let them know he was out, and I was their contact person from here on out. I credited them on their next few shipments, and everybody was cool. Illegal and legal businesses stayed and even referred to a few new ones. Now with this shit, I don't have any other choice. He already showed how he wants to handle shit. If I gotta pick between me or him, I'm picking me."

"It's something else I gotta tell you," I said, shaking my head. I hated Cade had put us in the position, but everything needed to be laid on the table. Our parents would grieve his death, and I know they would never heal, but if Cade had already tried to take Naeem's life, I know he wouldn't stop until he was dead and then come after me. I would rather watch my parents mourn one child than be one they were grieving.

"If you're going to tell me he fuckin' Yalonda, I already know that too." Naeem shook his head. "I been knowing, but I didn't care cuz she and I were through. When I broke up with her the last time, I meant that shit."

"The girls might not be yours," I said, ripping the band-aid off. There was no reason to sugarcoat the truth; my brother needed to know everything. If he found out something like this from anyone else, it would knock him off his feet, and he'd been off his game. Right now wasn't the time for that. Naeem ran his tongue over his teeth and nodded. I could see the tears form in his eyes, but he didn't let them fall. I was about to say something else, but Mama walked back into the room. She looked at me and then at Naeem and shook her head.

"Make sure y'all say a prayer before and after y'all do whatever y'all gonna do," Mama said, sitting beside me. "I know we aren't super religious people, but I do know one thing: prayer works. I have been doing it from the moment I found out about Naeem. I even had a few favors pulled; some special people were praying for you to come out of this. Whatever it is y'all got planned, make sure y'all pray."

"Yes, ma'am," Naeem replied, and I nodded.

CHAPTER 32

Exodus

"I NEED YOU TO FIND CADE," Paxton said as soon as I opened the front door. I stood at the door, knob still in my hand, and stared down at her as she looked up at me with a mug. I hadn't seen her in almost a week, which I was cool with. We texted and talked constantly, but she was busy spending time with Naeem and giving her parents a much-needed break. Naeem had come home last night, and even though he didn't want to, they'd all agreed that it would be better if he stayed at Paxton's. "Can you do that?"

"Let's try this shit again," I said, shaking my head and taking a deep breath. "I open the door, and you're supposed to greet me. Drop a kiss on a nigga's lips, hug me, you know, show some affection since you missed my ass."

"Exodus, I don't have time for all that right now." She sighed, and I continued to stare down at her, not giving a fuck. I licked my lips and waited. Paxton, stubborn ass, knew I wouldn't move from my spot until I got what I wanted. "Fine." She grabbed the collar of my shirt and pulled me down. The second our lips touched, I took control of that shit, pulling her close to me by her waist and driving my tongue into her mouth. She tasted like oranges, and I loved that shit.

"Now tell me what you need," I said once we pulled apart. Paxton wiped my bottom lip with her thumb and shook her head. "Come on now, Hitta, cuz the way my dick brickin' up right now, you only got about two more seconds before I'm pushing into your pussy."

"I need you to find Cade," she said. "Can you do that?"

"It's already done." I shrugged and smiled at her. "I have been waiting for you to come to me."

"Let's go then," she said, returning to her car. I didn't move from my spot, and she turned and looked at me. I knew she was going to have an attitude, but I didn't give a fuck. My feet didn't move because she told them to. "Exodus."

"Hitta." I said her name with the same attitude she said mine.

"Come on," she demanded, and I shook my head. "Why not?"

"Come in the house, Hitta," I sighed. Paxton mugged the hell out of me, and I tried not to laugh. This girl was so used to getting her way that she didn't know what to do when someone told her no. She opened her mouth to start to argue, and I walked away. She could talk to the damn front door for all I cared, but I wasn't moving because she wanted me to.

I dropped down on the couch and un-paused the TV so I could finish watching my show. The sound of the front door slamming shut echoed throughout the house when Paxton closed the door. When she entered the living room, she looked pissed off, but I didn't give a damn.

"Are you serious right now?" she fussed, pointing at the TV. I was watching Queen Charlotte on Netflix. At first, I thought that shit would be boring, but the way the Queen handled niggas had me crackin' up laughing the entire time. Her mouth was vicious, but the way she held her husband down was dope as fuck. "You're in here watching TV knowing I want to find my brother and kill him?"

"What you yellin' for, Hitta?" I asked, putting the TV back on pause. If she was about to fuss, I would miss some shit, have to rewatch it later, and put me behind on what I planned to do for the day. "I'm sittin' right here. Come check this shit out with me. Watch how this woman is loving her nigga and running shit."

"I don't give a damn about that bitch!" she yelled, and I chuckled. "Ain't shit funny either, Exodus!"

"Yeah, it is." I relaxed on the couch, stretched my legs out, and rested my foot on the coffee table. "You over there yelling and shit for no reason. We are not moving until I say we are."

"And what do you run, Exodus?" She crossed her arms over her chest, and my eyes rested on her titties. My dick started brickin' up in shorts, and I had to adjust them. "Huh, what?"

"Hitta." I chuckled and shook my head. "Chill with the yellin' like for real. I have never disrespected you, so don't start doin' that shit to me." I mugged the hell out of her and ran my tongue over my teeth.

"Then do what the fuck I'm askin' you to do, Exodus!" she yelled, not giving a fuck about what I just said. "You said you have my brother, then take me to him."

"No."

"And why the fuck not?"

"Because you movin' off straight emotion right now!" I snapped and stood up. I moved quickly, getting in her face and staring down at her. "I told you about that shit already! I said stop fuckin' moving on emotion because you ignore shit! If I said I got Cade, then what is that tellin' you? I got that nigga! I know where he is! I know that nigga unpredictable, and that got you a little shook. He already came after Naeem, so that shit means he could try to come after you or your parents, and that scares you, but as your nigga, I'm asking you to trust me! I told you I got you! I've been showing you that shit! Let me handle this shit!"

"I ain't scared of shit, Exodus!" she yelled.

"Then why are you crying?" I asked her and grabbed her chin. I wiped my thumb over the tears that rolled down her cheek. "Huh, Hitta? If you aren't scared, then why are you crying?" Paxton jerked her face from my hand and then quickly wiped her face. I laughed to keep my anger under control. I hated she wasn't comfortable enough yet to express her emotions. "Come sit down, watch a little TV with me and relax. Cade is at the warehouse. I had two of my cousins pick him up the other day. I haven't seen him yet but planned to go later."

"I want to go now," she said, and I shook my head. "I'm not asking you, Exodus; I'm telling you."

"For what?" I asked her, and she turned her head so she didn't have to look at me. "Nah, tough ass, tell me for what?" I grabbed her face again and made her face me. "Look at me when I'm talkin' to you." It took a few seconds, but she finally looked at me. It wasn't anger in her eyes when she looked at me, though. If anything, it was sadness and pain. Killing her brother wouldn't be as easy as she thought, and I needed her to understand that shit. "If you can't even say the words, how you think you gonna handle the action?"

"I've killed before," she stubbornly said. "Cade won't be my last body."

"Nor will he be your next," I told her, and she rolled her eyes. "Paxton, you not killing that nigga. I know you don't want to hear that, and it's cool that you don't like my words, but at the end of the day, my word is just that. You can be mad, even fuss at me later, shit hold off on giving me pussy for a day or two, but I ain't changing my mind."

"If you don't let me do this, I'll never forgive you," she said.

"And if I do, you'll never forgive yourself. You can hate me for the rest of your life, and I'll be cool with that, but you're not about to hate yourself," I countered, then kissed her lips and let her face go. "Now come on and watch this Queen lady roast folks." I went back and sat down on the couch. Paxton's stubborn ass stayed in her spot for a few minutes before she walked out of the house. I heard her car pull out of the driveway before I turned my show back on and kept watching. I wasn't about to chase behind her ass.

"Yeah?" I answered my phone not even thirty minutes later.

"Yo' girlfriend pulled up in the driveway," Krude said, laughing. "I'ono what you did to her, but she's out there talking to Megan, and they look like they are getting hyped."

"This fuckin' girl, man," I sighed and stood up. I cut off the TV and grabbed my truck keys off the table. "Don't let her leave. I don't give a damn what she says or how badly she shows out. I'm on my way."

"I got some chloroform in the garage," Krude said.

"Nigga, do not use that shit on my woman!" I yelled, got into my truck, and started it. Krude's house was about fifteen minutes from my spot.

"Then what the fuck I'm gonna use?" he questioned with an attitude. As I pulled out of my garage, my phone connected to the blue tooth, so I dropped it into my lap. "I don't hit women, so I can't knock her ass out, and the way Megan looks, she might beat my ass if I try to stop them."

"Nigga, how the fuck does Paxton even know where you live?" I asked, speeding down the street.

"I don't know!" he fussed with an attitude. "I just got out of the shower and was feeling a little sexy and shit with the towel wrapped around my waist and water running down my body, so I went to look for her and couldn't find her in the house. I could hear voices, though, so I checked outside, and there they fuckin' were."

"They haven't left, have they?" I asked.

"Nah, man," he replied. The distinctive sound of blinds being closed echoed through my truck. "Shit, man, I think they saw me."

"Nigga, are you in the blinds?" I yelled.

"I was," Krude replied. "I'm running back to my room now. Megan, not about to cuss my ass out for bending her shit trying to look through them."

"Nigga, I swear I hate you." I sighed and shook my head. Krude's big ass worked my fucking nerves so damn bad at times. "You are a grown-ass man, peeking through the blinds at your crib and watching your girlfriend talk to her damn friend."

"First off, nigga, I'm still in my towel, so I wasn't about to open the blinds up. Second, I'm doing you a fuckin' favor telling you where yo' crazy ass girlfriend is. And third, it ain't just Paxton outside; it's Golden too!"

"Why is Golden there, nigga?" I pushed down on the gas and weaved in and out through cars. Megan, I could deal with, she talked big shit, but I knew she wouldn't do too much crazy shit. But Golden, I knew, didn't give a flying fuck about shit. She was raised by a pimp, best friends with a damn maniac, and in a relationship with a damn trigger-happy nigga. Golden had absolutely no fear and knew it was niggas behind her that would quickly kill for her without a second thought. "Is Trigga with her?"

"Nope." Krude laughed.

"So, she by herself?" I asked, turning down the street. "Cool, I can handle that."

"Oh no, nigga, I didn't say she was alone."

I pulled up, threw my truck in park, and got out. My eyes landed on Paxton, who was standing next to Golden and Megan talking, but it was the nigga behind them leaning against his car that had me shaking my head. "No, absolutely fuckin' not, nigga! Take yo' ass home before I call Nyla!"

"She the one who sent me." Memphis smirked, then took a pull of his blunt. "She said, and I quote, 'Megan is to not go anywhere without me by her side,' and who the fuck I look like, not listening to my wife?"

"Then why Golden here?" I asked, pointing at her short ass.

"Oh, I'm trying to turn over a new leaf and not kill women, so I brought my best friend." He shrugged like the shit wasn't crazy sounding. "Trigga said she got one body; then she gotta come home, though."

"Memphis, you my nigga, but nah, homie, this ain't it," I said, shaking my head. "I appreciate you sliding through, but y'all can go." I turned to look at Paxton, who looked mad as hell. "Get in the truck, Hitta."

"Are you taking me to Cade?" she asked, crossing her arms over her chest. "Because if you aren't, we have nothing to discuss."

"Get in the truck, Hitta," I said, pinching my nose's bridge. "Like legit get in the fuckin' truck."

"Unless you are taking me to Cade, then no."

"Get in the truck," I repeated and stared her down.

"Unless—"

"GET. IN. THE. FUCKING. TRUCK!" I roared, cutting her off. I got in her face and dared her to say something else. I was tired of playing with Paxton, and she knew it from the look on her face.

"Aye, big cuz," Krude said, pulling at my arm to get me back up from Paxton's face, but I didn't move. "Like for real backup."

"Nah, Krude," I fussed, snatching my arm from his grip. "She wanna be so fuckin' tough all the damn time instead of listening." Paxton tried to sidestep me, but I cut her off. "You don't fuckin' listen, bro! Like at all! You pulled up here, getting rah-rah with Megan and pulling these two muthafuckas into shit! Memphis and Golden are killers! They don't do this shit on a whim! Memphis stepping out on the permission of his wife isn't a joke! Golden being here on the strength of Trigga ain't a game! It's nigga that step hard for her! They will light this fuckin' city up if even a fuckin' hair is out of place. Memphis's wife is pregnant, due any minute, yet she lettin' him move. If one thing happens to that nigga, I gotta answer for that shit! Not you! Me!" I slapped my chest. "That's what you are not getting! It's not a bitch bone in my body, but I'd let them niggas end me if that keeps you safe! You out here going off emotions, and I told you from the beginning that going off emotions wasn't the damn move! But you don't listen!"

"I just want revenge for my brother," Paxton said through clenched teeth.

"And I told you I had you!" I yelled. "I told you it would be taken care of! As your nigga, it's my job to take care of that!"

"You aren't my nigga!" Paxton yelled. I stepped back and stared her down. My anger was going to get the best of me, and I was going to break her fuckin' neck if I didn't. "I've been telling you that! You and I aren't together! We fuck! That's it, that's all!" Paxton stepped into my face and mugged me like I wasn't shit. "You keep saying I don't listen, but you aren't either! We are not together! I don't look at you as nothing more than a piece of dick I can bounce on when I need a fix."

"What?" I laughed. "You serious?"

"Yes." She nodded. "We are not together."

"Yo, this is why you and Mahogany are such good friends because y'all both slow! She was moving the same way with Focus, talking about they weren't shit, and now you are doing the same to me? You are fuckin' funny as hell for that shit. Stop playing with me."

"I'm not playing."

I looked over at my cousin and then at Memphis before shaking my head.

"We weren't a we." She waved her hand between our bodies. "You were doing you, and I was doing me."

"Are you fuckin' serious right now?" I wiped my hand down my face, dropped my head, and shook it. When I lifted it, Cross and Judge stood behind Paxton. I already knew that Krude called them to try to calm me down. Everybody knew I wouldn't touch a woman unless I had no other reason, but the feelings I was feeling right now had me ready to change my mind. I chuckled and shook my head. This wasn't the move for me. I wasn't the type of nigga to deal with shit like this. And I damn sure wouldn't deal with a woman like this. If I were just some dick, she would bounce on, then so be it. I was washing my hands of her ass. "Take her to the warehouse."

"Ex, man, hold up," Judge said, shaking his head.

"Nah, she wanna be so fuckin' tough; take her to the warehouse and let her handle the shit her fuckin' self," I told my cousin. I took one final look at Paxton before walking away.

"Ex!" Cross called out to me.

"Take her to the fuckin' warehouse!" I yelled. "And make sure her payment is secured before she pulls the damn trigger."

CHAPTER 33

Paxton

"YO' tough ass, let's go," Krude said. I turned to look at him, surprised to see the serious look on his face. Krude usually smiled and laughed, so seeing him serious made me step back. "Nah, no backtracking now. Let's go."

"Krude," Megan called out to him.

"Nah, baby," he said, shaking his head. A woman and a man stood next to him. The woman I remembered from the club opening a few weeks ago, but the man I'd never seen before. He was tall, probably taller than Krude, but shorter than Exodus. His skin was the color of warm chocolate, and he had an oval face, full lips, and a thick beard. His eyes were just as dark as his skin. He was built and more muscular than Exodus and Krude, but he wasn't overly jacked. He wore a pair of gold and black-framed glasses and was dressed in black. "Ex said to take her to the warehouse so that she can finish this shit, so that's what I'm doing."

"He didn't mean that," the woman said, shaking her head. Seeing her in the sunlight, I saw the similarities between her, Exodus Krude, and Corinthian. There was no denying the entire DeCorte bloodline and their similarities.

"Ex doesn't say shit he doesn't mean," Krude replied, then turned and looked at me. "Let's go, Paxton." He pulled his keys out of his pocket and hit the key fob to unlock his truck. We got in, and he pulled off. My heart was beating so hard in my chest that I thought it would break through my ribs. I wasn't scared, but more so nervous. I was going to handle this shit with Cade and then help my parents mourn the loss of their child, but I wouldn't regret it. "You know, I always thought you were smart."

"What?" I looked over at Krude, confused about what he was talking about.

"I thought you were smart, but shit, now I'm not so sure," he replied, shaking his head. "That shit you pulled back there at the house proved otherwise."

"Me wanting to protect my brother and take care of a problem shows that I'm not smart?" I asked with a humorless laugh.

"Nah." Krude glanced at me, then returned to the road. "The fact that you haven't listened to shit Ex has said makes you not too bright. That nigga said he had it, yet you are trying to control shit. Then to top it off, you just embarrassed that nigga in front of other people?" He chuckled and shook his head. "That shit is not easily forgiven."

"I'm not asking for his forgiveness," I replied, and sucked my teeth.

"Now I see why you and Mahogany are friends." He chuckled. "She swore she didn't ask Focus to do shit yet reaped the rewards of all his actions."

"Mahogany's situation with Focus is completely different from the one I have with Exodus," I argued.

"You asked him for help, did you not?" he asked me, and immediately I shut my mouth because I had. "Oh, you forgot? You called that nigga and asked for his services, and he gave them free of charge and without thought. He only asked you to do one thing, which was not working off emotions, and you couldn't do that shit. He has been doing this well before any of us for years and hasn't gotten caught. He's smart with his moves, so if he said no emotion, he was saying it for a reason, yet you couldn't listen. I'm not even going to say you couldn't; I'm going to say you wouldn't. You went straight off your emotions like a madman."

"How is he going to tell me not to work off emotion when that's all he's done when dealing with me?" I asked, and Krude shrugged. "No, since you know it all, explain that to me."

"What did he do that was fueled by emotion?"

"He burned down a restaurant, killed the owner, pulled a gun at a woman at a clinic," I said, counting each incident off on my fingers. "Shall I go on?"

"Did you die, though?" he asked me with a laugh. "Like that nigga was doing shit for you, really because of you. Exodus doesn't do shit without thinking, so if he did all that, it was because of you."

"So it's my fault?"

"That nigga likes you, shit he probably loves you, so yeah, it's your fault. Answer me this: When have you ever seen Ex not in control? Like the nigga is calculated as hell in everything that he does, but when it comes to you, he doesn't think. It's a straight reaction to everything and to making you happy. If he said let him handle it, you should've let him do that. Your brother has been sitting in that damn warehouse since Naeem woke up. That morning, he chilled with your parents and had Cross and Judge pick his ass up."

"Exodus doesn't know my parents," I said, shaking my head.

"Yes, he does." Krude laughed. "Nigga, bring yo' mama food every morning and chop it up with her. Yo' pops too."

"What?" I took my phone out of my purse and texted my mom. She replied, confirming what Krude was saying, and even went into detail about how he'd unknowingly taken care of Naeem's medical bills for them. I dropped my phone in my lap and shook my head. "Why did he do that?"

"As I said, he more than likely loves yo' ass," Krude answered, even though I wasn't talking to him. "You fucked that up, though. That shit you pulled at my spot and then not listening to him, got him hot."

"I was only venting to Megan," I started to explain. "She was on the phone with Nyla, and shit just started going left."

"Nah, you don't owe me an explanation," he said, shaking his head and cutting me off. "I ain't your nigga. I don't have shit to do with y'all and how y'all move. Understand, I'll handle that shit with Megan."

For the rest of the ride, I sat staring out the window. Krude turned the music up and sang along to every song. His voice wasn't the greatest, but I needed him to keep himself distracted so I didn't have to talk.

Me: Did you know Exodus was visiting my parents at the hospital?

Mahogany: I wasn't sure, but I figured he was because Tobias mentioned it.

Me: I didn't know (facepalm)

Mahogany: Oh hell, what did you do?

Me: I kind of went off on him.

Mahogany: Why? For him visiting your parents? That's not something to go off about. If anything, it's sweet.

Me: No, not that.

Mahogany: Then what?

"We here," Krude said. I looked up from my phone to see us pull up in front of a large warehouse. We'd been driving for nearly an hour. His other two cousins pulled up, and we all headed inside. "Your phone, keys, and purse gotta go over in one of those bins." Krude pointed to a table that had mental boxes on it. "Tell Cross your size, and she'll get you a jumpsuit."

"What do I need a jumpsuit for?" I asked, looking around.

"Helps make sure we don't have any DNA evidence on us," Cross said with a shrug. "It's a safety protocol thing."

"And the metal containers?" I asked, nodding toward them.

"Same thing," Cross answered. "Nine designed them. Once you place your phone in there, they connect to his system, and he erases your location over the last twenty-four hours and rewrites it to make it seem like you were never here."

"Whose idea was all that?" I asked, putting my phone into a case.

"Ex's," Cross answered. "Now give me your size."

"Sixteen," I said, and she nodded. Without words, she walked to a locker, pulled out a small bag, and handed it to me.

"Put it on over your clothes and shoes. It has a hood to cover your hair."

"Thank you," I said, nodding.

"No reason to thank me," she said, shaking her head. "I'm going to be completely honest with you. You shouldn't be here. You might have a few bodies under your belt, but it's different when you have to kill your flesh and blood. Trust me, I know from personal experience. You should've let Ex handle this."

"He's my brother," I said, shaking my head. "If anyone is going to kill him, it will be me."

"Follow me then," she said and headed toward the back. The hallway was long; maybe every seven feet was a door; at least twenty doors had to be on each wall. The warehouse was big, probably more extensive than I could ever imagine; I had no doubt there were more rooms. What got me was each door was painted with a color, letter, and number. The door that we stopped at was painted green and labeled E-20.

"Aye, Cross, did you get paid?" the man from earlier asked. He stood at the end of the hallway with a bored expression. "Ex said she pays before pulling the trigger."

"Charge it to my account, Judge," she replied. Judge nodded, then walked away. "Come on."

She put in a code to the door and pushed it open. The sight of Cade in a pair of shorts tied down to a metal chair made my blood run hot. He lifted his head, looked at me, then smirked. My brother's eyes were cold; if anything, he looked at me as if I were the enemy, not the person raised with him. We hadn't been the closest at times, but nothing in me would have told me he would have tried to kill one of us before this.

"It took you long enough to get here," Cade said, shaking his head. He tried to lean back in the chair, but who'd ever tired him up had it to where he couldn't move. "I was starting to think you wouldn't show up."

"I've been busy," I replied, shrugging. I looked around the room, trying to get a good look at it. The room was small, maybe a twelve-by-twelve square with a metal table in the middle. Three small tables were in one corner with what looked like tools on them; Cade was in a chair not too far from the long table. A hose hung from the ceiling, and there were no windows, but the bright lights shining down from the ceiling gave off enough light. I could hear a soft hum from the AC blowing into the room, and a camera was posted in the upper corner of the room. All the walls and floors were concrete. "You know, taking care of Naeem and our parents."

"Of course you have," he sneered. "Taking care of that weak-ass nigga like the world revolves around him. You, Mama, and Daddy been kissing his little ass since he came home from the hospital."

"You jealous of Naeem Cade?" I questioned, slightly surprised. Cade was damn near ten years older than Naeem. When he was born, nothing in our lives changed; adding a baby into the equation just got a little more hectic. "You did all this cuz you were jealous of him?"

"Jealous of what?" he asked with a laugh. "Naeem got what I gave him. He was cool with my hand-me-downs. It didn't matter what he was either, clothes, food, bitches; he gladly took it all."

"Then what is the problem?" I couldn't help but ask. "If you thought Naeem was good with everything, then why try to kill him?"

"Cuz that nigga was fuckin' up my money!" he roared and jumped like he would get out of his seat. The chains wrapped around him weren't going to break, though. "He got fuckin' nosey and started looking into shit he wasn't supposed to!"

"So you shot him?"

"Hell yeah!" he laughed. "If that bitch behind you hadn't faked me, I would've made sure he was dead, then came after you next."

CHAPTER 34
Exodus

"KILL that nigga so my sister doesn't have to," Naeem said, standing on my porch and giving me the same look his sister had a few hours earlier. He wore ball shorts, a beater, tall socks, slides, and a backpack. He looked better than I expected after being in the hospital for damn near a month. His left arm was still cast, but I figured that was coming off soon. I'd sent Corinthian to Paxton's house a day after his release to care for his hair and beard. I sighed and shook my head. "Legit Exodus, don't let her have to be the one who ends his ass."

"Yo' sister grown Naeem," I replied, crossing my arms over my chest. "I can't control her."

"I'm not asking you to control her." He looked weak and could barely stand on his own two feet. I stepped back and let him in. Slowly, we walked over to the couch and sat down. Naeem was pushing himself too hard, and if he weren't careful, he would end up back in the hospital. Why this nigga thought they could take a few bullets and be in a coma for damn near a month and bounce around like it was nothing was beyond me. "Look, I know you don't know me like that, but I know you have been chillin' with my parents and in some kind of relationship with Paxton, so I'm asking you as a man not to let her pull that trigger."

"Paxton is-"

"Stubborn as fuck, hardheaded, and doesn't listen," he said, interrupting me with a laugh. "I know that. Shit, we all do, but Paxton loves hard, man. This shit with Cade is fucked up. I will be the first to admit that I didn't expect him to switch up on me like he did, but he has, and I know my sister. She took that shit personally; she swears she my damn mama."

I grunted instead of responding, and Naeem shook his head.

"How about this," he said, pulling his backpack off and opening it. "I asked Corinthian your fee, and she had to hit up a few of your cousins to get the correct price, but it's all here." He stacked money on the table in front of him. "I even added to it because it's a rush job."

"I can't take your money, Naeem," I said, shaking my head. I could tell he didn't nearly have enough to cover my fee, but I wasn't going to tell his ass that. He needed to feel like a man, and I would let him.

"Why not?" he asked me, slightly surprised. "You're a killer, right? I'm paying you to kill somebody."

"It ain't about the money," I sighed. "Yo' sister said she takin' care of it."

"I don't want her dealing with Cade!" he fussed. I mugged the shit out of him, and he took a second to calm himself down. He shook his head and sighed. "Paxton don't need that on her conscience. Her taking Cade's life will fuck with her for the rest of her life. I can't have that for her."

"She made her decision."

"I thought you were her nigga." Naeem softly laughed. "From the damn minute I woke up, Mama and Daddy kept talking about your ass. I mean, shit, I felt a little jealous for a second because they didn't let up. Then I saw Paxton and how she talked about your ass, and I was like, oh wait, this nigga actually might mean something. Paxton never talked about a nigga, not even the one she swore she was engaged to." Naeem looked me up and down. "Pops said you were different. Said from the jump, you moved differently. He knew a killer when he saw one, but he said with you he trusted his daughters' safety." He pushed up out of his chair with a grunt. "I guess he just meant physically cuz from the way you are moving now, ain't no way he meant mentally. I hope the next nigga my sister ends up with can protect her like she needs."

I watched Naeem slowly walk out of my house. My eyes returned to the stacks of money still sitting on the table. Naeem may have been young, but he knew how to issue a challenge. He'd paid me, even though I didn't accept the money he left on the table. But his reaction to Paxton dealing with Cade rubbed me the wrong way. I grabbed my iPad off the couch next to me and pulled up the security cameras at the warehouse. I flipped through the channels until I found what I was looking for and unmuted the speaker.

"You swear that nigga walks on water and don't even know half of what he was doing," Cade said to Paxton.

"What don't I see?" she asked.

"Everything!" he yelled. "You are so fuckin' blind to that nigga; you swear he innocent! That nigga ain't shit!" When he turned to face the camera, I shook my head. This was the same nigga from the pawnshop. Now, getting a good look at him, I could see the similarities between him, Paxton, and Naeem.

"You tried to kill him for what exactly, then?" Paxton asked her brother. I shook my head and stood. It didn't matter why he tried to kill him; the fact of the matter was he had, and that wasn't forgivable. I switched camera angles and got a good look at Cade for the first time. I let out a small laugh and shook my head. He was the same nigga I'd seen at the pawnshop a few weeks ago. I cut off the iPad and headed to my truck.

"Yeah?" Krude answered his phone as I drove.

"Don't let her kill him," I said. The drive to the warehouse from my spot would take about forty-five minutes, and that was if I didn't hit traffic. "You hear me, Krude?"

"Yeah, I heard you," he replied with a laugh. "I thought you said you didn't give a fuck what she did. Now you changin' your mind?"

"Krude," I grunted. "Nigga, stop being argumentative and do what I'm about you. Go in that room and drag her out if you have to."

"Oh no, nigga, I'm not putting my hands on her." He laughed. "I am not going to deal with your shit later today when you calm down and realize I had to touch her ass. No, nope, figure something else out."

"Genesis!" I yelled and punched the steering wheel, causing my truck to swerve slightly. "I'm tellin' you to go in there and stop that damn girl from killing her brother! Ain't no changing my mind about how you do it!"

The only response to my outburst was the line beeping, indicating Krude had hung up. When I called back, I went straight to voicemail, and I knew that emotional-ass nigga had blocked me because I yelled at him. I was going to rock that nigga when I saw him. I pushed my truck, being mindful of any cops on the road, and headed toward the warehouse. When I pulled up a little under thirty minutes later, I parked, got out, and slammed the door closed. I put the code in the door and stepped inside to find my cousins standing in the middle of the room, going at it. Cross was yelling at Krude, sitting at the small table in the middle of the room with a bored look. Judge sat next to him with his head buried in a book. Paxton was knocked out on the couch next to the table. I walked over to her and checked her over. My eyes landed on a big-ass bruise that was on the right side of her face.

"Who hit her?" I roared, turning to face my cousins. Cross glanced over at Krude, who was staring at me like I was a fuck nigga. Judge pushed up from the table and shook his head. "Krude, you hit her?"

"Didn't you say by any means necessary?" he asked with a smirk. Without thinking, I rushed over to my cousin. Judge and Cross quickly moved out of the way while Krude lifted his hand and pointed a can at me. "Nigga if you take one more step, I will spray your ass with this bear pepper spray." I stopped moving because he looked serious as hell.

"Why the fuck did you hit her?" I yelled, slowly making my way over to him. Krude didn't think shit through, so to know he'd knocked Paxton's ass out pissed me the fuck off. "She's a woman, man!"

"I didn't hit her ass," he grunted, and I stopped moving. "The fuck, I look like hitting a woman. I won't even hit Cross's ole manly ass, and she's related to us!"

"Then how did she get that bruise on her face?" I asked.

"She fell after I used my chloroform," he said, shrugging. I looked over at Cross, who sighed and nodded. "I just want you to know she's strong as fuck too! I thought I had the upper hand and snuck up behind her and covered her face, but she elbowed the shit out of me. If she weren't your girl, I would've boxed the fuck outta her ass." He set the mace on the table and lifted his shirt to show me the bruise that was forming on his side. "When Megan asks me what happen, I'm just callin' you, and you better explain everything to her ass."

"How long has she been out?" I asked, looking over at Paxton. I didn't give a fuck what Krude was talking about as long as he didn't hit her.

"About twenty-five minutes," Judge answered. "Based on her size and the amount of chloroform that Krude used, she should be out for another twenty minutes."

"You saw how much he used?" I questioned him, and he nodded. "Why the fuck did you let him do it, then?"

"Didn't you say to stop her?" he asked as if I was slow. "That seemed like the safest bet. I wasn't going in there to try to talk her out of killing him."

"You thought it was a good idea?" I said to Cross, ignoring Judge. "I thought you were the smart one!"

"Fuck you too nigga!" Judge fussed. "If you'd killed that nigga when we first snatched him up, we wouldn't be having this conversation! Don't come in here fussing because you fuckin' love this girl and not thinkin' straight!" I turned back to Judge and stepped in his face. "I ain't Krude nigga. I'll box your ass with no problem for stepping to me wrong."

"Oh, my fuckin' goodness," Cross fussed as she came to separate us. She pushed between our large bodies and shook her head. "You two are going to give me a headache! Ex, you need to calm the fuck down." She pointed at me. "We let Krude do it because he had the damn chloroform, and I was tired of hearing him whine. Judge watched him the entire time, so chill." She turned toward Judge. "Go over there and read your damn book or something. We all know this nigga isn't thinking straight, and we talked about this."

Judge and I stared each other down for a few seconds, and then he returned to sitting in his chair. He picked up his book and went back to reading. He occasionally looked up at me and smirked, but no other words came.

"You got some smelling salt?" I asked Krude. He dug into his pocket and then threw me a small pack. "Appreciate it." I popped the packet as I walked over to Paxton. It took a few minutes for her to wake up after using it. I hated that movies and TV shows made it seem like all you had to do was pop it and then brush it under someone's nose, and they would instantly wake up. Paxton started coughing, and I helped her sit up. It took another five minutes before she had her bearings. "You cool?"

"He knocked me out with something," she mumbled, rubbing her forehead.

"Chloroform," Krude proudly replied, and I shook my head. "I been wanting to use it for a while now."

Paxton pushed off the couch and looked around before turning her attention to me. "Give me your gun," she said, putting her hand out. "I know you don't want me to do this, but I need to."

Instead of arguing with her, I opened the metal cabinet in the corner of the room and grabbed a gun. I checked the clip and then handed it to her. I knew everyone expected me to argue with her, but I didn't have it in me yet. I wanted to see what he had to say; once he did and Paxton still wanted to kill this nigga, then I wasn't going to stand in her way.

CHAPTER 35

Paxton

WE WALKED BACK to the room where Cade was being held, and I took a deep breath before pushing the door open. Exodus hadn't said a word since I asked him for a gun. I was prepared to argue with Exodus about how I needed to do this, but instead, he was silent. Cade looked up at me when Exodus closed the door behind us.

"You back again?" Cade asked, shaking his head. "You do too much talkin' for me, Paxton. If you are going to end my ass, do it; otherwise, stop wasting my fuckin' time." He looked over at Exodus, and a flicker of recognition flashed across his face before turning to look at me.

"I just wanna know why," I said, shaking my head. "After that, I'll put two bullets into your head and go on with my day."

"You ain't gonna like my answers." He laughed.

"How you know?" I asked.

"Cuz I know you, Paxton," he replied. "You looking for some deep shit as an answer, which you aren't going to get."

"Tell me anyway," I said as I walked around the room. I hadn't moved from my spot by the door the first time I was here. Now, I was roaming. The room was sterile; nothing was personal except for the scriptures on the wall. Those had meaning; I glanced over at Exodus, leaning against the door with his arms crossed over his chest. His eyes stayed locked on Cade as if there was a chance he could escape.

"Shit, simple, I wanted to run it all," Cade answered. "Letting you run the company put good money in my pocket, but I wanted to make more."

"And fuckin' around with Yalonda?"

"She gives good head." Cade shrugged. "I have been fuckin' around with her for years. Well, before she started fuckin' with Naeem."

"Where is she?"

"I don't fucking know," he replied. "I've been looking for her for weeks; she's been MIA. But understand, I planned to kill her ass if I caught her. She has been playing with my head for years."

"The girls?" I asked. Cade's smile blossomed, and I knew he would kill them if he got the chance. "They don't have to die because of some shit their mama has done."

"They aren't mine, so I don't give a fuck," he said, not giving a fuck. "Shit, I'm doing everybody a favor if you wanna be honest. They aren't Naeem's either. That nigga can't even have kids, so I don't know why he was frontin' for so long like they were his." My face twisted up in confusion. "Oh, you didn't know, huh? Yeah, that nigga is shooting blanks. He found out when he was a teen, nigga sterile, yet was claiming those girls."

"They could've been yours."

"They weren't. I got a DNA test on them a couple of months back." He shrugged. "That bitch been running foul for a while, so I don't have no sympathy for her ass. She'd been collecting child support from Naeem, me, and another nigga for years. She got what was coming to her."

"You're fucked up," I said, shaking my head. "Like for real fucked up."

"And you think you're better than me? He laughed. "Be for real about the shit. You have popped how many niggas? Huh? Too damn many to fuckin' count." His eyes cut to Exodus, and he smirked. "And you fuckin' with a known killer. That nigga got so many bodies I doubt even he knows the exact number." He turned back to me. "So why the fuck are you judging me! At least I don't hide my shit! I wanted power! I wanted niggas to see my name or face and know I was that nigga! Running that business helped me get both, but I wanted more!"

"But was it worth your life!" I yelled. "Huh, Cade? Was getting all that power and money worth your fucking life! Because we both know how this ends! One of us isn't walking about this room! One of us will have to sit next to our parents at the other's funeral and then watch them mourn! One of us, and by one of us, I mean me!"

"Then kill me!" Cade yelled back. "Flipped that fuckin' safety off and blow my fuckin' head off or shut the fuck up because this back-and-forth shit is boring the fuck outta me!" He thrashed against the chains. "And understand, if you don't, I won't hesitate to kill you! I'll kill Naeem and our parents without a second thought! Then after that shit, I'll go home and sleep through the fuckin' like a damn baby!"

I flipped the safety off the gun in my hand and walked over to Cade. I pushed the barrel into his forehead and stared down at him.

"Pull the trigger," Exodus said from behind me. When he moved from his spot against the door, I didn't know, but I could feel his front pressed against my back. "That nigga doesn't get to live. If you have to pick between you or him, pick yourself. He told you why he did it; it ain't nothing left to say."

"My mama told me to pray," I said softly. "She said before and after I decided I needed to pray on it."

"There are six things that the Lord hates, seven that are an abomination to him: haughty eyes, a lying tongue, and hands that shed innocent blood, a heart that devises wicked plans, feet that make haste to run to evil, a false witness who breathes out lies, and one who sows discord among brothers. Proverbs chapter six, verses sixteen through nineteen. That nigga doesn't deserve a prayer, Hitta. He's content with his decisions and will easily take your life if given a chance."

"Kill me, bitch!" Cade yelled with cold eyes.

I turned and looked at Exodus. I couldn't do it. No matter how hard I wanted to try, I couldn't take my brother's life. "I-I-I-" I stuttered. I handed him back the gun and buried my face into his chest.

Bam

I jumped at the sound of the gun going off and then the sound of his blood spilling onto the floor.

"Cleanup will come, take his body into the woods in another state and make it look like a carjacking," Exodus said. I nodded my head. He gently moved me from him and stepped back. "Cross will take you home."

A few seconds later, I heard the door open and close, and I turned to Cade. I took one final look at my brother and left the room. Krude and Judge sat at the table in the middle of the room. Krude was talking, and Judge sat there reading his book.

"You ready?" Cross asked, coming from the other side of the building. The jumpsuit she wore was covered in blood. "Give me a few minutes to change, and then we can go."

"Okay," I said, nodding. I looked around the room, trying to see where Exodus was, but he wasn't around.

"He's gone," Judge said without looking up from his book. "Cross, he said your payment is already in your account."

"Did he say where he was going?" Cross asked.

"Nope, and I didn't care enough to ask," Judge answered.

CHAPTER 36
Exodus

"YOU KNOW, I always thought you weren't wrapped too tight, but seeing this shit makes me realize I didn't realize how off you were." Krude laughed as he sat down across from me. I looked up from my paperwork and mugged his ass. Krude threw his hands up like he was surrendering and laughed louder. "For real, what kind of nigga are you?"

"What do you mean?" I asked as I set my papers on my desk. "I'm just a businessman."

"Nigga, you for real!" he shook his head. He cut his eyes at the closed door, then sat back and got comfortable. "Correct me if I'm wrong, but isn't this the restaurant that you tried to burn down and then killed the owner and his cousin because of Paxton?" I sat there staring at Krude, and he shook his head. "Nigga, I know you hear me."

"I do." I nodded. "But you said correct you if you were wrong. You weren't, so I didn't."

"Nigga!" He threw his hands in the air.

"Wait, hold up," I said, cutting him off. "I didn't try to burn it down anything, so you did get that wrong."

"You set it on fire in three different spots!" he fussed.

"Yeah, but I wasn't trying to burn it down."

"Then what were you trying to do?" He twisted his mouth to the side and crossed his arms. "Just add some razzle dazzle to the décor or something?"

"Yeah." I chuckled and nodded my head. "It needed an upgrade, anyway."

"Oh, so that's what you did?" he questioned. "You upgraded the building?"

"Shit, the entire thing." I shrugged and returned to reading the report in front of me.

"You twisted as fuck." He laughed.

A few weeks after Qumar and his cousin's bodies were discovered, his sister sold the business. I was joking around with Focus and said I was interested in buying it, but Focus saw another source of income and jumped on it. It didn't take much to convince me to invest once we saw the finance reports. After we bought it, I chalked up the money to renovate the entire building, which had been a smart move in the long run since we would have a more lounge vibe than a restaurant. It had been Focus's idea to keep the original name but add the two to it.

"Man, whatever," I said, shaking my head. "What are you doing here?"

"Shit, just came to check on you." He shrugged. "You haven't been to the warehouse in a few." He stretched his long legs in front of him. "The others were afraid to ask you, so I came as a tribute."

"The fuck they scared to ask me for?" I questioned, surprised.

"Cuz you have been biting folk's heads off the last two weeks," he replied, and I grunted. "Ever since that shit with Paxton and her brother, you haven't been acting the same."

"How have I been acting?"

"Shit, not normal." He shrugged. "Like, even Madea asked about it yesterday when I talked to her, and you know it's not like her to ask us about each other."

"I'm cool, Krude," I said, running my hands over my face. "I have just been focused on ensuring this place does well."

"You talked to Paxton?" he asked, and I shook my head. I hadn't seen or spoken to Paxton in almost three weeks, and that shit worked my nerves, but I wasn't about to beg her ass to be with me. Like she said at the warehouse, we were just fuckin'; she looked at me for dick. "Oh, you don't know she is dating some nigga?"

"What nigga?" I said, mugging the hell out of him.

"I'ono," Krude replied. "She was on the phone with Megan the other day, and they were talking. She said something about going on again with some nigga named Yuri." He smirked. "Nigga name sound gay as fuck, but shit, my parents looked at me and said, 'oh this nigga looks like a Genesis,' so who the fuck am I to judge?"

"Did she say where they were going?" I asked, knowing I didn't need to know.

"Oh, no, I didn't hear that." He shook his head. "I'm working on giving Megan her space when she's on the phone and shit, so I left out the room."

"Then why the fuck did you tell me for?" I questioned with an attitude.

"I wanted to see if you cared," he said, then stood up. "I see I'm right, so my work here is done."

"Get the fuck outta my office," I said, turning back to my paperwork.

"I'm leaving." He laughed. "I'm going to enjoy the show that's happening out there."

"What show?" I asked, cutting my eyes at him.

"Yo' girl out there threatening to kill everybody." He shrugged. "I'm guessing she hasn't done it yet, though."

"The fuck are you talkin' about?" I jumped up from my seat and rushed out of my office. Krude stupid ass was behind me cracking up like he'd just heard the best damn joke in the world. I stepped into the lounge and looked around. It was clear except for a small group of people near the bar. I made my way over to the bar; the few employees there took one look at me and made themselves ghosts. "The fuck is going on!" My eyes landed on Paxton, who had her gun pointed at Naeem.

"Just tell me the truth!" Paxton yelled at her brother as he stared her down. "This whole time, you were fuckin' playin' me! Just admit it!"

"Wasn't nobody playin' you, Paxton," Naeem said, then sucked his teeth. "I told you everything you needed to know. That other shit didn't matter."

"It mattered, Naeem!" she screamed. "Cade died because I thought he tried to kill you and was coming after me next!"

"He did!" Naeem yelled, then stood up. That weak look he was giving off when I saw him last was gone. He looked like he hadn't just been fighting for his life a month ago. "That nigga came after me. He shot at me over some bullshit!"

"Was it bullshit, though, Naeem?" Paxton shook her head like she knew her brother was full of it. "Cuz I've been looking over the reports, and things still aren't adding up. Money is still missing!"

"The fuck you lookin' over reports for?" Naeem growled. He took a small step toward her, and I stepped forward. He looked over at me and smirked. "This doesn't have shit to do with you, nigga. From what I have been hearing from our parents, y'all broke up, so back the fuck up so I can handle this shit with my sister."

"Keep thinkin' that shit," I replied. "Understand, the second you get too close to her; your parents will bury a second child in less than sixty days. I was nice enough to let your parents bury Cade so they could have some closure, but you won't be so damn lucky."

"Nigga, I paid you to handle that." Naeem laughed. "You work for me." He looked me up and down like I was a little nigga. This nigga had balls the size of Texas to talk to me like he was.

There wasn't any need for words, so I stepped over the table that separated us and got in his face. "I work for who?" I asked him as I grabbed him by the collar and pulled him to me. "Because the last time I checked, the little money you left on my table doesn't make me roll out of bed on a nice day. Now answer your sister's question since you are so fuckin' tough suddenly."

I pushed Naeem away from me and turned and looked at Paxton. She looked good as fuck, and as much as I wanted to snatch her ass up and take her to my office, I wasn't about to do shit. I looked her up and down, then stepped back. This was their family issue, wasn't shit for me to worry about. "Handle this shit." Paxton's cold eyes swept over me before she gave me a quick nod. "Anything you break will be billed to you."

"Nigga, you are so fuckin' cheap!" Krude laughed next to me. I cut my eyes at that nigga to see him bent over, cracking up. I couldn't stand his ass. "She over here about to kill somebody, and you talkin' about billin' her!" He wiped his hands down his face and shook his head. "Nigga, you are so fuckin' funny!"

"Nigga, shut up," Naeem said to Krude. My cousin looked over at him, still laughing, and shook his head. "Fuckin' clown."

"Let me introduce you to my biggest fuckin' joke, then," Krude replied. "He pulled his gun from his back and flipped off the safety. "My cousin and your sister might have thought your life had some meaning, but I don't."

"Let her handle it, Krude," I told my cousin. He looked over his shoulder at me and lifted his brow in question. "This her shit. Let her handle it."

"If you don't kill this nigga, I will," he said to Paxton, then mugged the fuck out of Naeem before stepping back.

"She not gonna kill me." Naeem laughed and shook his head. "I'm her brother, I'm allowed to fuck up and do stupid shit, and she's gonna forgive me." Naeem shrugged his shoulder and smirked at me. "Ain't that right, big sis?"

"No," Paxton answered, and Naeem turned to look at her with surprise that she disagreed with him.

"What, you mean no?" He mugged her. "From the jump, it's been you and me. Now you are switching up on me? Why?"

"Because you tried to play me," she replied. "This shit with Cade trying to kill you went further than just a little bit of money missing and him fuckin' around with Yalonda." She shook her head. "It took me a minute to see it, but when I did and started digging, I knew I was going to have to kill you."

"Oh yeah?" He smirked, then sat back in his seat. "Tell me what you figured out, then."

"You have been stealing for years, probably since you were a kid and Daddy had you working for him," Paxton said. I could see the hurt in her eyes as she looked at her brother. They were close, closer than she and Cade were, so I knew this was fucking with her mind. "At first, I thought I was trippin' because the reports that you gave me from your accountant were consistent, so I hit her up. She was confused as fuck, but because she was about her shit, and you paid for her services with the company card, she sent me her original reports. You know the ones that you hadn't altered?"

A flash of guilt swept Naeem's face, and I shook my head. This nigga was a piece of work. "That bitch lying," he said, trying to figure out his next move. "Show me that shit if it's different."

"Why so you can lie some more?" Paxton laughed and shook her head. "You know what the fuck you did, so let's not play like you don't."

"Go on somewhere, Paxton," Naeem said, waving her off. "You yapping your gums like I'm supposed to care."

"You are!" she yelled.

"I did what I had to do to handle my shit." He laughed. "Cade was a means to an end. He was doing shady shit; I caught him; you knockin' him off was just a consolation prize. Now, unless you want Mama and Daddy to know their daughter killed their son, you might want to step back and play your part like you have been doing."

"My part?" She laughed. The fact that she hadn't corrected Naeem about her killing Cade hadn't slipped past me, either. She wanted that nigga to think she pulled the trigger. "Nigga, what is my part?"

"The one I'm letting you play." He shrugged. "Shit about to change."

"Excuse you?" Paxton reared back as if he'd hit her, then laughed softly. "Naeem, you're about to see a whole new side to me, and I promise you, baby brother, it's not one you will like."

"Paxton, ain't nobody scared of you." Naeem smirked and shook his head. He sat forward, resting his elbows on his legs, and gave his sister a soft smile. "I have been letting you think you run something, but I can see now that it was my mistake." He reached behind him, pulled out his gun, then rested it between his open legs. "So let me break this shit down to you one time so we never have this conversation again. The company is mine; I'll run it like I want. You can stay on or step off, but I don't give a fuck either way." He shook his head.

"Don't overstep your boundaries if you want to say cool. That was Cade's problem. He overstepped, and I was tired of that shit."

"So y'all were in on it together?" she asked with a laugh.

"In the beginning, he started getting greedy, and I couldn't have that."

CHAPTER 37

Paxton

NAEEM SAT across from me like he was the world's biggest boss; all I could do was shake my head. I was going to have to kill his ass, too, and that broke my heart, but just like I knew if I let Cade live, he would have killed me. I knew it was the same way for Naeem. From the moment I read over the reports from the accountant Reggie, I knew my brother had played me. Exodus's words about taking my emotions out of all this and just looking at the facts ran through my mind constantly. I was looking at everything initially, knowing that Cade had come after Naeem, and he had banked on that.

"Why?" I asked, knowing that his answer didn't matter. I knew why, or at least I thought I did. They wanted to power, just like Cade had said. "Was it because Cade messed with Yalonda?"

"Shit, nah." He laughed. "I knew from the jump that they were fuckin' around. I wasn't a fool; I used Yalonda just like she used me. After a while, we had a cool little thing going on. She finessed a few niggas for me, and I let her keep her life."

"She's alive then?" I asked because she still hadn't been seen.

"Nope," he replied. "I killed her the day I paid that nigga to kill Cade." He nodded at Exodus. "I thought I was taking care of everything in one day, but now I see I was wrong."

"What about the girls?"

"Dead." He shrugged. "I don't believe in witnesses." My eyes cut to the girl sitting next to him. "They weren't mine anyway, so it wasn't a hard decision."

"Wow," I replied. My brother was heartless. He'd raised those two girls or at least pretended to, and I could've sworn he loved them too. I ran my hand over my face to keep myself from crying. Even if he didn't love them, my parents and I did. There was no way in hell I would tell them they were dead. I would rather they think Yalonda ran off with them than break their hearts from knowing their son killed them.

"It's all a part of the game, big sis," Naeem said. He sat back, crossed his legs at his ankles, and draped one of his arms over the back of the couch. "Things change, and people die. It's life. You learn and move on."

"It's fucked up, is what it is," I said, and Naeem shrugged. "So, what was the endgame for you? Have Exodus kill Cade, you kill Yalonda, and then you and Xavi run the company? If I was on board, then cool, but if I wasn't, you'd knock me off?"

"Almost," he said, shaking his head. "I was going to kill Xavi too. He was starting to get cold feet and back out of shit. I don't have time for disloyalty on my team."

"You're one to talk about loyalty." Exodus laughed. Naeem mugged him, but Exodus didn't give a damn. "You want loyalty from niggas but crossed your own blood? Make that shit make sense. Especially since the most loyal person on your team was your sister!" he took a step toward Naeem with a menacing look. "She was out here knockin' niggas off. Split her time between sitting with you and working so your parents wouldn't always have to be at the hospital. She looked for and eventually killed Cade, then sat next to your parents at his funeral, knowing they were mourning a child who wasn't shit all out of her loyalty to you!" he mugged Naeem. "Now you are sitting your no-good ass in my business, throwing words around like loyalty when you've been the most un-loyal nigga the entire time!"

"Nigga, nobody, asked you for your opinion," Naeem said,

mugging Exodus. He turned from him to look at me. "It's your choice, Paxton, either make money or have Mama and Daddy mourning your death." He glanced over at the woman sitting next to him and smirked. "Baby, you decide. Is my sister loyal enough to sit next to us?"

"It doesn't matter if you think I'm loyal enough to sit with you because I already know you aren't loyal enough to sit next to me," I said, shaking my head at my brother. I moved around the table that separated us and sat down to face him. Naeem started to move, but the sound of a safety being flipped and a gun barrel pressed against his temple stopped him. I looked at Cross at his side and smiled at her. "I was wondering how long it would take you to pull that."

"I was waiting for the right time," Cross said, then shrugged.

"The fuck is going on?" Naeem sneered, looking between us.

"You see, Naeem, you weren't as smart as you thought," I said, crossing my legs. "You've always had this habit of running your mouth when you thought you were the smartest person in the room. I can't lie, though, if it hadn't been for Exodus telling me to step away from my emotions, I wouldn't have seen everything for what it was." I glanced over at Exodus, who stood next to Krude with a blank expression on his face. The hard look in his eyes softened momentarily before I turned back to Naeem. "You want to know what I found out?"

"Yeah." Naeem smirked. "Since you are so fuckin' smart, let me know what you know."

"You have been stealing from the company for years; we both know that. And you would've gotten away with it if it wasn't for Cade. He figured it out, and knowing him, he wanted a cut. Y'all split it for a while, but Cade was Cade, and just a little cut wasn't enough after a while, so he started doing his own deals. That went on for a while, then you wanted to expand your private empire and started hitting up accounts that he already had deals going with. When you found out you were being left out of deals that pissed you off, you started thinking of ways to get him out. You ran your mouth to Xavi, not knowing he was in on the side deals with Cade. Xavi started giving Cade a heads-up, which pissed you off because it looked like Cade had outsmarted you. That's when you sent Yalonda his way to cause some problems; since you already knew about their past, it was smart. But when you realized that wasn't going as planned, Yalonda was running game on both of y'all." I shrugged. "I guess she was smarter than you thought."

"Not smart enough not to end up dead," Naeem said through clenched teeth.

"That may be true, but she played you just like you tried to play her," I replied. I didn't sympathize with any adult in this situation, not even myself, because I knew what my brothers were capable of. I got comfortable and didn't think Naeem would do me dirty; that would never happen again. "But like I said, you almost got away with it all." I shook my head and stood. "Once I read those reports and started piecing together what everyone around me was saying, I realized you weren't shit, just like Cade. The only difference was Cade never hid how selfish he was. If it didn't benefit him, he didn't care, and we all knew that." I bent down so that Naeem and I were eye to eye. "I could handle his deceit because I knew who he was. It was you that broke my heart. You would've gotten the world from me, but you'd rather steal it. But it's cool because you'll never get to do it again."

"You'd kill me, Paxton?" Naeem asked, slightly surprised. I'd never as much as raised my hand to Naeem growing up. I didn't yell at him and hated seeing him hurt as a child. For a brief second, a flash of my little brother, the one I loved more than I loved myself, crossed my mind, and my eyes filled with tears. "Huh, you'd kill me?"

"No," I answered honestly as I stood. "I'm not going to kill you. I'm not that heartless. I couldn't kill Cade just like I can't kill you." I shook my head at the sly smirk that spread across Naeem's face. "I paid her to do it." I nodded at Cross. "You see, little brother, you pillow talk too much too. You told Cross your entire plan without realizing I'd sent her there to keep an eye on you. All you saw was a beautiful woman, and you wanted to impress her. I don't know how many times I told you in the past that a pretty face would be the death of you. It looks like I was right, huh?"

I turned and started to walk away. Cross and I already had an agreement. We had a heart-to-heart When she took me home after Exodus killed Cade. She'd pointed out things that Cade had said and even given me a separate finance report they'd run. When I read over everything later that night, I was surprised at how much had been left out of Naeem's report. I called her the next day and asked her to look into Naeem for me. She'd agreed; first, she looked into his business reports, then into his street activity. The more she dug up, the more I cried myself to sleep. My brother had played me; he'd used the trust and loyalty he knew I had for him and played me. I ASKED CROSS TO PRETEND TO BE INTERESTED IN HIM because I knew how mouthy Naeem could be when he was interested in someone. They'd gone on dates and hung out a couple of times, and Naeem started running his mouth. He'd ended up telling Cross damn near everything, and once I'd heard enough, I was ready to end it all. Me barging in on their date and questioning Naeem was all Cross's idea.

My eyes briefly locked with Exodus's as I passed him. He gave me a slight nod before turning back to Cross and Naeem.

"You know my cousin over there is good with scriptures and all that, but I have an art form of my own," Cross said to Naeem as I walked through the empty lounge. She laughed softly. "We haven't formally been introduced. My name is Cross, and I'm the last person you would've ever wanted to meet."

I pushed open the door and walked to my car. I already knew that Cross planned to torture and then kill Naeem. When I asked her to kill him, she informed me that her method of killing was torture, and after hearing Naeem say he killed the girls, I had no sympathy for him.

CHAPTER 38

Exodus

"SO YOU'RE mad at her for doing what you told her to do?" Madea asked as she moved through the kitchen. She grabbed the spoon she was looking for, returned to the stove, and started stirring the greens she was cooking. I let out a small grunt, and she began to laugh. "I don't see the problem, Exodus."

"It ain't that I'm mad at her for listening," I said, then rubbed my hands over my face.

"Then what are you mad about?" She laughed. "Because from the outside looking in, that's what it looks like."

"She said I was a dick appointment to her," I fessed up, and Madea laughed harder. I sucked my teeth and crossed my arms over my chest; of course, she would think this shit was funny. "For real, Madea?"

"Exodus, honey," she said after finally collecting herself. "That girl is giving you the same amount of blues you gave women in the past."

"It ain't the same," I said, shaking my head. "I was upfront with Paxton when I stepped to her. I told her we go together."

"And?" Madea put the lid on her pot and turned to face me.

"And what?"

"You told that grown-ass woman y'all go together and what else?"

"I gave her dick, took her on dates, cooked for her, spent time with her people." I counted off on my fingers everything. "I wasn't fucking around with another bitch or giving anyone else my time."

"And," Madea said again.

"What else was a nigga supposed to do, Madea?" I threw my hands in the air and sighed. "I thought that's what females wanted. A nigga that was upfront with everything. I was upfront with Paxton and told her we go together."

"I think y'all got the slow gene from y'all granddaddy's side," she said, shaking her head. Mahogany walked into the kitchen and sat next to me. She rested her hand over her stomach and looked between us. Madea grabbed a small plate out of the cabinet and fixed Mahogany a small plate. Only Mahogany could get Madea to come into town and cook for her. Any and everyone else was told no without a second thought. "Tell your friend he can't boss that girl into wanting to be with him."

"Who?" Mahogany questioned before taking a bite of her pork chop. "Paxton?"

Madea nodded, and Mahogany cut her eyes at me before smiling at me.

"Don't start your shit, man," I sighed.

"I'm not starting anything." She laughed. "If anything, I think y'all deserve each other."

"What?" I questioned, surprised. I didn't talk to Mahogany about what Paxton and I had going because I didn't want to put her in the middle of anything. She was friends with both of us. "Why do you think that?"

"Because y'all act just alike." She shrugged.

"She's stubborn, hardheaded, bossy as fuck, does what she wants to, hot-headed," I countered, and both Mahogany and Madea started to laugh. "The hell y'all laughing at."

"You are too!" Madea replied. "Exodus, I love you with everything in me, but you are no better. You just met your match and don't know how to react." She fixed a second plate and set it in front of me. "Let me tell you something; then I'm going to sit down and relax. You were a dick appointment to her because you never asked her what she wanted. Just like Focus took away Mahogany's choice in their situation because he thought he knew better, you are taking away hers. Did you ever ask her what she wanted?"

"Nah." I sighed and wiped my hands over my face again. Madea gave me a knowing look, then set the plate she fixed in front of me.

"Eat," she said, pointing to the plate. "Let me be until I say otherwise."

"She told you," Mahogany said once Madea was gone.

"You know you're not any help, right?" I chuckled. "I have your back, and you let her talk crazy to me." I took a bite of my food and groaned in satisfaction.

"I'll let her keep doing it, too, if she keeps cooking like this." Mahogany laughed. I shook my head, and she shrugged. "But for real, you like Paxton? Like, want to be her boyfriend?"

"Fuck yeah," I said, nodding. "I didn't expect to, but I can't even front that's my heart, man."

"Then go tell her," Mahogany said like that shit was simple.

"Mahogany," I sighed as I stared at her. Having a female best friend was cool until they expected you to read their minds. Mahogany looked up from her plate with a lifted brow. "How the fuck am I supposed to tell that girl I want to be her nigga? Paxton doesn't like all that grand shit, and let's be honest, I'm not doing all that shit either."

"How did you show her you were interested in her?" she asked, rolling her eyes.

"I ate her pussy on the living room table," I answered with a shrug, and Mahogany just stared at me with a slow blink that made me laugh. "Our shit wasn't romantic, it started as lust, and I want more." I shrugged. "I like kicking it with her; we vibe. Her pussy good as fuck, and she not scared of a nigga."

"I hate being best friends with a man," Mahogany sighed. "I swear you are all slow as fuck at times. Look, I will do you this favor, and after that, you're on your own." She got up from her seat and walked into the living room. I finished eating my food and cleaned the kitchen before entering the living room. Mahogany was on the couch next to Focus, who started laughing when he saw me.

"The fuck you laughin' at, nigga?" I asked, sitting across from them.

"One said you slow," he answered. "But I been knowing that shit."
He shrugged. "You ready to go?"

"The fuck are we going?"

"Cash in on One's favor," he said, then got up from the couch. He
kissed Mahogany's forehead and then grabbed his keys off the table.
"Bring yo' ass, nigga."

I mugged the shit out of a smiling Mahogany, then got up and
followed Focus out of the house. We got into his truck and headed east.
The entire ride, I kept trying to figure out what the fuck we were about
to do, and by the time we pulled up in front of Paxton's house, I was
confused as hell. Focus parked on the street; then we got out. "Don't
say shit; let me do all the talking," he said after ringing the doorbell. A
few seconds later, Paxton pulled the front door open; she was dressed
in a pair of yoga shorts and a sports bra. I looked her up and down but
didn't say a word.

"What's up?" she said to Focus. Her eyes bounced over to me
before going back to him. I let out a small laugh and shook my head.
Focus mugged me for a second, then turned back to Paxton.

"Watch out, man," Focus said. He stepped around Paxton and
walked into her house. A few seconds later, he returned, looked us
over, and walked back to the truck.

"The fuck you going?" I called out to him.

"My woman said to leave your ass here until y'all figure this shit
out!" he yelled before climbing into his truck. "Plus, it's a nigga in
there. You can handle that shit, though!" he slammed his door closed,
started his truck, and pulled off.

I turned around to face Paxton, who was leaning against the door
frame with a smirk on her face. I mugged the shit out of her, pushed
past her, and stepped into the house.

"The hell are you doing!" she screamed as I entered the living
room.

"Where the nigga at!" I yelled as I pulled my gun from my waist. "I
swear on everything whatever nigga you got in here gonna die in this
bitch."

"There is no one here." Paxton sighed and sat on the couch. "Do you think Focus would've left if there was?" I stared at her as I ran my tongue over my teeth. "If you think I'm lying, check the house."

"If I find somebody, their death is your fault," I said, walking away. I checked her entire house with no damn shame. I felt like the police executing a search warrant; I flipped over mattresses, pulled shit out of her closet, pushed open shower curtains, and kicked over anything that a nigga may have been able to hide behind. I came back down to the living room, out of breath, hot, and still annoyed.

"Told you no one was here," she said without looking from the TV. "Emotional-ass nigga did all that for nothing."

"I'm emotional?" I asked with a laugh. "You're one to talk."

"You are." She laughed. "From the beginning, you have been telling me to keep my emotions in check, but all you do is move on yours. Not one damn thought ever passes through your mind because you are going straight off emotions."

"Fuck you, Paxton," I said, shaking my head. I pulled my phone out of my pocket and hit up Krude to tell him to come to get me.

"Nigga, what did you say?" Paxton said.

"You heard me." I looked up from my phone to see her jump off the couch and enter my space. "Move out my face before I fuck you up."

"Get your disrespectful ass out of my house!" she yelled, and I stood up. I towered over her tiny ass and smirked at her. "And whatever you fucked up in here, you're going to replace."

"I bet you the fuck I don't," I said, stepping around her. "You better be lucky I didn't shoot this bitch up."

"You are so fuckin' toxic!" she yelled, and I shrugged. I was damn near at the front door when a pillow hit me in the back. I turned around, and I swear God had a nigga's back because if I hadn't, I wouldn't have known she planned to launch a small table lamp at me.

"You throw that shit at me if you want to," I growled. "I'll break your damn neck." Paxton hesitated for a second, then launched it at me. I sidestepped it. "The fuck is wrong with you!"

"Get out!"

"I'm trying to fuckin' leave, but you keep throwing shit!" I laughed and shook my head. "You're crazy ass fuck, man! Like for real crazy as shit!"

"And what are you?" she asked and came and got in my face. Her little ass thought she was scaring a nigga, which made me laugh harder. "If I'm crazy, then what are you? Because you have done nothing but show your ass the last few months. You've killed people, held people at gunpoint, burned a damn restaurant only to buy it later. You spent time with my family unknowingly. What the fuck did you do all that for if you weren't crazy?"

"I'm in love with your ass!" I yelled, not giving a fuck. If she wanted to know the damn truth, she would get it. "I did all that shit because I'm in love with you! From the night you pulled your gun at the fuckin' club, I have probably been in love with you!"

"Why didn't you say something?" she asked, sounding confused as fuck.

"I did!" I threw my hands in the air. "I told you we go together! I brought you breakfast, dicked you down, killed niggas for you. That nigga Memphis said that was romantic shit!"

"It's not." She laughed and shook her head. "I don't know how he got Nyla if he was doing shit like that."

"Krude said kidnap yo' ass," I said, then wiped my hand down my face.

"Don't listen to Krude either," she replied.

Her doorbell rang, and we both cut our eyes at the door. "Open the door, nigga. I know you in there!" Krude yelled, and I groaned. When I hit him up, he said he was less than five minutes away; I didn't believe him because Krude had no concept of time. "Come on, let me in, or I'm gonna pee in her damn bushes." Paxton pushed past me and pulled her door open. "I thought so; point me to the bathroom."

"Down the hall to the left," Paxton said, pointing. He took off in the direction that she pointed to. We stood silently staring each other down until Krude returned from the bathroom.

"Paxton, the police ransacked yo' spot, or you get robbed?" he said, looking around. "Cuz yo' shit fucked up."

"No, your cousin did that looking for someone," she answered.

"Oh," Krude replied with a shrug. He pulled his phone out of his pocket and started taking pictures.

"The fuck are you doing, nigga?" I asked.

"Getting proof that I ain't the only crazy one in the family." He laughed. Once he was done, he put his phone away and turned to me. "You ready to go?"

"Yeah." I nodded. I looked over at Paxton one last time, then we left. I wasn't about to beg her with me. If she wanted a nigga, she would have to figure out her shit and then come to me.

"Where yo' car at?" Krude said once we pulled off.

"Mahogany's," I answered.

"Good, cuz I'm heading that way anyway to get some food. I heard Madea threw down in the kitchen."

"She did."

"Cool," he said, nodding.

CHAPTER 39

Paxton

"YOU DON'T GET to tell me you love me and then walk away," I said, jumping out of the car. I drove like a bat out of hell to catch up with Krude's fast-driving ass. The entire drive over, I kept going over what I would say. Nothing made sense; my words kept getting jumbled, so I went with the first thing that came to mind.

"What else was I supposed to do?" Exodus countered as he shut Krude's truck door. He barely looked at me, so I stepped in his way so he had no choice. "Move; I don't have time for your shit."

"You don't get to walk away from me!" I yelled, getting in his face. Exodus looked me up and down but didn't say anything. "You have to give me a chance to reply."

"What you gotta say!" he yelled. "I told you how I felt! I told you I love your stubborn ass! If you aren't telling me that shit back, we have nothing to discuss!"

I bit into my bottom lip to keep from laughing. He was pissed, like pissed, to the point he was yelling, and I swear I was the only person I'd ever heard him yell at. He wiped his hands down his face and shook his head. He always told me I was emotional, yet he was the most emotional man ever. It was cute because I knew no matter how pissed I made him, how many times he threatened me, Exodus never, and I mean, never made me fear him, which is why I knew he would never hurt me.

"Get the fuck outta my way," he said, trying to sidestep me, and I blocked his path away. "Move, Paxton."

"Tell me again," I said, not trying to hold back my smile now.

"What!" he stepped back like I swung on me.

"Tell me you love me again," I said, stepping into his face. I grabbed him by the collar of his shirt and pulled him down so we were at eye level. "Tell me again, Exodus."

"No," he said, then rang his tongue over his teeth.

"Tell. Me. Again."

"No." He shook his head.

"Nigga, if yo' emotional ass don't tell her you fuckin' love her!" Krude yelled from beside us. "The entire car ride over, all you did was talk about how you loved her ass, and she ain't say the shit back. She telling you to say it again, and you over here being stubborn." Krude threw his hands in the air and shook his head. "Madea! Tell this crybaby ass nigga to tell this crazy ass girl he loves her so I can make me a plate!"

"Krude, mind your damn business!" I glanced over my shoulder to see Mahogany, Focus, Exodus, and Krude's grandmother standing on the porch. "Bring your ass in this house so you can get a plate and leave them the hell alone! I swear your granddaddy dropped you on your head too many times when you were a little one."

"Madea, that nigga dropped me?" Krude asked, surprised. "Like for real dropped a nigga?" He made his way to the porch, and all I could do was shake my head because he was a damn fool. Mrs. DeCorte grabbed him by his arm and dragged him into the house. Mahogany and Focus followed behind them, laughing.

"Now, back to you," I said, turning to face Exodus, still staring at me with a cold look. "Tell me again."

"No," he repeated his answer.

"Exodus," I sighed and shook my head. "You're being emotional, and I don't understand why."

"I told you why!" he fussed them and stood up to his full height. "You pissing me off playing dumb."

"Emotional-ass nigga," I taunted because I knew he would spaz out, and I needed him to repeat the words. I had to hear them when I wasn't upset and ensure my reaction to them were real.

"I'm emotional because I love you!" he yelled, pinching the bridge of his nose.

I waited a few seconds to see if the feeling of hearing the words disappeared, and it didn't. My heart beat against my chest, and excitement coursed through my veins. This man loved me. His crazy ass loved me!

Exodus turned to walk away. "I love you too!" I said to his back. He stopped walking and turned to look at me with a confused look. I walked over to him, pulled him down, and kissed him. We fought for control before pulling apart.

"We go together now for real," Exodus said after ending the kissing. I let him go and headed inside the house. I found everyone in the living room. Mahogany and Focus were on one couch talking, and Krude and Mrs. DeCorte sat across from them on the phone. Krude was fussing, and Mrs. DeCorte was trying to hide her laughter. She looked up at me and then got up from the couch.

"I guess I can say we have officially met now," Mrs. DeCorte said as she hugged me. "That grandson of mine hasn't stressed you out too much, has he?"

"It's nothing I can't handle," I replied, and she nodded.

"Madea, granddaddy said get yo' ass on this phone," Krude said, standing up.

"That man didn't say that." She laughed and took the phone from him. "Excuse me for a second." Mrs. DeCorte left the living room, and I took her spot on the couch.

"Y'all good now?" Krude asked, and we nodded. "Cool, cuz you niggas are toxic as fuck." He turned to look at Mahogany and Focus. "You know that nigga destroyed her house cuz yo' ass said she had a nigga in there?"

"He what?" Mahogany asked, surprised. She turned and looked at Focus. "I said to drop him off and make his stay not lie."

"I did what I had to do, One," Focus said, leaning back on the couch to get comfortable. "You don't get to pick how I handle shit."

"She threw a lamp at the nigga." Krude laughed. "They deserve each other."

———

When I got home, I showered, washing the smell of work off my skin and hair. I checked myself over in the mirror, loving the feeling and sexy look of the black corselette and suspender belt bottom I paired with some black gladiator heels that laced up to my calf. My hair was wild and free around my head, and my face was lightly beaten. Since I was on my Olivia Pope vibe right now, I grabbed my black cape coat from my closet and headed out.

I pulled into Exodus's driveway, checked myself in the mirror one last time, and got out. I walked to the front door with a new pep, unlocked it, and stepped inside. The lights were off, but I walked through the house without problems. I made my way upstairs and to the primary bedroom. A small smile tugged at my lips at the sound of the shower running as I entered the room. I took a seat on the end of the bed and waited. The entire house had been redecorated, but the bedroom had the most drastic look. Gone were the white bed, dresser, couch, and plush rug. Now, in its place was massive all-black furniture. The water shut off, and my ears perked up as Exodus hummed while he moved around the bathroom. A short time later, the door opened, and he stepped out wrapped in a towel, and my pussy instantly throbbed.

"What are you doing here?" he asked, looking me up and down. His eyes were hungry, and I felt my body get hot when he licked his plump lips. Instead of answering him, I stood and unbuttoned my coat and let it drop to my feet. Slowly, I strolled over to Exodus and squatted in front of him. His dick pressed against the front of the towel, and I reached up to pull it down. Exodus didn't take his eyes off me as I kissed my way up his thigh, over his pubic hairs, and down his dick. When I got to the tip, I slowly worked my tongue over it, loving the taste of his pre-cum that seeped out. I opened my mouth gracefully and swallowed as much of his dick as possible. I had no mercy on him as I went to work. I hollowed out my cheeks and worked him over.

"Shit," he hissed and shook his head. Exodus reached down and ran his thumb over my cheek, and in all the years I'd been giving head, this was the first time I felt powerful and beautiful. "You are amazing." That was all the encouragement I needed. I braced my hands on his thighs and deep-throated Exodus. He dropped his head back and looked up at the sky. I could feel the drool running from my mouth, but I didn't care. I wanted this to be nasty and dirty even so that he would know to never play with me again. "Damn it, Hitta." His leg twitched under my hand, and I sped up my movements. My jaw would probably hurt tomorrow, but hearing him groan in pleasure was well worth it. When I started humming, he lifted his head and stared at me with a sexy smirk. His nostrils flared, and his breathing changed, and I knew he was close. "Swallow my nut." He put his hand on my head and started to fuck my mouth. If any other nigga would've said that to me, I would've stopped right then and there, but it was something about how Exodus spoke that had me wanting to follow his directions. "Fuck!" He bit into his bottom lip, and then the warmth of his cum hit the back of my throat. "Let me see." I pulled back and opened my mouth to show him it was empty, and he nodded. "Now stand the fuck up." With ease, I rose to my full height, and he looked me up and down. "I don't know what I did to deserve that shit, but whatever it was, understand I'm going to keep doing it." He wrapped his hand around my neck and pulled me close to him. Our lips brushed against each other, and he reached between my legs to touch my hot pussy. "Get in bed."

"No," I said, shaking my head. Exodus looked down at me with a mug on his face. "I'm in charge this time." I stepped away from him. "You get on the bed." Exodus climbed on the bed with a low laugh and laid on his back.

"My only request is that you leave that sexy-ass shit on," he said when I untied my corset. I stared at him, debating if I wanted to. The way that Exodus stared at me as if he appreciated the outfit made me leave it on.

I climbed into the bed, slowly kissing him as I moved up. His dick looked so hard that if I hadn't swallowed his cum, I would have sworn that he hadn't cum not even two minutes earlier. I twirled my tongue over the head of it before dropping two soft kisses on it and moving up his body. My eyes swept over his tattoos in amazement. They were beautiful, and later at another time, I would ask about what they all meant, but right now, I needed dick. Since I still had my heels on, I climbed onto his lap and rested on my knees. The tip of his dick teased at my opening, and for the first time tonight, I was glad I went with the crotchless panties.

"I have a few rules," I said as I kissed my way up his neck. "You ready for them?"

"You can say whatever you want, but I probably ain't gonna give a fuck," he roughly replied as he kneaded my ass. I bit into his neck, and he groaned.

"You already know the first rule is I'm in charge," I said, kissing his jaw. "Rule number two is you can't take control." Exodus laughed, and I smirked. I knew he was one of those niggas that liked to be in control, and him handing it over was going to be hard for him. "If you can't handle it, then I can leave." I pretended to move, and he tightly gripped my waist. I raised and looked at him. Exodus searched my eyes for a few seconds before nodding, and I smiled. "Good, now, rule three will be the most important of them all."

"What's that?" he asked. I teasingly started to lower onto his dick, and it took everything in me not to drop down on him. "Hmmm, Hitta, what's the most important rule?"

"Make me cum." I lowered myself fully onto him and let out a deep breath. Exodus's dick felt like heaven. He filled and stretched me in the most pleasurably painful way possible. "Can you do that, Exodus?" I started to rock my hips and bit into my bottom lip. I wanted to moan so bad from the slow rock I was doing but held it back. "Hmmm, can you do that?"

"With pleasure," he replied and grabbed onto my neck to drag me to kiss me. Like the other times we kissed, we fought for control, but he let me win this time. I pulled back, and he put his hands behind his head. "Show me what you got." I found the rhythm I wanted to use and rocked back and forth on his dick. Even though I was doing most of the work, Exodus fucked me from below. I reached back and unlaced my shoes. Once they were off, I planted my feet on the bed and started moving. Now that I had my balance, I had no problem working Exodus dick. Without taking his dick out of me, I spun around and got into the reverse cowgirl position. I grabbed Exodus's ankles and bounced on his dick. "Shit." He ran his hands over my ass.

"Fuck, I'm about to cum," I moaned and shook my head. Exodus spread my ass cheeks and pushed his wet thumb into my asshole. I let out a whimper. "Fuck!"

"Nah, don't slow down," he growled. "Look up." He pulled his thumb from my ass and grabbed my hair to make me look up. The sight of me staring at myself turned me on even more. "Look at your sexy ass working my dick." Exodus raised, making me lean forward, and he pulled his legs from under me. We ended up doggy style, and my rules went right out the fuckin' window. He pushed down on the small of my back, making me arch, and went to work. "Throw that ass." He spread my cheeks again, and I felt his spit roll down my asshole.

"Fuck, you feel so good!" I moaned. Exodus smacked my ass, and I hissed at the sting. I could feel my orgasm building, and I knew he could, too, from how he began pushing inside me. "I'm about to cum."

"Do that shit then, cuz it won't be the last one of the night."

"Fuck!" My walls started to spasm, and my eyes rolled into the back of my head. I buried my face into the covers to try to control something, but he pulled my head back.

"Nah, tough ass, let me hear that shit," he taunted. Like the first time we had sex, my body started to shake, and my head got hot. "Yeah, there it goes. Let that shit out."

"Exodus!" I whined because what he did to me felt too good to do anything else.

"Nah, don't get to whining now." He used his other hand to reach around and press on my clit. My knees started to buckle at the intense feeling spreading all over my body. "Let that nut go!"

"Shit!" I yelled as I did what he said. My orgasm swept through my body, and my arms gave out on me. But Exodus didn't care. He kept working me over, pushing into my pussy with so much force that I found myself coming off one orgasm to be pushed right into another one. This nigga was trying to kill me. That was the only logical explanation for what was going on. But then again, my dumb ass had come over here thinking I was running shit. He'd already shown me he wasn't one to play with when it came to sex, yet I was a hardhead and thought it was a one-and-done type of thing. I was wrong, like dead ass wrong. I reached my hand above my head and tried to tap out after my third orgasm hit me.

"You tapping?" he asked, pulling out of me. I thought he would let me live for a second, but I saw him stroking his dick and smirking over my shoulder. "Huh, you tapping?"

"Yeah." I nodded and pushed my hair out of my face.

He got out of bed and shook his head. "That shit is cute." He laughed.

"What?" I asked, rolling over to my back. My breathing was hard and uneven, but I didn't give a damn.

"That you thought I gave a fuck," he said, grabbing my ankle. "You said you wanted to cum. I let you, but I didn't say how many times I would you before I said I was done." Exodus dragged me to the edge of the bed and pushed my legs apart. He dropped to his knees, and his mouth latched on to my pussy before I could even blink twice.

"Shit!" I yelled and grabbed onto the covers. I made a mistake coming over here, but Lord, if I was going to die, at least I was going out the best way possible.

CHAPTER 40
Exodus

"HITTA!" I yelled, moving through the crowd. This fuckin' girl was going to make me choke her ass out. I tapped Krude on his shoulder as I passed him and threw my head toward the direction I knew Paxton had gone. "Hitta!"

"Man, what the fuck yo' girl do this time?" Krude asked, looking around. "Who is she with?"

"Cross," I replied, and Krude threw his hands up in frustration. How and when their friendship had developed was beyond me, but Cross and Paxton were close as hell. Usually, I would be down with my girl and family, linking up and being tight, but Cross and Paxton were short-tempered.

"I swear on everything nigga once you find her ass, you better drag her the fuck up outta here, take her home, dick her down, and get her pregnant," Krude fussed. Out of the corner of my eye, I saw a group of people rushing from one side of the club. "That's the only way you gonna calm her ass down!"

"I'll think about it." I chuckled and headed toward the other side of the club.

"Ain't shit to think about!" Krude yelled. "Megan got me pregnant right now!"

"Go to hell, Krude." I laughed.

"For real!" He said with a serious expression, "Why do you think I have been behaving?"

Instead of encouraging the conversation, I ignored him and pushed through the last crowd of people trying to get away. When my eyes landed on Paxton pointing her gun at Niecy, I let out a small laugh. From what I could tell, she had been lying low since Paxton had hemmed her up a few months back.

"I knew you were a jealous bitch!" Niecy yelled, and I shook my head. She didn't take her life for granted, and that shit was obvious.

"Bitch, I don't want that nigga!" Paxton replied with a laugh, and I felt my face twist up because what the fuck did she mean she didn't want that nigga? Who was the nigga? Because I knew it wasn't me. Paxton turned her gun to the nigga sitting zesty as hell on the couch next to Yalonda and mugged the shit out of him. It took me a second to recognize him, but I laughed when I did. This was the nigga that I beat up a few months back at the restaurant I shared with Focus. "Darryl, tell this bitch to stop playing with me. Don't worry; I warned her last time, and she didn't believe me."

"Hitta." I laughed and walked toward her. "Baby, give me the gun; you don't gotta kill her cuz she's slow." I reached for the gun, and Paxton mugged the hell out of me. "For real, baby, we talked about this emotional shit, right? We agreed to think things through before we start shooting."

Paxton stared at me for a few seconds before slowly nodding; she handed me her gun. I was proud as fuck that she wasn't letting her anger get the best of her.

"See, nigga, this is the shit we're on now," I said, looking over at Krude. I saw a blur move past me from the corner of my eye. I turned around in time to see Paxton jump over the table that separated her and Niecy and rock her shit. I stood there completely in shock as Paxton beat Niecy up. She didn't give her a chance to even pretend like she was going to defend herself. Paxton stomped Niecy into the ground, and when Darryl jumped up from his seat, I grabbed him by his throat. "Nigga, you got a death wish?"

"That's my fuckin' girl!" Darryl yelled like I was supposed to give a fuck.

"Nigga, let your woman take that ass whoopin' like you took yours," I replied, mugging the shit out of him. "I'm pretty sure I owe you a bullet." I flipped the safety off the gun I got from Paxton and pushed the barrel in between his eyes. "Say your fuckin' prayer now!"

Bang. Bang

I took my eyes off Darryl but didn't move my gun from its spot to look at Paxon. "Hitta, where the fuck did that gun come from?" I asked her.

"These thighs, baby," she said, smirking at me. She stood over Niecy's body with blood splattered over her clothes and face. "Where else would it be." I should've known that she was carrying, especially since she was dressed in a black bodycon dress that had a high split. When we stepped out earlier, I thought about getting her home later and fucking her. Now, I knew I would have to check her before we stepped out of the house in the future.

"That shit is so sexy," I said, shaking my head.

"You niggas are crazy," Krude said, laughing. I looked over at him and shrugged. "Kill that nigga you got so we can call Kino and get shit cleaned up."

I shot Darryl between the eyes and let his body drop. I looked over at Paxton and smirked. "Let's go, Hitta," I said, and she nodded.

I took her hand, and we all walked out of the room. Kino and his crew would clean up, and I would drop Khrisen a few stacks for the damages. We went through the crowd; no one looked in our direction.

"Damn it, Cross!" Krude yelled from behind us. I turned in time to see my cousin pointing her gun at Nine, who was towering over her. "Do not shoot that nigga!"

"Tell him to get the fuck outta my face," Cross replied.

"We know him!" Krude fussed, then turned to face me. "Tell this damn girl we know this crazy ass nigga!"

"Cross," I called out to her. "He cool."

"He knows I'm not the one to play with," Cross said, putting her gun away. I watched as Nine looked Cross up and down. He was interested as fuck, which was the only reason she was still alive right now.

Just as crazy as Cross was, Nine was worse. If he let her pull her gun on him and even walk away, it was a reason for it. "Make that the last time you walk up on me."

"I can't promise that," Nine replied with a smirk. He looked her up and down again before turning to look at me. "We got some business to discuss."

"Hit my lane later," I said, nodding. Nine walked away without another word. "Let's go."

"They have a history?" Paxton asked me as we continued our way to the truck.

"Not that I know of, but Cross is secretive as fuck, so they might," I answered with a shrug. I unlocked my truck and opened the passenger door for Paxton. "Get in." After she got situated, I closed the door, rounded the truck, and then got in.

"Drop me off nigga," Krude said, jumping into the back seat. "My baby mama is waiting on me."

"Baby mama?" Paxton laughed and turned in her seat to look at Krude. "Megan is not pregnant."

"Nah, she knocked me up," Krude replied. I took my eyes off the road for a second and glanced up at the rearview mirror to see his dramatic ass rub his flat stomach. "She ain't ever getting rid of me now."

"You niggas are crazy," Paxton said, laughing. She turned around in her seat and shook her head.

"Say's the woman covered in blood because she got mad at her gay ass ex and his girlfriend," Krude replied, and I chuckled. "If anything, we, as in Exodus and me, are the sane ones, and we have to deal with the consequences of our prayers manifesting."

"What are you talking about now, Krude?" Paxton asked him with a laugh.

"We prayed for y'all crazy asses," Krude replied. Paxton sighed and rolled her eyes. "When we were younger, our granddaddy said pray for the type of woman we wanted, and we did. Every fuckin' night before we closed our eyes, we would pray for y'all big head asses; now, at the time, we didn't know it was y'all but shit, look at us."

"Whatever, Krude." Paxton laughed.

"If you don't believe me, ask that nigga," Krude grunted.

Paxton looked over at me, and I nodded my head. "Yeah, Hitta, I prayed for you," I replied with a small laugh.

When we got to a red light, she leaned over the armrest and grabbed my face. "I love you, Exodus," she said before kissing me. I pushed my tongue into her mouth to deepen our kiss. The sounds of people honking didn't make me pull back from her.

"If you niggas don't drop me off with my woman so I can go love on her and not be jealous in this damn back seat!" Krude yelled and hit my seat. We pulled apart and laughed. "This damn girl covered in blood, and you slobbin' her down! Nasty ass niggas!

"Shut up, Krude." I laughed and pulled off. "You are being dramatic as fuck right now."

"Nigga, are you serious?" he yelled. "Y'all, the most emotional-ass people I have ever met!"

"I love you too, Hitta," I said, ignoring Krude. She looked over at me and smiled at me. Yeah, she looked crazy as fuck, with blood splattered all over her face and clothes, but I didn't care. If I was going to be with anyone, it may as well have been somebody who would keep me on my toes.

"Oh, now you gonna ignore me?" Krude complained. "Just treat me like I'm not worth shit; it's cool. I bet you'll be callin' my phone when her ass cussin' you the fuck out or throwin' shit at you. See if I answer."

"You will need nigga." I laughed. "Just like I'll answer when you call me on your bullshit with Megan."

"I'm not callin' you for shit," Krude replied. "Me and Megan are expecting a baby; we've matured."

Me and Paxton exchanged looks, then burst out laughing. He was lying like a muthafucka, but I would let him have it for now.

"Ay, Ex." Krude got out of the truck but didn't close the door. I turned around in my seat and looked at him. "You see that shit between Cross and Nine?"

"What shit, man?" I questioned because I knew how Krude's mind worked. He would make something out of nothing and have Cross and Nine coming after his ass for pissing them off.

"They in love nigga." He smiled, and I shook my head. "Watch what I tell you; it's gonna be some shit with them."

"Get the fuck outta here, nigga." I laughed. Krude reached over and dapped me up before closing the door and walking into the house.

"You think it's something with Cross and Nine?" Paxton asked.

"Oh yeah, baby, they go together." I laughed.

"For real?"

"Shit I'ono, Hitta." I glanced over to see a surprised look on her face. "All I know is we go together." I shrugged, then reached over to turn the volume up. Focus's latest song blasted through the speakers, and I sang along. "I'd light the whole world on fire for you."

"Oh, that's where you get the bad habits from, huh?" Paxton questioned with a laugh.

"Over you, baby fuck yeah," I replied with a laugh because shit, it was the truth. Over her, I'd be the most emotional nigga in the world. Wasn't no being logical or thinking shit through. When I got to a stoplight, I looked over at her. "Hitta?"

"Yeah?" she replied without looking up from her phone.

"Would you shoot me?" I asked her, thinking about our conversation from a few months back.

Paxton looked up from her phone with a confused expression on her face. It took her a second to figure out what I was talking about before she smiled and leaned over the armrest. She rested her forehead against mine and asked, "What do you think?" She dropped a few quick kisses on my lips and then pulled back.

"You know I never cashed in on the rest of my hours," I said, and Paxton rolled her eyes.

"You have cashed in on those plus a million more," she replied.

"No, I haven't," I said, shaking my head. "I know I still have some left."

"How many?" she questioned.

"Shit, I don't even know, but we might as well start over at this point." I turned my attention back to the road. "You cool with that?"

"Does it matter if I am?" she asked with a laugh.

"Nah, not really." I smirked. "Because we—"

"Go together," she said, interrupting me. "I know, Exodus."

"Our baby gonna be named Charnise."

"What?" I questioned with a laugh.

"I'm just putting it out there," he said, then reached over and tried to palm my stomach. "You and Krude gonna be pregnant at the same time." He looked over at me and smiled. "Shit gonna be dope as fuck."

"Go to hell, Exodus." I laughed.

The End

Want to be a part of the Grand Penz Family?

To submit your manuscript to Grand Penz Publications, please send the first three chapters and synopsis to info@grandpenz.com

Made in the USA
Monee, IL
03 October 2023

43901354R00129